the DOLLMAKER

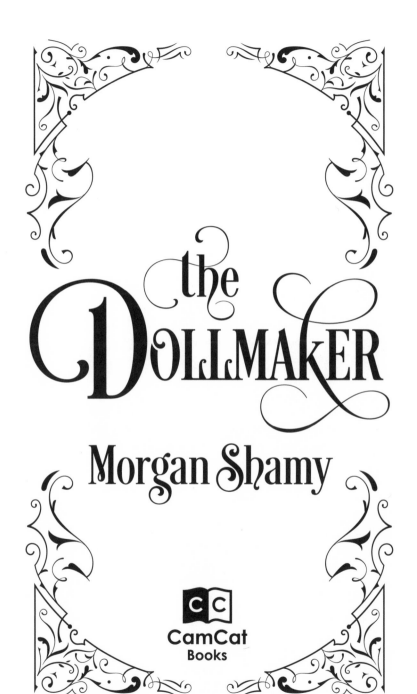

the DOLLMAKER

Morgan Shamy

CamCat Books

CamCat Publishing, LLC
Brentwood, Tennessee 37027
camcatpublishing.com

Hardcover ISBN 9780744308624
Paperback ISBN 9780744308648
Large-Print Paperback ISBN 9780744308686
eBook ISBN 9780744308709
Audiobook ISBN 9780744308716

Library of Congress Control Number: 2022944733

Book and cover design by Maryann Appel

5   3   1   2   4

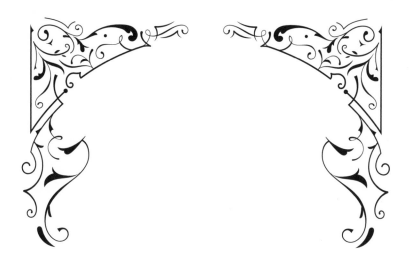

FOR MY UNCLE DEAN,
WHO'S MADE MY LIFE PURE MAGIC.

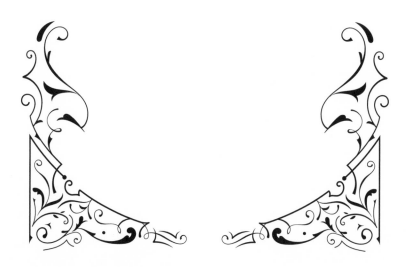

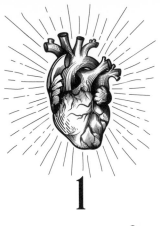

1

Standing on Air

Newport, Rhode Island, 1920

Fingertips stretched at length, gliding through the air, smooth against the heavy beat of the music. Necks stretched long and slender, and feet pattered on the floor, pointe shoes clicking. With thinly muscled legs and tiny waists, the girls in the old studio wove in and out of each other, jumping in time with the music. Shadows shifted over their white tutus and pink silk tights, their bodies reflected in the large mirror that hung on one side of the room.

Dawn Hildegard tilted her head sideways, expelling a constricted breath. She stood off to the side, her loose gray dress drab in the room. Next to the girls, she was a goose surrounded by swans. She fiddled with the silk scarf around her neck and analyzed the girls more closely, checking for injuries.

She zeroed in on the ballerina in the center of the room with her curls pinned tightly into her golden bun. Early-morning sunlight filtered in through the tall windows in the corner, highlighting the soft bones of her face, her lashes long and dark. Color dotted the ballerina's cheeks from exertion, but she seemed to float through the room, dancing as if it were effortless. Rose Waterford was the prima in the company; no one touched her grace and extension.

Even though the other girls in the company looked unearthly with their slender frames and porcelain skin, Rose exceeded them all. The *Newport Gazette* had called her "poetry on air" after her performance in *Giselle* last season.

Dawn studied Rose more closely. She was favoring her right leg, a slight limp as she moved from position to position. Her feet must have been bothering her again.

The ballet master, Caldwell, paced at the front of the class, tapping a wooden stick, yelling at the girls to stay in time with the music. His jaw was cut strong along the sides of his face, his dark hair a curly mop on his head. His open white shirt exposed his chest, sweat running down his bare skin.

"Stop, stop." Caldwell waved to the pianist, and the music ceased, the deep notes hanging in the air. He faced the girls head on. "A corps de ballet needs to be *one*. Like puppets on a string, you need to all move in sync. I expect perfection, and perfect is *not* what I'm getting." A single dark brow lifted as his eyes slid to Rose. "Except for you, Miss Waterford."

Pink flushed Rose's cheeks, but she kept her head level. The girls around her shifted their weight, some sneaking a glance at her.

"That's enough for now." Caldwell motioned for the girls to leave, his New York accent coming through. He'd only been the ballet master for about a month but clearly had command over the girls. "We will resume rehearsals on stage tonight for *Coppelia*. Rose, if I could have a word?"

The room seemed to exhale at once, and the girls departed, grabbing their hand towels from the barres. They brushed past Dawn, their thin muscles flexing as they walked, their chatter drifting behind them. Dawn shifted out of the way, letting them by. She peeked at herself in the dusty mirror in front of her. She hated the way her eyes resembled two black bruises, as if she hadn't slept in a week. Her dark hair hung in tangles over her face, where the other girls kept their curls pinned tightly to their heads. The color of her stained dress matched her demeanor, muted against the morning light.

She wasn't surprised she was sleep deprived; being Dr. Miller's assistant was an endless job, often calling her to visit patients' homes in the dead of night. She had shown up on the Browns' doorstep just after midnight to aid in Mrs. Brown's labor—twins—one of which was a breech delivery. The blood and screams still swirled inside her head, and she shivered.

Of course she was lucky to have the position at all, as it was rare for a woman to have such an apprenticeship. But the title ate through her core, sitting heavy in her stomach. It wasn't enough to be an apprentice. She wanted her *own* practice. She wanted freedom to heal, not just be the moral support. She closed her eyes for a moment, trying to breathe, before peeking out. She would get what she wanted.

Caldwell and Rose spoke quietly for a moment, Rose with her feet turned out and Caldwell with his sweaty hair hanging over his forehead. He rubbed his chest as he spoke, a small smile on his lips. Dawn overheard words like *exquisite* and *perfection*, but Rose only nodded in response, conveying thanks. Caldwell lifted up a hand and brushed her cheek, and Rose's dark lashes fluttered down, stark against her pale skin. Dawn's mouth twisted downward at the corners, her brows creasing.

Caldwell's gaze flicked to Dawn in the corner, and he lowered his hand, clearing his throat.

"I'll see you tonight, Miss Waterford."

Rose backed away as Caldwell exited the room, and as her eyes caught Dawn's, a smile lit her face.

"Dawn!" She rushed over and took her hands. "I'm so relieved you're here. I'm in so much pain." She drew Dawn over to a chair on the side of the room, planting herself down, and Dawn slung her medical pouch from her shoulder.

"Is it the feet again?" she asked.

Rose nodded, unlacing one pointe shoe. She slipped off the shoe and wiggled her stockinged toes. Dawn bent down and picked up her foot, analyzing it.

"It's swollen, that's for certain," she said. She pressed into the ball of her foot. "Soaking it with salts would be best. I can give you turmeric for the pain." She dug through her pouch. "Here." She handed Rose the herbs sealed in a small glass container.

Rose gripped the container and held it to her chest. "You're a lifesaver. I don't know what I'd do without you."

"Anything for my best friend." She smiled back, but it felt forced. Dawn took in the shadows beneath Rose's eyes. She hadn't noticed them earlier. Rose's engagement was wearing on her. "Are you all right?"

Rose bit her pink lips, the color matching her cheeks. "Any day could be my last day," she whispered. "Dancing. Performing. All of it. I don't want to give it up, Dawn." Moisture gathered in her eyes, but she blinked it away.

Dawn set her satchel down and took Rose's hands. They were unusually cold. "Then don't. You don't have to marry Chester. Don't let a man get in the way of what you want to do."

Rose shook her head, tightly squeezing her eyes closed. More tears gathered in the corners.

"You know that I need the money to support my great-uncle. He's done everything for me. He raised me when no one else would take me in. I'm lucky to have an engagement at all—especially to someone with money. I would be destitute without this marriage."

It was true. After her parents had died in the war, Rose didn't have anything. Marrying Chester was her only hope of survival. Being in the company didn't pay, and once young women in this town reached a certain age unmarried, they were looked down on by society. Once she was married, she'd be a sophisticated lady. She'd have to rear children. Dancing would be a thing of the past.

Dawn used to have money, until her father gambled it all away. But she didn't care about that. The poorer she was, the more men wouldn't want her. Marrying a man would destroy her chances at doing what she loved. And she would rather die a gruesome death than give up her dream of owning her own practice. She'd promised herself she'd never be tied down and forced under a man's rule.

Both Dawn and Rose were only twenty-one, yet it was ancient compared to the girls who had already come out into society. Dawn had been a debutante six months earlier and still hadn't secured herself a husband, much to her mother's dismay.

"Things are going to be fine," Dawn said. "I'll make sure of it." Rose lifted her eyes, her perfect lips pouting. Dawn gave Rose a tight hug and pulled back. She opened her mouth to say something about Caldwell stroking her cheek, but he'd done it numerous times before. Maybe it didn't bother Rose. It was normal for a director to get close to his dancers, wasn't it?

Dawn stood and dusted off her knee-length skirt. "I should get going. Dr. Miller wants me to remove a splinter that Johnny Wilson caught in his hand. I need to get it out before it becomes infected."

"You really should be doing more than removing splinters," Rose said, wiping the tears from her cheeks. "You're much more talented than that."

"Tell that to Dr. Miller." She couldn't hide the disdain in her voice. "Besides, I don't have a choice." *Not right now anyway.* The work that Dr. Miller did was "a man's job," where she was only allowed to do work suited to "a woman." Which apparently included delivering babies and removing splinters.

It was as if her schooling had been a complete waste. She'd been lucky enough to procure a position at the University of Geneva for her residency. Dr. Miller had connections, even though she'd been only seventeen at the time. She owed everything to him. Without him, she'd never have had the chance to live her dream. She'd been the only female student in her program, but had excelled quickly, completing her training in record time. Not that it mattered. Training or no, she was still viewed as inferior in the eyes of the public.

Dawn sighed and swung her satchel over her shoulder. Thoughts of starting her own practice came to her mind again. Maybe she could do this sooner rather than later. She knew she would have future patients, as the dancers here at this school preferred a female doctor. But she couldn't afford it. And her parents would never allow it while she was under their roof. She'd have to figure out another way.

She gave Rose one last smile before leaving.

Fresh air hit her nose as she left the rehearsal hall and stepped into the theater's courtyard. Brick walkways cut through green grass on a long expanse of lawn, large oak trees interspersed through the area, black lampposts lining the walkways. Red, yellow, and orange leaves splashed through the area like a child's finger painting, brightening the muted light from above. Thin clouds stretched over the sky, moving fast behind the towering theater.

Dawn peeked up at the ominous structure with its Victorian spires shooting into the sky. Statues of twisted creatures adorned the exterior, along with intricate carvings that lined the stone walls. It seemed to bend and warp above her, growing in size until she blinked and looked away. She had never been to the ballet, and the thought of seeing Rose onstage made her chest ache with longing. But because Rose's wedding was next week, she might not get a chance.

Dawn quickly headed down the pathways, making her way across the courtyard. She kept her medical pouch close to her side, her loose dress swishing, her canvas shoes quiet on the walk. Several people were gathered underneath the trees, conversing. Ladies in low-waisted dresses and cloche hats batted their eyes at men in silk shirts with handkerchiefs and fedoras.

Johnny Wilson was probably furious she wasn't there yet. He was a butcher right in town, who treated people worse than the animals he slaughtered. She had tended to a wound of his last year—a knife accident—and when she refused to give him opium, he slapped her across the face. She believed in herbs over opiates, as the stronger drugs were addictive.

A breeze skidded across her shoulders, and she tucked her scarf closer around her neck. Her feet crunched on the fall leaves, the cool air clearing her head. She was continuing across the lawn, toward the wrought-iron gates that surrounded the courtyard, when Chester appeared in front of her.

She stopped in her tracks, digging her heels into the grassy lawn.

"There you are," he said. A smile crooked his young face, and he leaned against a tree trunk, arms crossed. "I knew you would emerge at some point." His pin-striped suit was tailored perfectly against his lean frame, his shoes shiny.

She bit down hard on her lip, forcing her gaze away. Dawn wanted nothing to do with Rose's betrothed. Yes, Rose needed the marriage to survive, but he was the perpetrator. He was a dirty cheat. She marched past him, keeping her eyes straight forward.

"Whoa, wait up." He pushed off the tree and fell into step beside her.

She kept walking. "Hello, Chester. Meet any new girls lately? How's your love life?"

An image of Chester stepping outside a brothel flashed to her mind. She'd been walking home after visiting Mrs. Smith's fevering baby, when Chester had staggered outside, shirt open, two scantily clad women on his arms. He'd clearly been drunk—slurred speech and mussed hair. The women's hands had been all over him. Rose would be devastated if she knew.

"That's what I wanted to speak with you about," Chester said, rushing to keep up with her.

"There's nothing to talk about." She'd already decided she couldn't tell Rose. As much as she supported Rose's dancing, and she didn't want her to give up her dream, she couldn't watch her become destitute. She needed to be taken care of. If Rose knew about Chester's lies, she would refuse to marry him and then her whole future would be ruined. She'd lose the opportunity to take care of herself and her great-uncle.

Chester scratched the back of his head, his fingers running through his sandy hair. Deep dimples popped out of his cheeks.

"I really like her," he answered. "Might even love her."

"You sure have a funny way of showing it."

"Dawn." Chester grabbed her arm and drew her to a stop. She glared at him, her mouth glued into a straight line. "Our engagement party is in two days," he said. "I don't want anything to ruin it. Can I trust you with this?"

She stared back at him, taking in his expectant face. The face of a liar. The face of a cheat. It was common for men to have affairs with a variety of women, but this was Rose.

Sweet, innocent Rose.

"I already told you, I'm not going to say anything. You know as well as I do that Rose needs this."

Chester visibly relaxed. "Thank you." He paused for a moment, his dimples popping out in his cheeks again, before he said, "How are you? I know it's the anniversary of your brother's—"

"I'm *fine*. Good day, Chester." Although their families used to run in the same circles, that didn't mean he was her friend. And she didn't want to think about her brother now.

She started away when a yell echoed down from the courtyard. More shouts erupted, and Dawn glanced back over her shoulder, her brows pushed together. A loud creak sounded on the air, and her eyes widened.

"Look out!" Dawn shouted.

A large tree limb broke off from one of the massive oaks in the courtyard, crashing straight down onto a man who was standing underneath the tree. The branch nearly missed the woman next to him, and she clasped her gloved hands over her mouth before she screamed.

Dawn's heart took off, and she sprinted forward with Chester by her side. Men and women had gathered around the scene, and the man underneath the large branch was writhing in pain, though he kept a surprisingly cool face.

The large limb was as thick as a man, and at least a couple hundred pounds. It was clearly too heavy to move off by himself, and a circle of men rushed forward, including Chester, who removed his coat and rolled up his sleeves. On the count of three, the men hefted the branch off of the man; all the while the woman next to him continued to scream.

"My Frederick! He's as good as dead! I can't believe I'm to become a widow. We've only been married a week."

Frederick rolled his eyes at his wife's cries. "I'll be quite all right, dear, just let these men help me and quit your whimpering." The color had drained from his face.

The men were able to roll the limb off of Frederick, but he lay panting hard, wincing.

"Doctor! We need a doctor," his wife cried.

It was as if a jolt went through Dawn, electrocuting her straight to her middle. She pushed her way forward, shoving a couple men out of the way before kneeling in front of Frederick.

"I'm a doctor," she breathed. "I'm here to help you."

Looks were exchanged around her, but Dawn didn't pay them any mind. The town was small enough that she knew the usual faces the odd looks belonged to.

Frederick's lips were tucked inward, cringing through the pain. "Aren't you a little young to be a doctor?"

Her lips lifted up wryly. "I thought you'd oppose the fact that I'm a woman." She scanned his body.

"As long as you can heal me, I don't care what you are." He hissed as Dawn touched his side.

She lifted up his shirt and felt along his torso and stomach, pressing into his soft flesh, before she analyzed his shoulder. His wife had finally stopped screaming, but she was staring down at Dawn like she had grown a second head.

"You have broken ribs and a dislocated shoulder," Dawn said. "I'm going to have to pop the shoulder back in, but I'm going to need you to sit up. Do you think you can do that? It'll hurt."

Frederick's mouth turned down, but he gave a slight nod. More sweat shimmered on his brow. "A little help?"

Chester jumped in to help and guided Frederick upward, keeping him straight with his arms.

Dawn squared Frederick's shoulders and gently took his injured arm, straightening it out before him. She positioned it at the right angle, and Frederick cried out in pain. Dawn was used to the cries of human suffering, as she'd learned to not let them affect her. She zoned in on the task before her, seeing nothing but flesh, blood, and bone. Frederick was a specimen, nothing more, an object needing to be healed. If she let herself think of him as a person—as a man with hopes and dreams, a man with a family—she wouldn't be able to focus. The world blurred in her vision, Frederick crisp and clear before her.

Without warning, she shoved the arm up and in, and the expected "pop" sounded. Frederick curled over, whimpering.

"I feel like such a weakling," he finally said. "But it's feeling better."

"It'll feel worse tomorrow." She zeroed in on Frederick's pale face. "We need to get you to Dr. Miller's clinic. Fixing a dislocated shoulder is the least of your worries. We need to bind up your ribs, and by the look of discoloration on your abdomen, you could be bleeding internally."

Frederick paled further.

"No!" His wife stepped in. Her blonde ringlets bounced. "Absolutely not. We'll take you to a *real* doctor, Freddy." She shoved Chester aside and helped Frederick to his feet. He hissed, limping on one foot. "If anything's wrong, it's because *she* touched you." She threw Dawn a dirty look. "Come on."

The crowd departed, more people giving Dawn strange looks, until she and Chester were alone. A light breeze drifted in, chilling Dawn's skin. Chester stared out in front of him, mouth pressed downward.

"You saved his life," Chester said quietly.

She shook her head. "No, he's a dead man walking."

And he was. Without proper medical care, he wouldn't last a day.

2

⸢Black Tide⸣

Dawn unwrapped her scarf from her neck as she stepped inside the main entryway of her home. She ran her hands along the silky material, her fingers lingering at the bottom. The white satin was as pale as her skin, and she marveled at the stitching that swirled along the edges of the material. It was the nicest thing she owned. It made her feel as if she could stroll in Brenton Park with a gentleman on her arm.

Not that she wanted a gentleman on her arm.

She paused in the small entryway, taking in the dusty chandelier that hung above her, tarnished to a greenish brown. Ripped carpet ran up the stairs to the few rooms that sat there, including her own tiny bedroom, adjacent to her brother's old room. A parlor was over to her left—peeling paint on the door frame. Rustling came from the back kitchen, where Mrs. Cook was probably bustling around.

They didn't have the luxury of employing a butler, valets, maids, or a chef, but Mrs. Cook did what she could around the house for the small penny she was given. She'd only been employed with the Hildegards for about a month, but already she felt more like a mother to Dawn than her own.

She'd been the one who had stitched Dawn's scarf, as a welcoming gift.

She again admired the fine material.

"Mrs. Cook, is that you?" Dawn called out. "I'm home!"

Dawn brushed her skirt and headed down the narrow hallway to the back kitchen, her footsteps clicking on the hardwood floor. When she pushed the door open, Mrs. Cook had her back turned to her, bent over, removing a pan of tea cakes from the oven. Warm spice hit her nose, and Dawn inhaled, letting the smell settle into her chest. She could live in this kitchen.

Mrs. Cook spun around and nearly dropped the pan. She abruptly set it on the table, removing her hot gloves. Her hand flew to her chest.

"Child, you scared me." The wrinkles around her mouth deepened as her eyes narrowed. A red rash spread across her cheeks, and Dawn eyed the small bumps.

"If you used a cold compress and chamomile oil it would help with the rash," she said. "I think I have some on me." She dug into her pouch, but Mrs. Cook motioned her down.

"No, child. Sit. I'm perfectly fine. Just the sun. Madam has me working in the garden lately."

Dawn tightened her lips but plopped herself down at the table. She snatched a bite of tea cake from the pan and closed her eyes, chewing, nearly moaning from how hungry she was. She couldn't remember the last time she'd eaten. Probably twenty-four hours ago.

Mrs. Cook crossed her arms over her large chest and clicked her tongue. "You know, I was a nurse in the war and even the soldiers didn't look as haggard as you. That doctor has you running ragged."

Dawn sighed, snatching another bite of warm cake. "I'm fine," she mumbled, relishing the flavor on her tongue. "I just need to eat the rest of these tea cakes and I'll be good to go."

Mrs. Cook huffed. "I don't like you being out and about. You know it's not safe right now." She eyed the newspaper on the table and scooted it over to Dawn.

Silence stretched as Dawn peered at the headline.

The Dollmaker Strikes Again.

Dawn stopped chewing, her mouth parting slightly.

"He's back?"

Mrs. Cook nodded.

Dawn swallowed hard, the cake sticking in her throat.

Everyone was talking about the Dollmaker.

He was a serial killer—a man who killed young girls and hacked off their limbs, only to sew their different body parts back together. It was said each "masterpiece" he created was made up of at least eight different women. These creations were found suspended in different positions throughout the States, their eyes blank and bodies dressed as if they were beautiful dolls. It was like *Frankenstein*—Dawn had loved that book as a child, but the thought of a man taking different body parts and sewing them together made her blood curdle.

"It's not safe for any young woman to be out."

Dawn shivered but shook her head. "As if the Dollmaker would come here to Newport."

"He's traveling," Mrs. Cook said. She pointed at the paper. "He started in New York and he's traveling north. There have been three murders since his last masterpiece."

Masterpiece.

She hated to admit it, but a sick part of her was fascinated. From what she'd heard, the man's amputations were an art. Clean and clear cut, done with perfect precision. Dawn was already fascinated with the human body as is, and his skill only intrigued her further.

Footsteps pounded down the hall, and the kitchen door swung open. Dawn's mother barged into the room, a slender finger pointed in front of Mrs. Cook's face.

"I have a guest!" she said. "*What* is taking so long? How difficult is it to provide nourishment to our guest? Are you completely useless?"

Mrs. Cook stilled, and a lump bobbed in her chubby throat. "Coming right away, madam." Her eyes darted toward Dawn before her gaze shot back up to her mother.

Dorothy Hildegard was the epitome of fashion—or at least she tried to be. A burgundy scarf was wrapped around her bobbed hair, the same brocade necklace she always wore strung around her neck. It was the only piece of jewelry she owned that spoke of money. She'd sold most of her possessions after Dawn's father had bankrupted them. She wore a handkerchief dress and a fur shawl, with gloves that stopped at her wrists.

She lived in a pretend world, acting as if they had piles of money sitting in the next room.

Her mother's eyes slowly slid to Dawn, and they lit up. "There you are. Get up. You have a guest!" She gave her the same smile she did whenever she had a potential suitor for Dawn.

Mrs. Cook hustled backward and began placing the little cakes on a platter.

Dawn sprang up from her chair. *Not another one.* "A guest? Who?"

Her mother crossed her arms, and her mouth pulled up into what Dawn knew was her version of a smile. "Arthur Hemsworth. He's quite excited to meet you. Now get up."

"Arthur *Hemsworth*? That dirty old man?" The Hemsworth name was the wealthiest in town. She knew there were several Hemsworths, but she had met only Arthur. "I can't be here!" She scrambled around as if searching for her coat. "I need to leave."

Dorothy marched over and gripped Dawn roughly around the wrist, yanking her toward the door. "I should have you change, but your appearance will have to do."

Dawn tried to wriggle out of her hold. "Stop." She struggled further. "You're right, I shouldn't be seen right now. I'm not put together."

Dorothy pushed open the parlor door and shoved Dawn forward. She stumbled, catching herself on the sofa. Her fingers gripped the tufted leather, and her eyes immediately connected with Arthur Hemsworth's.

An old man, probably in his seventies, sat on the edge of his seat with his cane planted in front of him. Wrinkles folded over his face as he frowned, gray wisps of hair swooped back over his balding, pockmarked forehead and scalp. A finely tailored suit lined his impossibly skinny frame, and his knuckles stood out where he gripped the cane, large veins in his hands.

Dorothy nudged her in the side and mumbled, "Curtsy, smile, do something."

Dawn shifted away, throwing her a glare. Her gaze settled back on the old man. "Mr. Hemsworth."

Arthur's dry lips pulled up into a smile. His eyes sparkled as he looked her over, his gaze stopping on her bosom. "I look forward to our future time together."

Dawn stiffened, before subtly leaning into her mother. "*What* is he talking about?" she asked out of the side of her mouth.

"Mr. Hemsworth has agreed to marry you," her mother said, chin lifted. "It'll be a small ceremony next week." She lowered her voice and whispered, "Don't mess this up. You came out into society *six* months ago and you still haven't snatched a husband. This is your last shot. And Arthur Hemsworth is *very* rich." She straightened and gave Arthur a smile.

Arthur's gaze continued to roam over Dawn's body with a hungry look, and Dawn placed her hands on her abdomen, trying to breathe. Everything she had ever hoped for tumbled down in her mind like a landslide. Her practice. Her dream of being a doctor.

Owning her own clinic. It was all going to be taken away in an instant—by this old, dirty man.

"No," she said outright, voice trembling. "I won't. I'm sorry."

Arthur's face faltered, and his heavy-lidded eyes narrowed. Dawn knew she was acting like a child, but she didn't care. She'd stomp her foot and cry if she had to. Nothing could make her marry him. She wasn't sure how she had the ability to move, but she strode past the old man and swept out of the room, exiting to the front entryway. Shaking, she threw open the front door. Her mother shouted after her, but she stormed forward until something made her stop dead in her tracks.

A man stood before her, his hand raised like he was about to knock, a long black coat gliding along his lean frame. Dark eyes peered down at her, the shaded light from the trees deepening his defined bones. He had pockets for cheeks and sleek black hair that was combed smoothly against his head. He fixed his face into a glare.

"Is this the Hildegard residence?" he said curtly.

Dawn faltered back, blinking. She peeked behind her to the door, then faced him again.

"Who are you?"

His lips pressed tightly together. "I asked if this was the Hildegard residence."

She swiped a hand through her tangled hair while staring him down. She'd had a long day. First, waking up groggy from lack of sleep; second, the spectacle in the courtyard, and then finding out her life was being planned out for her. She didn't like this man's directness, and she wasn't about to let him make her day any worse.

"Is there something I can help you with Mr.—?"

The man puffed up his chest before exhaling. "I am Gideon Hemsworth. I was told my uncle was here."

Dawn's brows shot up to her forehead. "Arthur Hemsworth is your uncle?"

"Great-uncle, yes."

She swallowed down her surprise. She didn't know why he was here, but it couldn't be good. Anyone related to that disgusting man was bad news.

"Here to celebrate his engagement?" she said. "I hear some poor girl is being roped into marrying him."

"More like the other way around," he said darkly. "Now, will you show me to my uncle? You look like you work here, that you know your way around."

"Like I work . . .?" She peeked down at her loose gray dress before peering back up at him. She held in a smile. "You're right. I *do* know my way around here, and I can assure you that the residents of this house *don't* want you here."

Gideon kept his weight planted into the ground, and his severe eyes attacked her once more. "It appears that I'll need to make sure the residents of this house know how their *help* is speaking to me." His lips flattened. "Though I don't know how they can afford you."

He looked over the Hildegards' small stone apartment jammed between identical adjacent homes.

"If you'll excuse me." He brushed past Dawn and let himself into the house without another word. She stared after where he'd disappeared, her brows pressed firmly together. The nerve of that man. Assuming she was the *help*? Just because she didn't dress like . . . like Rose.

Gideon Hemsworth.

The name stuck in her throat. She couldn't get the image of his face out of her mind. She had never met someone so distinctive-looking before. She was used to conversing with many different people in her line of work, and they all blended together in a sea of ordinary faces. But Gideon Hemsworth . . .

She shook her head. He was Arthur Hemsworth's grandnephew. He was the enemy.

Shivering, she marched down the front steps, shoving him from her mind. She wanted nothing to do with anyone who had that last name.

⁂

Dawn entered the town square, wishing she had grabbed her scarf. Sunlight pounded down through the fall air, but it did nothing to warm her bones. She rubbed her arms as she made her way across the cobblestone road. Small shops were squeezed tightly together in a variety of colors. A bakery, a toy shop, sweets—there was even a fortune teller, across from Dr. Miller's office. Flowers hung from the balconies, and a large fountain roared in the middle of the square. People bustled to and fro, laughing, shopping; children darted around their mothers' skirts.

Years ago she'd had the money to shop freely, but she couldn't remember what it was like to walk into a fabric shop and pick out the finest materials. But she didn't care about material things. She cared about helping people. And wearing the finest silk wouldn't do much good while tending to a bloody patient.

She hurried across the square, edging past a group of women huddled around a newspaper.

The breeze blew in, rustling the paper, and she peeked over at the headline.

Dead body found in Jamestown.

Dawn halted in her steps, another breeze whooshing into her from the side. Jamestown was only three miles away. Mrs. Cook was right. The Dollmaker was traveling. She shivered, the shakes rocketing down her body. Sights and sounds blurred together as she stared at the paper.

"That's four murders so far," a woman said. She pointed at the paper. "He started in New York and he's headed here." The woman had a stoop, and Dawn analyzed her posture. It wouldn't be hard to fix if she manipulated her spine.

The woman next to her squealed, her gloved hand flying over her mouth. "It says she had an arm missing. Can you imagine?"

"I wonder how he kills them," another whispered.

"I hear he plays with his victims before he sets them on display," another woman whispered. "You know . . . sexually."

"He does not!" the first woman whacked her in the arm. "Don't be absurd!"

A third woman shrugged. "It's what I heard."

"He has to be out of his mind."

"He could be anyone."

"He could be here right *now*."

The women squealed again, and another set of shivers spread along Dawn's back. The Dollmaker couldn't be traveling to Newport, could he? Why would he come to their small town? Nothing happened here. Nothing but gossip. She shook her head and strode past the women, continuing to head across the square, but little goosebumps still covered her arms. She opened the door to Dr. Miller's office. A bell jingled when she walked in.

Inside, a long workbench stood against the far wall, and shelving lined the other three walls. Various bottles of herbs and medicines filled the shelves, along with books on anatomy and surgical procedures. An operating table sat in the middle of the space, its sheets clean and white under the lamp that hovered overhead. Dr. Miller always made sure that the entire room was disinfected, including all the tools that were spread out across the workbench.

He was away on business—Mr. Roper's foot needed to be amputated from stepping on a nail earlier this month—and no matter how hard Dawn begged to come and assist, he refused, not only because he thought Mr. Roper wouldn't approve of a woman assisting but also because a young lady shouldn't be exposed to such things.

So Dawn read. If she couldn't experience medical procedures in real life, she would read about them until she could open her own practice. She brushed her fingertips along the books that lined the shelves, stopping on *Treatise of the Operations of Surgery*. She had read it earlier this week when Dr. Miller had first heard about Mr. Roper's condition. She recalled the text of the book. "Cut quick with a crooked knife before covering the stump with the remaining skin. Have the patient bite down on a piece of wood for pain relief when ether isn't available. If the wound is only in the flesh, you may bathe it with brandy and cover the part with a compressed dip in a warm wine quickened with spir vini."

She could almost see the flesh before her—feel the knife in her hand. Her heart sped at the thought of cutting away the infectious disease that could shorten someone's life. She was the one who held the power to heal.

The bell jingled as Dr. Miller walked in, his mustache turned down. His gray hair stuck out to the sides, wispy behind his ears. Wrinkles creased his mouth as he pursed his lips. He set a couple bags on the floor.

"Sir, I didn't expect you here so soon," Dawn said. "How did it . . . how did it go?"

He shook his head, lines around his eyes. "It was too late when I got there. The fever took him." He walked over to the sink and rinsed his hands before wiping his face.

Dawn swallowed down the lump in her throat. "His family?"

"Left six kids behind. Lives out of town on a large farm. It'll be impossible for his wife to keep up on her own. She'll need to remarry or sell."

Dawn bit down hard at the injustice of it all. Who was to say Mrs. Roper couldn't handle the farm on her own? It was her land as much as Mr. Roper's. And now she had to give up her whole life because her husband was dead? It was unfair that she had to lose the man she loved because medicine wasn't advanced enough—because they didn't get there in time.

"I see that look on your face," Dr. Miller said. "It's the same look you had when I hired you."

"It's just not fair," she said.

Dr. Miller wiped his hands off with a towel and moved over to the vials of different herbs and medicines on the shelving next to him. "The world wasn't made for women, Dawn. I'll agree with you there. The world has a skewed view of what is proper and improper. If I hadn't been old friends with your father, I wouldn't have hired you. But I do see something in you, and I knew you'd be of great use to me."

"Then let me help you," she said. "*Really* help you. Let me show you how I can truly be of use. You hardly trust me."

Dr. Miller raised a tangled brow. "You're lucky I'm letting you be my assistant as it is, but even though you've finished your schooling, there is a line. The line is there to protect you, and I won't cross it. Even though I have different beliefs from my fellow men, it doesn't mean I'm going to put you in harm's way. There are many people out there who don't want a woman touching them. Even though it's the twentieth century, there are still superstitious folk who believe a woman healer might be dabbling in dark things."

"Like a witch?" Dawn laughed. "That would be the fortune-teller across the square, not me. The Salem witch trials were a long time ago, and like you said, it's the twentieth century."

He shook his head and straightened out a few vials. "If I were really trying to protect you, I'd send you home and forget this nonsense, but for some reason I'm a madman and have a soft spot for you." He smiled a warm smile. He paused on one vial and turned. "But maybe I'm just enough of a madman to bend the rules a little bit."

Dawn's heart quickened. "Really?"

"I have a tonsillectomy tomorrow. Would you like to assist me?"

"Yes," Dawn said quickly. "Definitely yes."

"Good. Then you can make sure my tools are sterile and that we have plenty of ether on hand. Now if you'll excuse me, I need to rest, lest I accidentally slit that poor boy's throat tomorrow."

He turned and headed toward the back room behind his office, where a small bed was made up. He spent more nights here than he did in his home. It was the job.

"Good night," Dawn said, her voice rising at the end. She coughed, clearing her throat. Hopefully, she hadn't caught anything from visiting Mrs. Smith's sick baby earlier this week. No, she always made sure she wore gloves and a mask when handling the sick.

Dr. Miller waved good-bye and disappeared behind the far door. Night had begun to descend, and she thought she'd better get home. Crazed Dollmaker or not, it wasn't safe for a young lady to be out alone after dark. She quickly ducked out of the office and made her way back, hoping Arthur Hemsworth and his insufferable nephew had left.

3

The Gift

The next day, excitement buzzed underneath Dawn's skin as she stood in the studio watching the girls dance. She came to check in on Rose to see if her feet were feeling better. White tutus swished before her; pointe shoes were quick on the ground. The girls circled one another, arms floating through the air, with Caldwell pounding a stick hard on the floor, keeping tempo. The morning light slanted in on their flawless faces, heads turning side to side as they glided together.

A golden curl had escaped from Rose's bun, cascading down her back. Dawn smiled at the sight. It was the first time in a while she hadn't seen Rose done up perfectly, from her lips to her lashes to her hair. Just the small flaw made her seem human. When they were little, they'd play outside for hours, and Rose always took great care not to soil her dresses, while Dawn always came home with green and brown stains on her stockings and skirts.

Rose flittered around the studio, her carriage light and wraith-like. The rest of the girls struggled to move in sync. A couple bumped into each other, and Caldwell tapped his stick harder. They were all orphans like Rose, and clearly not living up to the standards of the theater. Dawn couldn't stop thinking about the tonsillectomy she was to assist with later that day. It would be her first real surgery since medical school, and her palms itched in anticipation. She could almost feel the cool steel in her hand, the weight of the heavy knife. She imagined herself hovering over the patient, preparing for the incision.

"No!" Caldwell yelled. "Stop!" The music ceased, and he tapped his stick harder. "Land your pirouettes in fifth. Use your spot to bring the turn fully around. Dig your standing legs into the floor!"

Rose peeked back at Dawn and gave her a small smile. Dawn waved back and pointed at Rose's feet, lifting her eyebrows. Rose gave a soft nod, before turning back to Caldwell. Good. Her feet were feeling better.

Knowing that Rose was feeling better, Dawn decided it was time to prep for surgery. Even though the procedure only took seconds, the preparations would take much longer. The instruments would need to be disinfected and arranged, the bedding cleaned, the ether prepared. Dawn spun to the door and rammed into something hard. Strong arms gripped her shoulders, pushing her back, and Gideon Hemsworth's face came into view. The young gentleman's expression seemed to falter, as if taking a minute to recognize her, before his dark brows pushed over his eyes.

"What are you doing here?" Dawn gasped.

The room paused, and Dawn edged away from him.

"Ah, Gideon, welcome." Caldwell marched forward with outstretched arms. "Ladies, I'd like to introduce you to the new owner of the theater, Mr. Hemsworth."

Dawn inched farther off to the side. Rose stiffened, her cheeks flushing. Whispers erupted through the room as Gideon straightened his coat.

He had bought the theater? What would he want to do with a theater? Wasn't he busy enough being the nephew of a dirty old man?

Gideon eyed Dawn for another moment before he faced the class. Shadows played off the fine grooves of his face, dark, like his tailored coat. He kept his expression grim.

"*Coppelia* is to open next week," Gideon said, "and I'll be assisting with all rehearsals to make sure everything is up to par. I won't sit back and watch like the other owners before me. You should expect to see me and be prepared to take my criticism. If you don't, I'll ask you to leave. I won't have a mediocre ballet theater on my hands."

Caldwell rubbed a hand over his chest, his white shirt open. His gaze skated over to Rose before it returned to Gideon. Sweat ran down the girls' faces and necks, their black tunics sticking to their skin. They stood frozen, waiting for Gideon to proceed.

He stared the group down for a few more moments, his angular features lit by the sunlight. He then cleared his throat and said, "Good day." He eyed Dawn once more. "You." He gripped her upper arm. "Come with me."

Gideon pulled her outside the studio, clicking the door shut behind them. Dawn stumbled after him into the hallway, her arm aching from his hold. She yanked away and rubbed the sore spot.

"I beg your pardon. What is wrong with you?" she asked.

"I'm in the right mind to ask you the same question."

Dawn folded her arms, lifting her chin a notch. "Oh?"

His lips flicked up to the side before they returned to their pursed position. "You're a clever one, aren't you? Determined to infiltrate my entire life for your purposes. First, with my uncle, then here with the theater. What are you doing here?"

"I have no idea what you mean. What with your uncle? You mean our nonexistent engagement?"

Both of their questions hung unanswered in the air.

They stared each other down, but she refused to answer first. The last thing she needed was to feel inferior to another man.

Gideon heaved out a breath, running a hand over his face. "I meant that I know who you are. You're Dawn Hildegard. You lied to me about being a servant. Probably so you could escape under my nose and not face me regarding your plan to steal my uncle's fortune."

Dawn blurted out a laugh. Tears sprung to her eyes and she covered her mouth. The large outburst was quite unladylike, but she didn't care. He already didn't think of her as a lady.

"First of all, I didn't lie about being the help. You *assumed*. And second, I want nothing to do with your uncle. He's disgusting and rancid and a foul human being."

Surprise lit Gideon's eyes, and his mouth opened some. "You do realize you are talking about my family."

Dawn kept her chin lifted.

After a moment, he said, "You're not wrong." His mouth twisted. "The old man *is* a beast, and half the time I can hardly carry on with him."

"Well, that we can agree on."

"Doesn't mean that I trust you. You can hate the old man and still want his money."

Dawn sighed, releasing her anger. She was tired of being mad. "You don't know me. If you did, then you'd help me get *out* of this engagement."

He eyed her suspiciously but didn't comment. Instead, he said, "You still haven't told me why you're here."

She tilted her head, not sure if it was a demand or not. "My job," she said. "I'm doing my job."

"Which is?"

"Oh, so now you want to know what I do instead of assuming I'm the help?" Her anger rose again. "You don't need to know any more about me. Only that I want nothing to do with your uncle or *you*. Now, if you'll excuse me, I have somewhere I need to be."

"And where is that?" He raised a thick, dark brow.

"I'm off to find another old man I can swindle money out of," she said and left.

⸻ ⸻ ⸻

A shudder went through Dawn as she exited the building. Heat pounded beneath her skin, and the cool air around her did nothing to stop the flush in her cheeks. She placed her hands over her face, waiting for the heat to subside.

Gideon had taken her by surprise. He'd flustered her when she was never flustered. No man made her feel inferior. She was used to men looking down on her, but she never let it affect her. Yet something about Gideon set her nerves on edge.

His distinct façade made him appear as if he would be good company, but he was abrasive and dark. She hardly disliked anyone outright, but he was number two on her list, right behind his uncle.

Shaking her head, she brushed off her skirt and made the trek to Dr. Miller's office. She really should have gone home to see if Mrs. Cook needed anything from town before heading to the clinic, but the thought of facing her mother kept her feet moving in the opposite direction. Her mother was furious that she'd walked out on Arthur Hemsworth the day before—she had given her a lecture the minute she returned home that evening—but Dawn had marched upstairs and slammed her door, refusing to talk.

Stepping out of the theater's courtyard, she headed down the street, where leaves were scattered on the ground, the smell of refuse stinking in the gutters. Cars rumbled down the street—a luxury not all could afford. Dawn still rented a horse-drawn carriage when she needed transportation—though they were starting to become nonexistent. Gentlemen tipped their caps as she walked by. She kept her gloved hands linked in front of her, trying not to make eye contact. Even though it was the middle of the day, she knew better than to smile or give any man an indication that she might be interested in them. Women were taken advantage of in this town.

She turned another corner, heading past the local pub, when shouting erupted from inside. The door to the pub flew open and her father staggered out. His salt-and-pepper hair stuck out in all directions, and his clothes were rumpled. Another man followed him, waving his hands in the air and shouting. Her father ran back at the man, trying to ram into him from the front, but the man shoved him back, and her father toppled onto his backside.

"Father!" Dawn rushed forward, bending down next to him. She quickly checked his body for injuries, but there was only a nasty scrape on his cheek. She gently touched the side of his face, and he whacked her arm back.

"Don't fuss over me, child. I'm fine." His speech was slurred, and the smell of whiskey stung Dawn's nose. He tried to sit up, but Dawn pushed him back down.

"No, you're not. Let me look at this wound." Bits of dirt and stones were stuck to his bloody face. "You need to let me clean this up."

He pushed her away again. "I'm fine. I don't need any of your silly doctor stuff. You're already an embarrassment as it is."

Dawn jerked back, clamping her jaws together.

Her father scrambled to his feet and tipped sideways. Dawn gripped his arm, holding him upright.

"Let me help you home," she said.

This time, he didn't push her away. He mumbled something incoherent and Dawn pulled him along the sidewalk. They walked down the street, Dawn keeping a firm grip on her father, his footsteps meandering from side to side.

"You shouldn't be drinking," she said. "The prohibition is in effect. Alcohol should only be used for medicinal purposes." Though she believed it should've been avoided at all costs.

"It is medicccinal," he slurred. "You know my leg has hurt ever since the war."

The war.

She knew his leg only hurt in his mind, not physically. He blamed everything on the war.

"You're in trouble," he continued. "You've really done it this time, walking out on that suitor of yours."

"Arthur Hemsworth is not my suitor."

"To your mother he is. Already has your wedding dress picked out, she doesss."

His words slurred again.

"She wouldn't be trying to marry me off if you hadn't lost all our savings. And what was that about back there? You owe that man money?"

Her father frowned, mumbling something incoherent again.

Her hand tightened on his arm. "You can't keep this up. Drinking is bad for the liver. It's going to kill you."

"Like how you killed your brother?" He spat, tipping sideways again.

Dawn paused and the world skidded to a halt.

"Excuse me?" Her heart galloped in her chest, constricting tightly. "You know it's not my fault."

"Tell that to your mother." His eyelids drooped. "She loved him. She wishes it had been *you*."

Dawn inhaled sharply. Her lips went numb and she could hardly speak. "Well, it wasn't," she choked out. "And no one loved Joseph more than I did."

Her father started forward once more, and Dawn rushed to catch up to him.

"I know you don't mean these words, Papa. It's because you're drunk. I know you don't truly blame me for Joseph's death. Mother, I can believe . . . but . . ."

"Go along, child," he said. "Go off and play your games while you can. You'll be married soon enough, and it'll put all of this nonsense to an end."

Dawn paused on the small walkway as her father continued on. He could see himself home.

<center>~~~~~ ~~~~~ ~~~~~</center>

"I'm sorry I'm late!"

Dawn rushed into the clinic and removed her coat and gloves. She retrieved an apron that was hanging next to the door and wrapped it around her body. Brushing the loose strands of dark hair off her face, she focused in on the scene before her.

A boy sat on the operating table, his hair wild, like he had been rolling in the dirt. A woman who had to be his mother stood by his side, her hand on his bony back. Dr. Miller's mouth was tucked in to the side.

"This is Amos Johanson," Dr. Miller said. "We'll be performing his tonsillectomy today."

Dawn swallowed, her pulse thrumming. She moved over to the workbench where the tools and knives lay.

"I already disinfected them," Dr. Miller said.

She nodded, spinning back to the scene. "Shall we get to it then?"

The mother's hand tightened on her son's back. "Are you sure that it's safe?"

"It's a common procedure," Dawn said without waiting for Dr. Miller to speak. "It won't take more than thirty seconds per side."

The woman raised her brows at Dr. Miller. "Dawn is my assistant. She'll be helping today. It seems as if she's a little enthusiastic."

Heat warmed Dawn's cheeks, and she peeked over at Mrs. Johanson. She waited for the woman to object to her helping, but she didn't.

"Dawn, if you'll explain the procedure to Mrs. Johanson."

Silence fell, and Dawn twisted her fingers in front of her, before stretching them out straight. She cleared her throat. "We'll start by applying a few drops of ether onto a sponge to administer the anesthetic. Once Amos is relaxed, we'll remove each tonsil. It'll be quick and easy. I promise."

Mrs. Johanson nodded, but her chin quivered.

Dawn blew out a loud breath. "Let's get started then." She headed over to the basin to disinfect her hands, using a bar of lye soap to wash them. She snatched a pair of rubber gloves and snapped them on.

Dr. Miller motioned her forward, and Dawn brought the tray of instruments over to the patient, setting them on a small wooden table adjacent to the bed. Dr. Miller poured the ether onto the sponge and administered the anesthetic, and soon, little Amos was relaxed, mouth parted slightly. His mother hovered off to the side, her hands clasped over her mouth.

Dr. Miller took a tongue depressor, peered inside Amos's mouth, and grunted. He grabbed the forceps and they disappeared inside the young boy's mouth. He motioned for Dawn to hand him the blade. Even though it was only a few seconds, it felt like an eternity before Dr. Miller emerged with one red tonsil. Blood trickled out of the boy's mouth, running down his chin. Dr. Miller plopped the swollen tonsil into a dish before handing the forceps to Dawn.

"Why don't you try the other one?" Dr. Miller asked.

Dawn froze, staring at the tool before her. "Me?"

"Take it before I change my mind."

Dawn tentatively lifted her hand and took the sharp tool from Dr. Miller's hands. She placed it neatly on the tray before grabbing the forceps. She held steady, staring down at her patient. This was everything she'd dreamed about. Standing above a patient, ready to cut into human flesh and remove the disease from a body. She was a healer. It was what she did. Though her legs began to tremble, shaking, as if the earth were opening up beneath her. The young boy reminded her of Joseph, and suddenly it was all she could see. Joseph's frail body in front of her, cold and still, his eyes open and glazed. The air no longer pushing in and out of his lungs . . .

Dawn shook the thoughts away and gripped the forceps tighter, forcing herself to focus.

It was just her and the patient. Joseph wasn't here. She zoomed in on young Amos's face. Nothing else existed. Her mind focused until all she could see was the red infection, a swollen tonsil in the back of the boy's throat. She dipped inside and grabbed the remaining spongy red organ with the forceps and pulled it toward her. Taking the knife, she made a few small cuts, separating the tissue. She plopped the small chunk of flesh into the basin with a wet splat, bright red blood spilling outward.

The world rushed back, and Dawn focused on Mrs. Johanson's relieved face.

Dr. Miller crossed his arms, his mouth curving upward. "Well done."

"His throat will hurt," Dawn said, the adrenaline from the procedure slowly fading. "But for no more than a week or so. He'll be good as new soon."

Mrs. Johanson wiped her eyes. "Thank you."

She said it to Dawn, not Dr. Miller, and for the first time, something new bloomed inside her chest.

Appreciation.

4
Living Dead

T hank you.

The words resonated over and over again in Dawn's mind
as she made her way back home. Those two simple words Mrs.
Johanson had given her had taken root in the pit of her belly, slowly
growing like roots spreading outward, tangling with her veins.

Dark clouds shifted across the night sky as her feet clopped quietly on the cobblestones. The scent of rain hung heavy in the air, as
if the fat clouds above would burst at any moment. A slight breeze
skidded across the backs of her shoulders, and she tucked her coat
closer around her. She hated that her work often took her to walking
the streets at night. But she couldn't predict when patients would
need her help.

At the edge of the town square, a figure was leaning against a
lamppost. Its warm glow highlighted a man, his legs stretched out in
front of him. He tilted his head as she approached, his shadow in the
dim light a dark extension from the post.

Dawn skirted away from the man, edging along the shops that
lined the square, but the man straightened and stepped toward her.
She picked up the pace, but he followed, his lean presence still a

shadow in the dark. She picked up her feet and began to run—a man in the dark of night could never be good news—and the thought of the Dollmaker flashed to mind.

"Leave me alone," she called out. Her heart was hammering in her chest, and she tried to push out even breaths. Adrenaline had hit, and she knew it was just her blood circulation preparing her muscles to act.

"Dawn."

The name rang loud and clear through the night, the word slicing right through her being. She paused, her heart still thumping in her ears. She spun to face him.

"What do you want?"

Gideon emerged from the dark, the light from another lamppost highlighting half his face. It cast a warm glow over his features. His eyes were two dark hollows, matching his cheeks.

"Waiting for you. I asked around and discovered you worked with Dr. Miller. So you are a healer, then. I didn't believe you back at the theater."

"I'm a doctor, yes." She let out a shaky breath.

A smile played on the corners of his lips. "And what on earth would make you want to do such a thing?"

Why, indeed. She knew she was an anomaly—that girls her age were more interested in parties and finding wealthy husbands. She'd always been different.

Well, since her brother . . .

"And why should that matter to you?" she asked instead.

"Hmm." He took another step forward. "Answering a question with a question."

They stood in silence for a moment, another breeze pushing over Dawn's face.

"Tell me why you're here, Mr. Hemsworth."

"Gideon. Call me Gideon."

"All right. Gideon." The name felt foreign on her tongue, and she rolled it around in her mouth.

He linked his hands behind his back and slowly began to walk around her. His legs were long and lean, his head tipped downward.

"I need your expertise. I've already gone to Dr. Miller. And he won't help me."

"Expertise?"

"Medical expertise, yes."

A myriad of questions rose in her mind, but she clamped them down. "What do you mean?"

Gideon paused his circling and faced Dawn head on. "It's of a delicate nature. I'm afraid it isn't very proper."

Dawn held in a laugh. "If you haven't noticed, Gideon, I'm not your usual lady."

Something lit behind his eyes—amusement? Hesitancy? "No, you're not." He began his pacing again and said, "I assume you've heard about the murders?"

Dawn went cold. "You mean the Dollmaker?"

Gideon nodded. "I'm sure you've heard about his ... tastes."

She kept still, waiting.

"I need you to do some research for me. It's of a personal matter."

"What kind of research?"

He gripped her elbow and pulled her up against the nearest building. A large basket of flowers hung outside a door, their colors muted in the dim light.

"The Dollmaker clearly has medical knowledge or he wouldn't be able to do what he does. The amputations. The way he works with the human body."

"And what does that have to do with me?" Her pulse picked up.

"I have information on him. I've been studying him, and I need someone to help me."

"Help you with what? I still don't understand."

"Help me find him!" he burst out.

Blinking, Dawn edged back against the building. His sudden outburst shook her.

"I think I need to leave," Dawn said, and she hated the way her voice trembled. She didn't want him to know he had any power over her.

"Wait." Gideon held up a hand. "I'm sorry. It's just . . ." He heaved out a breath. "I just really need this, all right? The Dollmaker took something of mine and I need to make him pay."

Dawn eyed him suspiciously. "You mean," She swallowed. "A girl?"

"That doesn't matter. What matters is that I need a medical professional to help me find this man. He'd need medical tools. He'd need medicine—I assume. He'd need—" He broke off. "I've tried every avenue, and this is my last thought, my last resort."

There was a softness in Gideon that Dawn had never seen before. Where he had come off so cold and hardened in her first two encounters with him, he now was standing before her vulnerable, clearly desperate. But she wasn't going to help him find a mass murderer. Being tied to him socially would cause problems. She couldn't let consorting with a man ruin her reputation.

"I'm sorry, Gideon," she said. "I can't help you. Now if you'll excuse me." She brushed past him, but a chill had settled in her bones. The thought of finding that madman made her stomach twist, and she couldn't believe Gideon had asked her to help with such a thing.

"Wait, please," Gideon called after her.

But she continued walking, leaving him alone in the dark.

<hr />

Banging sounded from the front door of her home, and Dawn sat upright in bed. She heard shouting, and it took her a moment to realize it was coming from *inside* her house. Her feet met the cool floorboards before she quickly grabbed her robe, wrapping it around herself over her thin nightgown. She slid on her slippers and peeked outside her door, peering down the stairs to the frazzled woman standing inside her entryway.

She was speaking at an ungodly volume, and Mrs. Cook was waving her down, trying to get the woman to stop. Dawn's eyebrows shot up as she recognized Frederick's wife, from the courtyard the other day.

"Where *is* she?" the woman demanded. She pushed past Mrs. Cook, glancing around the home. "I need her now!"

"It's six a.m.," Mrs. Cook said. Her hair was still pinned to her head and her own robe cascaded to the floor. Her facial rash seemed extra red in the lamplight. "Come back at a decent hour."

"No!" Her eyes flicked around the space before they caught Dawn at the top of the stairs. "There you are! Get down here now. There's no time to waste."

Dawn wrapped her robe tighter around her body and slowly moved down the stairs. "Is Frederick all right?" The vision of the tree limb crashing down on him surged to her mind.

"No, he's not all right. He has a fever higher than the fire in my hearth, and he's as pale as a ghost. His breaths are labored and . . ." She set a hand to her forehead. "I'm too young to become a widow."

The woman had said they'd only been married a week.

"Where is he?" Dawn asked.

"At home, of course. I couldn't find Dr. Miller, so you were my last resort. You have to help me."

Dawn was beginning to feel like everyone's last resort. Gideon had said the same words to her.

"Fine," Dawn said. "Let's go." She grabbed her coat off a hanger, along with her silk scarf, which she wrapped tightly around her neck.

Mrs. Cook's eyes widened in surprise. "You can't go out like that! In your nightclothes."

"I highly doubt Frederick will care how I'm dressed," Dawn said. She nodded to the woman before grabbing her medical bag. "Let's go."

Frederick's wife drove the automobile, which rumbled beneath them. Its headlights illuminated the streets in the dim morning light, and she took the turns as fast as the vehicle would go. Dawn had only ridden in an automobile once, when her father had borrowed one from a neighbor a few years ago.

The sun hadn't shown its face yet, and billowing gray clouds hung in the sky, the air blowing in the open windows. They approached a building on the outskirts of town, where the structures were packed tightly together, with steps leading up to every door. The car came to a stop, its brakes emitting a loud screech in the silent morning.

Frederick's wife jumped out of the car and rushed up the front steps, Dawn following behind.

The inside of the home was similar to Dawn's in layout—stairs leading up to the second level, a small main foyer opening up to other rooms—if a bit nicer. Where cracks and peeling brocade wallpaper lined Dawn's walls, Frederick's home was polished and pristine.

"In here," Frederick's wife said and led her into the downstairs back bedroom.

Frederick lay on a small wrought-iron bed with a striped mattress, his body seeming to have shrunk to half its size since she'd last seen him. No longer was he the lively man that Dawn had met in the courtyard but a shell of that person. Kerosene lamps burned on the side tables, casting an eerie glow on Frederick's small frame.

His thin chest rose and fell beneath his open white shirt, wheezing breaths echoing through the room.

"It seems to get worse every hour," his wife said.

Dawn turned to her and asked, "What is your name?"

"It's Gertrude," the woman said, wiping a tear from her eye. "Can you do anything?"

Dawn set a hand on her arm. "Gertrude, everything is going to be okay." She moved over to the bed and gently unbuttoned Frederick's shirt further. He stirred, his eyes glazed, barely focusing on Dawn.

"My savior," he choked out, wheezing again. A faint smile lifted his face.

The skin on Frederick's abdomen was a deep purple, a clear indication of internal hemorrhaging. Dawn had been right. She set a hand on his sweaty forehead. He was warm. Really warm. Dawn placed two fingertips underneath the line of his stubbled jaw, feeling his racing heartbeat.

"He's been vomiting," Gertrude said. "And every time he does, he curls up in pain. I have a maid, Clara, who says she has some healing knowledge, but she hasn't been of any help."

"We could use some wild geranium or birthroot," Dawn said. "That would slow the bleeding." But Dawn knew it would only slow the inevitable. She knew the look of death when she saw it. There was a scent heavy in the air, and it settled in her nose like poison. "But I think we should just use some laudanum. Make him comfortable." Her voice caught at the end. She didn't believe in using opiates, but she kept some in her bag just in case—for incidents like this.

Gertrude nodded, clearly not understanding what Dawn meant. "All right. Yes. Make him comfortable."

Dawn removed the small bottle from her bag and uncorked it, placing it to Frederick's mouth. His lips trembled, but he was able to swallow, his skin a sick shade of white.

Gertrude hung in the back, her face as pale as her husband's. "Now what?"

"Get me a cold washrag." Another attempt to make him comfortable.

Gertrude bustled over to a washbasin, dipped a rag into the water, and brought it over. Dawn spread it across his forehead, and he moaned. The two women stood over Frederick's body, Dawn wondering how to tell Gertrude that her husband was about to die—that there was nothing she could do—and Gertrude with her hands covering her face, tears still in her eyes.

She hated feeling helpless. She hated her lack of knowledge. If only she knew more. If only she had read more books, studied harder, maybe she'd know what to do. But she was certain Dr. Miller would be as helpless as she was.

Dawn zoned in on Frederick's body as she patted the washcloth over his face and neck. She could almost see the blood flowing through his veins. Earlier this week he had been full of life, full of color, and it had been taken away from him in less than a heartbeat. None of them knew how long they had. How fragile life was, like petals on a flower, blooming just long enough to show their beauty before it was too late. She could tell Frederick was a good man, and she suddenly wanted to know everything about him. She'd always forced herself not to care about her patients—she viewed them as specimens needing to be healed. It was too hard to think of them as people. But seeing Frederick lying there, she wondered what kind of void he would leave in this world. Did he have family? Would they miss him? What were his talents? Would he be forgotten?

It wasn't fair that death was inevitable. The thought that everyone had an expiration date sent a chill through her. When would she face the same fate?

Dawn and Gertrude stood over his body for a long while—long enough for the morning light to slant through the window. The sunlight streamed through the curtains, shifting over Frederick's sickly face, moving as if in slow motion, just like time passing, between them.

Just as Dawn's mind started to drift into a numb haze, Frederick's body suddenly stiffened and was wracked with shakes. His eyes rolled into the back of his head, the whites showing, his mouth open. A seizure. The bed rattled as his entire body thrashed back and forth. Dawn's heart spiked and she rushed over, turning him onto his side, pinning him to the bed.

Gertrude started screaming, her hands hovering over her husband. "Do something! You have to do something!"

"I'm trying!" Dawn cried. "The best we can do is wait it out!"

"What about that herb?" Gertrude yelled. "The birthroot or whatever it was. Do you have it?"

"Yes, it's in my bag, But—"

"Give it to him!"

Dawn shook her head. As much as she wanted to help Frederick, she knew he only had a short time left. "Gertrude, you need to prepare."

"Prepare for *what*?" Anger lined her face before fear hovered behind her expression. She threw herself over her husband as Frederick continued to thrash on the bed. Dawn still held him down. "You witch!" she yelled. "You did this to him!"

Dawn faltered, her hold loosening.

"You were there the day the limb fell. And now he's possessed with the devil. Look at him. And now you're refusing to help him!"

"No," Dawn choked out. "That's not true. Your husband is hemorrhaging. It's too late to save him. He—"

"Help!" Gertrude cried. She sprinted to the door and called out into the hallway. "Help! Clara, call the authorities." She whirled on Dawn. "I'll have you put away for this. I'll have them lock you away until you will regret what you've done here."

Dawn glanced back and forth from Gertrude to her flailing husband. Her breathing sped up, her mind raced, but she wouldn't back away from the bed. She had taken an oath to help others in need, and even though Gertrude was threatening her, she wouldn't leave Frederick alone.

Footsteps sounded from upstairs, beating in time with her heart. She peeked down at Frederick again, and his body stilled. His face slackened, and his breaths stopped. His eyes stayed open, and everything paused.

The heavy scent of death settled on the air, suffocating her, filling her lungs. Gertrude was still yelling, but Dawn barely heard it. Her voice was muffled behind the pulse hammering in her head.

"I . . ."

The footsteps pounded faster.

"Help!" Gertrude screamed.

Dawn snapped to attention and everything zoomed back into focus. Gertrude's body guarding the door. Frederick lifeless in bed. The rushing footsteps distinct. She hurried over to the door and shoved Gertrude aside. The woman cried out, still yelling, and Dawn bolted down the hall. A maid, who Dawn assumed was Clara, raced down the stairs, but Dawn threw open the front door and hurled herself outside. Fresh air attacked her face, clearing her mind, and she frantically took in her surroundings. Everything was silent. No sign of anyone nearby.

Dawn took off down the street, not caring that she was in her nightclothes and slippers. She would run home in her bare feet if she had to.

5

Cryptic

Dawn turned corner after corner, her lungs burning. She felt as if an invisible monster were chasing after her. Her thighs ached, and little rocks bit into the thin soles of her slippers. The city began to stir, a few passersby glancing in her direction. She edged as far into the shadows as she could, tucked up against the buildings. She had two choices: run into the town square to take a direct approach home or use a back alley to cut the running time in half. She didn't want to be out in public. Not like this. But she also didn't want to duck into the shadows of the city, where there could be unruly people around.

She decided to take the shortcut. Sliding in between two tall buildings, Dawn sprinted along the back road that would quickly take her home. The dark buildings towered above, seeming to loom over her as she continued to run. The word *witch* wouldn't leave her mind. People in this day and age should've moved past such superstitions. This was the twentieth century. Surely people didn't still believe in witches.

Laughter echoed up ahead and she slowed her pace, catching her breath. A few women lounged on the street, wearing dresses cut low over their bosoms with hemlines that showed their thighs. They sat on the front steps of an apartment building, some with cigarettes at their lips, smoke swirling into the cool air. Dawn paused across the street, cursing herself. She should've gone through the square.

"Oy," one woman called out. A headband was wrapped around her head over her loose curls. "I haven't seen you before. Rough night?" She let out a laugh, and the others chuckled along with her. Red lipstick was smeared on her cheek, her wide-necked dress fallen over her bare shoulder.

Dawn glanced down at her own attire and pulled her coat closer around her. They could clearly see she was in her nightclothes.

"What's your name, dearie?"

Dawn kept her lips in tight, rolling her neck uncomfortably.

"Come on, dearie. Don't be shy. You're clearly new, a young thing like you. Why don't you come on in and we can get you some breakfast? Almost all of our clients are gone for the night."

Dawn peeked past them at the brothel, its gray stone pillars carved in angular detail. *Clients.* She couldn't believe these women and what they did with men. She clenched her eyes shut. She would never marry. She didn't need to think of such things.

"I have somewhere I need to be," Dawn said. She kept her arms wrapped around her. "If you'll excuse me."

The woman lifted her brow but didn't object. Dawn took a step forward and tripped on a piece of trash. She fumbled upright and edged along the opposite building, making her way past them. But before she did, Chester staggered out, a woman wrapped around him like a bow, her hands running down his chest.

Dawn paused, mouth falling open. "Chester!"

Chester blinked, his gaze roaming until it paused on Dawn. He paled.

"Dawn? What are you—" He looked down at her attire. "*What* are you doing here?"

She wrapped her arms around herself tighter. "Your engagement party is tonight. You told me you were done with"—her gaze skated to the woman next to him—"these engagements. I thought you loved her."

Rose would be heartbroken if she found out. She was already being forced into a marriage of convenience when all she wanted to do was dance. But to be locked in a marriage to a man who wouldn't be faithful to her? Rose had cried for days when Dawn had accidentally broken her music box when they were children, imagine how she would react to *this*.

Chester shoved the woman off of him, and she staggered off to the side. "I do love her. I love Rose."

Dawn narrowed her eyes.

"I do," he reiterated. "Please don't tell her. This was the last time, I promise. I love Rose with all my heart."

Dawn crossed her arms, mouth pinched. "I'm going to tell her, Chester. I gave you a chance, and you failed. Good day." She spun on her heel and headed down the alley, where the sunrise shone up ahead. This time she walked slowly, with her head held high.

The events of the morning slowly faded away as Dawn bathed and got herself dressed. The fresh water on her bare skin had rejuvenated her, almost making her forget Gertrude's words.

Witch.

She pulled on a drop-waisted dress that hung just below her knees and slipped on her boots—she couldn't handle wearing the T-strap heels the rest of the women wore in her town.

She was to go into the office today and help Dr. Miller refill his medicine jars. She'd probably need to visit Nora, who supplied her with the herbs. Nora always seemed to have exactly what she needed right when she needed it. Sun streamed in through the open window as she pinned up her hair, its rays illuminating her dusty-looking glass. Dark curls sprang outward from her effort, and she tried to pin them back in. The strands matched the heavy shadows under her eyes. She needed to sleep more.

She wasn't invited to the engagement party tonight—she wasn't invited to anything since her father had made a disgrace of their family—but she needed to see Rose and tell her about Chester. Maybe she could use the information about his betrayal to get her out of the engagement. There had to be another suitor for her. There had to be another way for her to secure her financial future. Hopefully, she'd be at the studio.

Her thoughts drifted as images of their years-long friendship swirled inside her head. Sitting on Rose's bedroom floor, dressing dolls. Sitting in her parlor listening to the radio. Spending a weekend at her grandfather's estate in the country, running outside until dark. They would laugh for hours—things were always easy with Rose. No one else made her feel as if she could do anything. Even when things changed, Rose had been the only one who had stuck by her side.

Taking one last glance in the mirror and pinching her cheeks to get more color, Dawn headed down the stairs, her hand gliding on the rough wooden banister.

She paused.

Her mother stood at the bottom of the stairs, arms crossed. Lines creased the corners of her mouth, her lids lowered to slits. Her reddish gray hair was pinned tightly against her head, her usual burgundy scarf tight across her forehead.

"We need to have a talk, child," she said. Mrs. Cook bustled in, a broom in hand, but her mother waved her off. "Leave. Now!"

Mrs. Cook bowed her head and turned to depart, but not before throwing Dawn a sympathetic look.

"You're to visit Arthur Hemsworth today and apologize," she said. "He's agreed to see you."

Dawn's hand tightened on the banister. "I'm what?"

"You heard me. He's agreed to send a car and bring you to his home. You *will* apologize for your rude behavior this week."

Dawn set her chin, staring her mother down. "No. I'm not seeing that man. You can't make me. I refuse."

"I can and I will. I heard about what happened this morning at poor Frederick's home. Gertrude, that poor woman, called on me this morning. Word is spreading that you killed that man, and I won't have it. I hear she's going to the authorities. We *will* get you married before it's too late, and no one will take you."

"I don't care what people say about me. I'm not doing it."

Dawn continued down the stairs, brushing past her, but her mother gripped her arm. She yanked her toward her and slapped her in the face. Dawn flinched, the sting spreading across her cheek. Tears blurred her eyes as her mother kept a firm grip.

"The car is waiting outside now. Grab your coat. Mr. Hemsworth's valet will escort you."

Dawn continued to stare her mother down, unmoving, until her mother snatched her coat for her and shoved it into her chest. She yanked her toward the door and pulled her down the front steps to the vehicle waiting in front of them.

Before Dawn knew it, she was in the car. It started moving, giving her no chance to escape. She clutched her coat to her chest, her fate looming before her.

⁂

The driver pulled the vehicle to a stop and shut off the engine. He was a wiry man with a balding head and a kind face. He opened her door, but Dawn couldn't move to get out. She stared up at the manor before her, her heart thick in her throat. Mr. Hemsworth's house was set on a hill just outside of town, its green lawn stretching outward for at least an acre. Pillars ran along the front of the house, its large double doors carved in swirls. It was lined with white trim carved in intricate detail. The chauffeur motioned her out of the car again and she forced herself to exit, swallowing.

Large willow trees shifted in the wind as she moved up the front steps, still holding her coat in hand. Brass handles adorned the outside. Dawn picked up the cool door knocker, thumping it twice.

Silence stretched as she waited outside and peered around, searching for an escape. Maybe the driver would just take her home. He was still waiting by the car. Or she could walk home, though it would be several miles and would take her more than an hour.

Finally, the door peeled open, and a man dressed in a three-piece suit with wide lapels and high-rise cuffed trousers stood before her. He peered at her with an eyebrow raised, his back ramrod straight.

"Come on in, Miss Hildegard." He opened the door wider, sweeping his arm inside.

Dawn slowly moved forward, stepping into the main foyer. Every part of her itched to run, but she needed to face her fate head on—to end this once and for all.

A chandelier hung above, its golden legs stretching out like a spider. Two marble staircases cascaded in front of her, their shiny floors freshly polished. Several doors lined the entryway. Dawn shivered, wondering which door Arthur Hemsworth lurked behind. The thought of seeing that lecherous man again made her stomach lurch. She pressed a hand over her abdomen, trying to breathe.

"I'm Percival," the man in the suit said. "And I will escort you to our lord. This way."

Percival's long, skinny legs stepped forward, leading her to a far door at the end of the entryway. Dawn's shoes clicked softly, her footsteps echoing off the high ceiling. She peeked back at the exit and sighed.

Percival pulled open a polished wooden door and motioned her in. Inside, bookshelves lined the walls, with stacks of books thrown in disarray. A large mahogany desk was planted in the middle of the room, papers scattered over the top. A chandelier made of antlers adorned the ceiling.

Gideon hovered over the desk, head bowed, his dark hair sleek. His palms were flat on the top as he looked over a document. His mouth was pressed firmly together, eyes intent on the page.

"Miss Hildegard is here, sir," Percival said.

Gideon raised his head, his eyes connecting with Dawn's. A small smile played on the corners of his lips as he stepped out in front of the desk. He gave her a formal bow.

Dawn peeked back at Percival, confused. "I thought you were taking me to—"

"To my uncle?" Gideon finished for her. "No. He's upstairs, probably asleep in a drunken slumber. Your mother believes you're here to visit him, though."

Her eyebrows lifted in surprise. "Then what am I doing here?"

"I'm sorry for the pretense. But it wouldn't be proper for me to invite you over. I knew I had to go through other channels."

"You still haven't answered my question." She crossed her arms, her feet planted on the floor.

Gideon nodded to his servant. "Percival? If you will leave us alone."

Percival dipped his head and clicked the door softly shut behind him.

"Come, sit," Gideon said, moving over to a chair and pulling it out in front of him.

Dawn eyed the chair warily. "I already told you I wouldn't help you."

He held still, the morning light filtering in through the window. His jaw was tight, the light carving shadows on his face. "Humor me?"

"It's hardly proper for me to be alone with you."

He let out a humorless laugh. "From what I know of you, Dawn, you hardly care about propriety."

He did have a point. They stared each other down for a few moments before she sighed.

"Fine," she said. As she passed by him, a sweet smell wafted through her nose. It seemed familiar, but she couldn't pinpoint it. She lowered herself onto the chair.

Gideon's mouth flicked up as he sat on the corner of the desk, crossing his arms. He appraised her before saying, "I decided I need to be honest with you."

Dawn held her hands firmly in her lap, her back straight. "Oh?"

He nodded. "It took me a moment, but I realized that you were being honest with me, so I needed to do the same. I believe you that you aren't after my uncle's money."

"Well, I'm glad you have some sense," she said, her heart thumping.

Another smile lifted his lips. She didn't realize he had a sense of humor. From the moment she'd met him, he'd been nothing but grim.

"You have to understand that there have been many women over the years who were after his money . . . and mine." He lifted a brow. When she didn't answer, he continued. "I know you don't want to help me, but at least hear me out. Will you do that?"

Dawn sat in silence, a clock ticking on the far wall. The smell of dust and books mingled in the air around her, and she pushed out a breath. "Fine."

Gideon stood up and paced away from her. He ran a hand through his sleek hair, his mouth set tight again.

"I was . . . engaged once," he said tentatively. "Her name was Sophia—Sophie, for short. Sophie was . . . well, let's just say we were madly in love. She was my life. My heart. My everything." He swallowed, and a lump bobbed in his throat. "I met her two years ago at a theater in New York. She was a ballerina, and the most exquisite one I'd ever seen. I knew immediately I had to meet her. Since that moment, there was no one else for me." He swallowed again, vocal cords tight in his neck.

Dawn held still, listening. It felt strange to see such emotion from him.

"It was the week before our wedding when Sophie disappeared. She went out into town one day to buy ribbons for her bouquet and she never returned home. Her nanny was with her, but she lost Sophie somewhere in the crowd. It's quite busy in New York, and her nanny didn't know what to do but run home and tell her family what had happened."

A chill rippled through Dawn, ending in her toes. She was rapt yet afraid to learn what happened next.

"There were many who thought she ran off with another man, but I knew she would never. Sophie loved me as much as I loved her. Then, one day, I saw it."

"Saw what?" She held her breath.

Gideon paused and visibly swallowed. His whole body froze, as if the room had taken on an arctic chill. "I saw the Dollmaker's work."

Dawn couldn't move. She couldn't breathe.

He continued. "I was taking a stroll in Central Park when I happened upon a crowd. Women were crying, men were sick. I still remember the screams. I should've turned away, I should've walked in the other direction, but my morbid curiosity overcame me. I walked up to the crowd and saw what they were looking at. On a bench, right in the middle of the park, a . . . I don't know what to call her . . . to call *it*." He ran a hand over his face. "She was a girl, stitched together, with . . . different body parts from different young women. She was dressed in white lace, her skirt short, like a baby doll. Her face looked like it had been sewn to another person's head. Thick stitches lined the neck and where the arms and legs and joints connected. Different arms . . . different legs . . . different hands . . ." He shut his eyes, shuddering. "It was horrible."

"And what does this have to do with Sophie?" Dawn asked, paralyzed, though she already knew.

"It was the left hand that gave it away. It was . . . the thing was . . . it was wearing Sophie's engagement ring."

Dawn abruptly stood up from her chair, toppling it over. Her stomach wrenched, and she curled over slightly. She quickly gathered herself, not wanting to upset Gideon further. She knew it must've been hard for him to relive this.

"So what did you do?" she asked, trying to push out even breaths.

"Everything. I went to the authorities. I asked around. I gathered every document and newspaper I could on the man. I even stalked the streets at night hoping to find him. But everything has led to a dead end. No one knows who this man is."

Dawn squeezed her eyes shut.

The pain he must've experienced. And now he was after this madman?

"Gideon, I'm sorry for what happened to you, but you *shouldn't* get involved in this. If he finds out you are searching for him—"

"I don't care!" he burst out. "You think I care if that psychopath comes after me? I would welcome it. I have to take him down."

Dawn stilled, and she felt the blood leave her face.

"Will you help me?" he asked. "You're my last hope."

They stood, staring at each other in silence, her heart heavy in her chest. A myriad of thoughts ran through her head. She pictured herself poring over documents with Gideon. She saw herself walking the streets at night trying to find this madman.

She imagined him coming after her.

No.

She shook her head.

Her job. If she spent time with Gideon or was seen with him around town, rumors would spread. No one would take her seriously. She'd be no better than the ladies of the night.

"No," she said quickly. "Gideon, I feel awful for what happened to you, but I just can't . . . no, I can't get involved in this. I have a life. I have . . ." She shook her head again. "I wish you the best of luck."

Gideon's chest heaved up and down, his fists clenched tightly. He stood silent for a long while before he arranged his face into a blank mask.

"Fine," he said curtly. "You can see yourself to the door."

Dawn waited, expecting him to say something else, but he had turned his back on her and returned to the documents on the desk. Maybe she had acted too quickly. Maybe there was a world where she helped him. Maybe she should've told him she'd think about it. But she didn't owe him any favors. He was a man focused on only his own pursuits. She couldn't give him any of her time.

She waited for a few more seconds before seeing herself out.

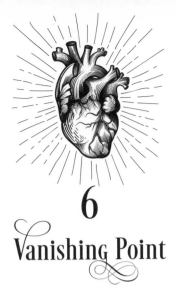

6
Vanishing Point

L ater that day, Dawn peeked inside Nora's shop, squinting in the dark. Candles were spread out over the space, flickering in the dim light. The flames cast shifting, dancing shadows on the walls as she stepped inside.

"Nora? Are you here?"

Herbs and trinkets lined the shelves that encompassed the room. Animal pelts, skulls, and other strange bones were strewn around, along with frogs in jars. Beads were hung in a doorway to the back. The room was eclectic and had an unearthly aura, as if Dawn had stepped onto another planet.

Rustling came from the back, and Nora emerged, her jet-black hair hanging in braids over her face and the neckline of her white robe plunging.

She glided forward, a human skull in hand.

"Dawn, I didn't expect you so soon. Have you run out of your herbs?"

Dawn eyed the skull, then pulled out her medical pouch and peered inside. "I am running low on turmeric and carbolic. I could use some lavender too."

Nora set the skull down on a nearby shelf, her long fingers running along it. She moved across the room, her white robe swishing over her bare feet, and started gathering the herbs Dawn had asked for.

"You seem different," Nora said. "Something has happened in your life."

Dawn blinked and drew her brows together. "I don't know what you mean."

Nora's mouth curved upward. "You've met someone. Someone who has made an impact on you."

Gideon's face immediately surged to mind, and she tried to shove it away.

"No," she said quickly. "It's just me. Unless you're talking about Arthur Hemsworth. The man my mother is determined to marry me off to."

Nora stopped and spun around. A fine line creased her forehead. "Perhaps, but I don't think that's it." Her eyes glazed over, and her expression went blank before her eyes cleared. "If you want some herbs that will kill the old man, I'd be happy to supply you with some."

Dawn let out a laugh, snorting. "I'll let you know if it comes to that."

Nora returned to the herbs, gathering a few vials that contained the ingredients. She passed them to Dawn, who then exchanged a few coins for her service. Nora gave a satisfied smile, her dark braids framing her pale face.

"You should come to a séance I'm having tonight. You might find it interesting."

Dawn's lips twitched. "Thanks for the invite, but I haven't slept for days, I'd probably fall asleep and wake the dead with my snoring."

Nora chuckled, waving her hand. "Fine. But I'm going to get you there one of these days."

Dawn smiled. "Good luck tonight. And thank you for the invite." She waved as she exited the front door. Leaving her shop took ten pounds off her shoulders. Though they were friends, there was something off about the woman.

In the town square, Dawn stepped into the fresh air, a buzz of noise around her. People bustled back and forth, shopping, walking down the sidewalks, crossing the cobblestone road. Ladies sold seeds on the corner, with a few selling flowers and other items. She took in the shops lined tightly together, including Dr. Miller's office just across the way. She wasn't needed today, but she could do some more reading. There was a book on cleaning out wounds she was interested in. She started across the street, keeping her medical pouch close to her side. She walked by a few shops and eateries. As she passed an alleyway, a movement caught her attention out of the corner of her eye, and she paused.

Caldwell had Rose in a firm grip, her body yanked up close to his. Rose struggled to get out of his embrace, her fur coat sliding off her shoulder. Caldwell pulled her closer, lifting a hand up to her face and stroking her cheek. Rose grunted and tried to shove him off, but his grip was too strong.

Dawn's heart took off, and she was paralyzed for a moment, before reality kicked in.

"Rose!" She threw herself into the alleyway, darting forward. "Get off of her!"

Caldwell's face faltered, before he zeroed in on Dawn. He fumbled back a step and straightened his coat.

"Healer," he said. He turned to Rose and gave her a small bow. "I'll see you in class later, Miss Waterford." He brushed past them without another word.

Rose clutched her coat to her chest, her wide eyes moist. Her lips trembled as she rushed into Dawn's arms. She embraced her tightly.

"Oh, thank you," Rose said. "I don't know what I would've done if you hadn't shown up."

Dawn took her arms and held her back. "*What* were you doing down here with him?" She peeked at the trash littered on the ground, the two buildings surrounding them high over her head.

"He said he needed to discuss the pas de deux," she said. "I didn't think . . . I don't know what he . . . he started talking about my engagement party tonight and that he wanted to meet with me. It felt . . . quite improper, like . . ." She swallowed down a hiccup.

"It's okay," Dawn said. "We won't let that happen." Though the thought of Chester burned through her chest. "Rose, there's something else we need to talk about. It's Chester. He—"

"No," she said. She shook her head and her blonde curls bounced. "I don't want to know. I'm already giving my life to him, he's already taking everything from me, I can't bear to think about it anymore."

She bit her pink lips, and in that moment, she looked as if she were five years old, eyes terrified as if a monster were under her bed. Dawn quickly pulled her into another hug, and her light perfume wafted inside her nose. Rose's thin body trembled, and Dawn held her tighter. She would do anything to protect her. She didn't deserve this fate.

Rose stiffened, and Dawn pulled back. "What's wrong?"

Rose lifted up a hand and pointed, her eyes widening. Screaming ricocheted from the square, and Dawn jerked upright. She peeked behind her. "What's that?"

Rose moved forward a few steps. "Something's happening."

The two girls moved swiftly back down the alley and emerged into the sunshine. A group of people had gathered, surrounding the fountain that roared in the middle of the square. A statue of a robed woman spurted water from her mouth, its peaceful sight a contrast to the screaming below it.

"Come on." Dawn marched forward, pushing her way to the front of the group. But she lost all confidence when she saw what had gathered the crowd. She clasped her hands over her mouth, faltering.

A young girl lay before her, lifeless on the ground, her eyes glazed and directed toward the blue sky. Her skin was papery and wrinkled, like it was starting to sink in on itself. A horrid smell wafted off her and people covered their noses. Her silk skirt was pushed up quite indecently, showing her thighs—or what was left of one of her thighs. Right above the knee, her bone was cut cleanly across, the skin folded neatly over. Whoever had amputated the lower half of her leg had known what they were doing.

Dawn spotted a tiny, folded piece of paper tucked into the girl's bodice. She quickly bent down and retrieved the note, pocketing it before anyone saw it. People gave her odd looks, but she backed away, leaving Rose staring at the horror. She fumbled with the note, opening it swiftly.

Another step of my ultimate masterpiece.

That was all it said. Her fingers shook, and she pocketed the note once more. She didn't know why she took it. It was an impulse.

"What was that?"

The voice came from behind, cutting straight through her core. She paused, knowing he was there, knowing she could never mistake that voice. She felt his presence hovering behind her, and she slowly turned.

Gideon looked as proper as ever in his silk shirt with a handkerchief and a black fedora tipped over his head. The color matched the deep hollows in his cheeks. He appraised Dawn with a quizzical expression, his hands tucked into his pockets.

"Nothing that is of your concern."

"Oh? I saw you pick that note up from the body. It seems like a clue. Are you really going to withhold it from me after everything I've disclosed to you about my Sophie?" Emotion caught at his voice.

Her hand hovered over her pocket, hesitating, until she sighed. "Fine." She retrieved the paper and handed it to him.

Gideon quickly opened the parchment, his eyes scanning back and forth, and lowered it.

"You're going to let this happen? You know this is the Dollmaker, right? How can you stand by and do nothing?"

"I . . ." She didn't have a voice. This was the Dollmaker? Of course it was. But still, she asked, "Are you sure it's him?"

He gave her a pointed look. "I'm keeping this. If you come to your senses and decide to help me, you know where to find me."

And he turned and marched away.

⁃⁃⁃

Dawn sat in her bedroom, gazing out her open window. She peered up at the moon. Little wisps of clouds stretched over the golden orb. Stars dotted the sky, and a cool breeze wafted in.

She hadn't had a chance to talk to Rose about Chester. Their engagement party was happening right *now*. Who knew how it was going? It wasn't often that she wished she were still considered higher class, but every once in a while, she couldn't help but dream of what it would be like to attend one of those parties. The dresses. The dancing. The food.

Her mother had put her in dance lessons as a child—back when they'd had more money. She'd even once had a few nice dresses— silks and laces, with bows and ribbon. She remembered trips out to her grandfather's estate with gardens that circled the stone home, and she'd spend hours running through the maze of flowers into the evening until the fireflies came out.

Her uncle owned the estate now but had cut off her father completely after he'd defaulted on the multiple loans her uncle had given him. Now they were left alone to fend for themselves, though her mother still wouldn't admit to their circumstances. She spent what little money they had on her own dresses, trying to look the part of a lady in high society.

Dawn peered down at her own loose white blouse and sighed. She really should have spoken to Rose. Chester was going to get away with his devious behavior, and Rose was going to have to live with it.

Thoughts of the events of the day cut through her mind, and the vision of the poor dead girl painted itself in her head. Her body hadn't yet started to decompose. How long had it been since the Dollmaker mutilated her? Who was she? What kind of life did she have? By the looks of her dress, she'd had money. It shouldn't take too long to identify her, if a report had been filed for her absence.

Another step of my ultimate masterpiece.

What did that mean? He had taken her leg, what else would he do? Was she only a piece of his next puzzle? The image of what Gideon had painted in her head of the girl stitched together with different body parts surfaced. Her stomach twisted, and she stood up from the window. She paced back and forth on her wood floor, the boards creaking. She knew her mother would yell at her for making such a racket, but she didn't care. Let the ceiling squeak.

Guilt ate at her insides for not helping Gideon. The look he'd given her today appeared in her head, the disappointment in his voice. He truly did think she could help, but she knew she couldn't. She was a healer, not a detective. But the amputation had been done with skill. The Dollmaker knew how to cut it just right. Perhaps she could ask around and find surgeons who traveled through the area. Tools would have to have been purchased between here and New York.

No.

It was absurd. She wasn't going to get involved.

She wrung her hands out in front of her, continuing to pace. She couldn't stay in here any longer. She needed to speak with Rose before it was too late. She'd never forgive herself if Rose lived the rest of her life in misery.

She crept into the hallway and clicked the door closed behind her. The stairs creaked as she descended, but there was no movement from the parlor. Her mother must have been asleep. She snatched her coat off the rack and buttoned up the front before retrieving her gloves and scarf, sliding them on. She slipped outside without being noticed.

Cool air stung her cheeks and she peered up at the sky, where a few more clouds had moved in. A gust of wind blew past her, and Dawn tucked her coat in closer around her. Drops of rain started to splatter down, but she didn't care. Rose was more important.

The lampposts' light reflected in the puddles on the road and Dawn edged around the water, keeping to the sides of the street. Silence settled in her chest. It was as if the world paused—there were no sensations around her. No noise. No hustle of everyday life. Just quiet, stillness, where she could finally think.

It was just her and the air around her, pushing in and out of her lungs. The crispness cleared her head, placing her senses on full alert and making her aware of every droplet on the ground, every splatter on her head. She could feel her blood traveling through her body, every beat of her steady heart.

Until she thought of the Dollmaker once more. With each step, the air cooled further. The puddles on the ground seemed *too* still. The night *too* quiet. She tucked her arms closer around her, new adrenaline coursing through her. What was she doing out at this time of night?

He could be watching her now.

But music drifted out from around the corner as she approached Rose's house, and thoughts of the Dollmaker fled. She clenched her fists tightly at the thought of Chester smiling and socializing at Rose's side. He needed to be called out on his behavior. This *had* to break up the engagement—and Rose would just have to suffer the consequences. She would make it right.

Dawn paused underneath the lamppost on the corner of the street, its flames burning from the gas underneath. From this angle, she could see that Rose's house was lit up, every window glowing. Laughter came from indoors, echoing in the night. Silhouettes moved over the windows. Dawn imagined glasses clinking together, stories being shared.

Gathering her nerve, she ran her palms along the front of her coat and stepped out into the dark street, heading toward Rose's house. She was doing the greater good. Chester needed to be stopped. Rose needed to be saved from this marriage. Her footsteps splashed in the shallow puddles, and she forced her legs forward before she lost her determination.

Rose's front door opened and a lovely silhouette ran out, curls pinned to the sides of her head, tiny waist, skirt hanging just below her knees. Her dress swished as she descended the front steps quickly, racing over to the nearest lamppost. Her gloved hands clung to the post, and Rose's form lit up in the dark, the dim light highlighting her long lashes and full lips. Her chest pushed up and down, her fingers tightening around the post.

"Rose!" Dawn called out.

Her head snapped up, and she squinted into the dark. "Dawn?"

Had something happened between her and Chester? Was the party too much for her?

Dawn kept on, crossing the street.

Suddenly, something darted from the shadows. Before Dawn could blink, a figure sprang toward Rose. The figure wrapped its arm around her waist and clasped a hand over her mouth. Rose flailed, trying to cry out, swinging her arms back and forth, feet kicking out in front of her, but the figure dragged her backward at a quick pace, tugging her into the night.

Dawn blinked, and then reality crashed in.

"Rose!" she screamed. She rushed forward, racing, feet splashing in the puddles. The figure disappeared behind the back of the building and Dawn bolted after it, heading down the alleyway.

"Rose!" she called again.

She paused at the end of the alley, head darting from side to side, chest heaving. Her eyes stretched wide in the dark, but the figure was nowhere to be found. Alarm bells clanged in her head. Where had they gone?

Had Chester snatched her? Someone else? She peeked back behind her, heart hammering.

Dawn took off back down the alley. She needed help. She raced up the front steps of Rose's home, pushing open the door. Her hair hung in strands over her face as she burst into the foyer. Ladies paused, while a few gentlemen slid their gazes over. Their noses crinkled and mouths parted.

"Someone help," Dawn choked out.

No one moved. They stared down at her with disapproving looks, eyebrows raised.

"Please," Dawn repeated.

She knew these faces from her childhood. She'd helped some of these faces with their ailments and broken bones. They *knew* her. Why weren't they responding?

A couple of men emerged from the crowd and started forward, rolling up their sleeves.

Dawn edged back. "No."

The men grabbed her by the arms and began to escort her outside.

"No!" she yelled once more. "It's Rose! Some man took her! He can't be too far. We need to find her!" She looked for Chester, but he wasn't anywhere to be seen. Why hadn't any of them noticed the bride was gone?

Giggles erupted and backs turned to her. The men continued to drag her while she yelled. The door slammed in her face, and Dawn stood on the porch alone. She whirled around, but all she found was silence.

She suddenly hated the silence.

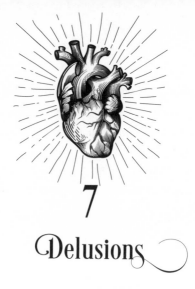

7

Delusions

D awn pounded on the door, praying he would be home. She wasn't sure if Gideon lived with his uncle or if he resided somewhere else. She prayed that Arthur Hemsworth wouldn't answer the door.

She'd already gone to the authorities and had given her tale of the events, but they'd looked at her as if she were crazy, even with the Dollmaker running around. An officer said they would look into it, but he'd hurried her along as if he were irritated. He'd have to believe her soon. It wouldn't be too long before everyone knew Rose was missing. Even though she was an orphan, she still ran in the right circles because of her parents' status before they died.

She pounded on the door again, her knuckles cold against the wood. They ached, but she kept pounding. She had used what little money she'd had to rent a carriage. It had dropped her off at the bottom of the estate where the road stopped, and she had run up through the rain across the long lawn, up to the Hemsworth manor. Finally, the door peeled open and Gideon stood before her, white shirt open to his lean stomach, hair combed back against his head. He had dark circles under his eyes, so Dawn knew he hadn't been sleeping. She was drenched, her dress soggy, her shoes completely soaked. Her jaw chattered as she wrapped her arms around herself.

"Our servants have gone to bed," he said. "What on earth are you doing here at this ungodly hour?" His eyes widened. "And soaked to the brim?"

Her body continued to tremble. "Please, can I come in?"

Gideon swung the door open further, his lips turned downward. "By all means."

Dawn moved swiftly past him, marching into the marble foyer. A single candle glowed on the side table, its flame flickering on the walls. Light spilled out from the open door just down the hallway from the foyer, where she assumed Gideon must have been.

"I need your help," she said quickly, her voice echoing in the massive space. "It's my friend. She's—" She hiccupped. "You have to help me. No one else believes me. I—"

"Whoa. Slow down," Gideon said. "You're going to catch your death. Let's get you dried off. There's a fire in my study. Come warm yourself." He turned and started heading down the marble hallway.

"I . . . I can't. It's quite inappropriate for me to be alone with you."

He paused, humor quirking his lips. "It's quite inappropriate for you to come waltzing in here at this time of night. And I'm not going to stand here and have a conversation in the foyer. Not with you looking like a wet rat."

Chills rocketed through her and her jaw chattered. He did have a point. She tentatively stepped forward, following him down the large hall. Inside the study, flames licked the fireplace. Gideon pulled out a chair for her to sit in. She lowered herself, peeling off her wet coat and laying it on the chair behind her. She leaned forward, rubbing her hands, and the fire instantly warmed her cheeks, shivers erupting down her back.

"Can I get you something to drink? Brandy? I obtained some for medical purposes. It would help warm you."

"I don't drink," she said. "It's bad for the liver."

His lips twitched upward as he moved over to the fire, leaning against the mantel. He waved a hand forward. "Talk."

A wave of embarrassment suddenly swept through her. She was sitting alone with a man, drenched, in the middle of the night. What if Rose wasn't really in trouble, and she was making a fool of herself? No. She'd seen what happened. Gideon was the only one she could turn to.

"It's Rose," she said quickly. "She's my friend. She—"

"Rose Waterford. Yes, I'm quite aware of who she is. I was invited to her engagement party tonight. Unfortunately, I was detained."

Dawn swallowed, her hands beginning to warm. "I witnessed someone take her. And I think it was him."

Gideon pushed off the mantel, slowly straightening. "Tell me more."

"I've decided to help you," she said. "If it is him, if it is this Dollmaker, then I can't let her die. I just can't. We *have* to find her."

Hope lit Gideon's eyes as his body stayed stiff. "You'll help me."

She nodded quickly. "Yes. Anything. I'll do anything."

Gideon nodded back, his jaws clamped together. The orange firelight played off his strong bones, hollowing them out. "Then we must start at once. But first, we must find you some dry clothes."

Dawn shook her head. "No. If we're going to do this, we're going to do it properly. I couldn't handle your uncle walking in on us—or your servants. If it got out that I was . . . indecent with you, it could ruin my reputation. And that would affect my credibility as a doctor. I won't let anything compromise that."

Gideon's face twisted as he began to pace in front of the fire. His hands were linked behind his back, his form long and dark. His jaw ground back and forth until he paused.

"I'll be your suitor then," he said.

Dawn froze. "Excuse me?" Her lungs suddenly turned to ice blocks. She didn't think she could get any colder.

"It's the only way we'll be able to spend time together," he said. "I'll visit your parents' tomorrow. I'll let them know of my intentions. They won't say no. I am worth just as much as my uncle."

Her throat had sealed off tightly. "That's ridiculous. I mean . . ."

"It's not as if I *plan* to go through with it. We both know we won't marry, but it'll give us some time to figure this out. And it'll be through the proper channels. And it'll get my uncle off your back."

Dawn hesitated, wringing her fingers in front of her. Pretend to be engaged to Gideon? Work closely with him? Become some sort of crime-fighting healer? It was ridiculous. But it *would* eliminate Arthur Hemsworth from the picture.

"I'll do it."

He gave one sharp nod. "Let me grab the car. It'll take you home. And I'll meet with you tomorrow."

Her bedroom door swung open, banging on the opposite wall. Her mother rushed in in a flurry, waving a card over her head. Dawn blinked, light searing her eyes, and she squinted up at her mother's hovering form. By the light slanting through the window, she could see it was late morning.

"Get up, child! Get up!" Her mother yanked her from her bed and Dawn swayed on her feet. Her mother pushed her over to the chair by the vanity and forced her to sit down. "I'll have Mrs. Cook come do your hair. We need to get you presentable for Mr. Hemsworth—not Arthur Hemsworth but Gideon Hemsworth, his nephew! He has made his intentions clear and wants to court you. I never thought. Not after what a disappointment you were!"

Dawn stiffened in her chair.

She had almost forgotten.

Now that it was morning, and the emotions of last night had subsided, a sick feeling planted itself in her gut. *What had she done?* She shouldn't have agreed to help Gideon. She couldn't put on a ruse in front of her whole family. She couldn't pretend to be charmed by him, care for him.

But Rose. Another wave of panic hit. Rose was gone. Her jaw chattered, and she clamped her teeth together, trying to calm herself. When she'd gone to bed last night, she'd heard her mother speaking from the next room about the authorities sending out a search party for Rose. Maybe she would be all right. Help was on the way.

A headache was creeping up. She needed lavender. That would help. But the thought of moving made her head pound twice as hard.

Mrs. Cook rushed in, her apron splattered with flour and her hat floppy on her head. Her rash was still splotchy on her face. She really needed to treat it before it became infected.

Mrs. Cook held a silk dress in her arms, the shiny material glistening in the morning light. "I've brought it, madam."

Her mother motioned her forward, taking the dress from her arms and examining the material. Dawn knew that dress. It was the nicest thing they owned. Her mother had worn it once but didn't fit into it anymore, and they hadn't had the money to get it tailored.

"Why is that in here?"

"Because you're going to wear it, child," her mother said. "If we are going to snag this man, then first impressions are everything. It's too bright for your dark hair, but maybe it'll give you a bit of color." Lines creased around her mouth.

The bright orange hurt her eyes, and she wasn't sure that it would give her any color at all. It probably would make her look sallower than ever. The dress was longer than the current style and it had bright yellow ribbons stitched into the slippery fabric. Dawn cringed but allowed Mrs. Cook to slide it over her head and button up the back. Her mother stood off to the side, tapping her fingers on her pointy chin.

"Is this really necessary?" Dawn finally asked. She eyed the dress again. She looked like a clown.

Her mother's eyes darkened as her lips pinched. "You've been the worst disappointment of my life. This will be the *only* good thing that will come from you, so don't mess it up." Her eyes flew to Mrs. Cook. "Hurry up and finish those scones. They have to be the best scones Gideon Hemsworth has ever tasted." She whirled away, striding from the room.

Mrs. Cook huffed. "I've had many employers in my day, but none so intense."

"*Intense*?" Dawn exclaimed. "She's the worst human being I've ever met."

Mrs. Cook set a hand on her arm. "Let me tell you something I used to tell a girl I nannied. Beauty comes from within. And your beauty will shine through. It doesn't matter what you're wearing."

Dawn turned to the mirror, staring at her dusty reflection. Ruffles were stitched into the dress in all the wrong places around the yellow ribbon with bows at the end. The orange wiped out her already pale complexion, making her look almost dead.

"But it's hideous," Dawn whispered. "I can't possibly wear this." The dress appeared much lovelier in her childhood memories of her mother wearing it.

"It'll have to do," Mrs. Cook said. "You can't very well see Mr. Hemsworth in your usual clothes."

Dawn opened her mouth to say that it didn't matter what she wore—Gideon Hemsworth was going to pursue her regardless of her apparel—but she snapped it shut, not wanting to already blow their plan.

"Now to your hair."

After Mrs. Cook had succeeded in pinning her hair in extravagant swirls that should only be worn at a fancy party, Dawn peeked through her dark lashes at the finished product. She looked like a doll—silly and made up.

Mrs. Cook's face turned wistful as she peered at Dawn through the mirror. "It's been a while since I've done anyone's hair." She swallowed, and moisture gathered in the corners of her eyes.

Dawn spun around in her chair. "You were talking about the girl you nannied? Tell me about her."

Mrs. Cook's mouth lifted a tad. "She was beautiful. The most beautiful girl I'd ever seen—your friend, Rose, reminds me of her."

Dawn stiffened at the mention of Rose. Her heart quickened, but she pushed out a steady breath.

"She was a dancer," Mrs. Cook continued. Her gaze drifted far away before she shook her head. "I must finish the scones." She bustled toward the door, then turned. "Your mother expects you downstairs and waiting."

Dawn let out a shudder, silence settling into her heart. She waited in her room, her hands over her stomach, trying to push out even breaths. A draft drifted into the room, cooling her heated face. She was suddenly aware of every detail around her. The clanging coming from the kitchen downstairs, the spider crawling on the wall in the corner, playful yelling echoing from down the street, the tingles that rippled down her arms in anticipation, her mother's voice prattling on.

She couldn't do this.

But she had to, she reminded herself. Rose needed her. Gideon would help find her. And being courted by Gideon would only give her more credibility, which would help her career. After all, wasn't that what mattered?

Yes, she assured herself. She could, in fact, do this.

It was better than being known as a witch. She would feign an attachment to him. She would do it for her future.

For Rose's future.

<hr/>

Dawn sat in the parlor, where her mother shoved a cross-stitch into her hands. She hadn't done a cross-stitch since the day her grandmother had taught her as a little girl. She stared down at the little x's and decorative embroidery she had started years ago. The stitching made her think of her work.

She envisioned a body in front of her . . . flesh and blood . . . a gaping wound. She imagined threading the skin with the needle, sewing flesh back together.

"Dawn!"

Dawn jerked to attention, dropping the cross-stitch in her lap. Gideon stood next to her mother's scowling face, tall and straight, his pin-striped suit fitted tightly against his lean frame. Light from the parlor windows shone inside, highlighting half of his face, casting splotchy shapes on his severe bones.

He stared down at Dawn with amusement on his lips, eyebrows lifting.

Dawn sprung to her feet, straightening out her skirt. The cross-stitch fell to the floor. She fumbled down to retrieve it, and her mother coughed, continuing to scowl.

"Mr. Hemsworth is here to see you," her mother said. "Mr. Hemsworth, would you please have a seat? We have fresh scones coming out of the oven now."

Gideon kept his eyes locked on Dawn. "No. No thank you. I'd rather skip the pleasantries, if you don't mind. I'm more in the mood for a walk. Miss Hildegard, would you accompany me on a walk through town?"

"Oh!" Her mother clapped her hands. "What a pleasant idea! A walk through town. With all those people." Her mother fanned herself. "It will be good for you to get out."

Dawn inwardly rolled her eyes.

"Shall we?" Gideon offered his arm, his brows still raised. His lips were quirked up, as if keeping in laughter.

"Let me fetch my coat." Dawn stormed past his arm and out into the foyer, where she readily buttoned up the brass buttons, hoping to hide at least half of her dress.

Gideon followed and opened the front door, sweeping his arm outside. The two walked down the street in silence, heading toward town. Houses lined the street, tight together, and several passersby glanced in their direction. Gideon kept his arms down at his sides, not offering his elbow to her, and she didn't care. They could drop the pretense now that her mother wasn't near.

"Nice dress," Gideon finally said.

"Don't. Don't even start."

"You look ridiculous."

Dawn huffed, lifting her chin. "You know it's my mother."

He let out a low chuckle. "If that dress is supposed to seduce me, it's failing miserably."

Dawn stayed silent. She wouldn't give in to his teasing. They continued to walk, Gideon's legs long in front of him. People continued to brush past, and a couple of ladies whispered in their direction. Cars and horse-drawn carriages rumbled down the street.

Gideon led Dawn down an alley, away from town.

Dawn pinched her brows together. "Where are we going? I thought we were going to the square."

"I'm taking you to my home. I've bought a house just outside of town so I can have a space to do my investigating. We need privacy."

"I thought we were going through the proper channels? I can't be alone with you!"

He gave her a sidelong glance. "You really don't expect us to work out in the open with ogling eyes?"

She kept her lips sealed tight. He did have a point.

They passed a few buildings, some crumbling and worn with age, trash littering the street. Everything dimmed as the sun disappeared behind the buildings, and Dawn rubbed her arms; the air was several degrees cooler in the shade. Voices echoed in the distance.

"An odd place for someone as rich as you."

He let out a laugh. "I don't want people to know I'm here."

They stopped in front of a building, and Dawn glanced around to make sure no one was watching. If anyone saw her entering a residence alone with a man, she would be ruined. She quickly rushed up the steps the second Gideon unlocked the door and pushed it open. Kerosene lamps were already lit, lining the narrow hallway that led to a door at the far end. A staircase ascended upward, but Gideon led Dawn down the hall. Shadows flicked off of the walls, shapes dancing as she followed Gideon's lean form. She kept her arms wrapped around herself, a chill creeping down her back.

"I spent the morning here trying to prepare for our session," he said. He pushed the door open at the end. "I've laid out every document and piece of information I could find."

Inside, more lamps were spread around the room. A large table was in the middle of the space. Papers were scattered and piled on top of one another, with several journals and books stacked in small towers. She noticed a pile of medical journals at the base of the table. A chaise stood on one side of the room, pictures of landscapes hung on the walls. It was warmer inside this enclosed space, with a fire roaring in front of her.

"Do you stay here?" Dawn asked, her voice loud in the quiet.

"I prefer to be on my own, yes, rather than live in my house in town or at my uncle's estate. People . . . they expect too much of me.

I don't like being looked at. I don't like being judged. As if my life was perfect."

His life *was* perfect, Dawn thought. To have money. To have status. To have freedom. But then she remembered his Sophie dying, and she shook the thought away. He did have his demons.

"Well, let's get started then, shall we?" Dawn marched over to the table. The sooner she began with Gideon, the sooner they would find Rose. Her throat tightened at the thought of her, and she forced herself to breathe. She was still alive. She *had* to be alive.

Gideon stepped in front of her, and she nearly rammed into his chest. He was close—too close—inappropriately close, and the sweet smell he gave off attacked her senses. She flinched.

"I know I've practically forced you into doing this," he said, "but I will give you the opportunity to back out if you must. What you're about to see isn't pretty."

Dawn stared into his eyes. Sweat shone on his forehead. He held her gaze with such intensity, her mind blanked out, until she composed herself. She took a step back, clearing her head.

"I'm perfectly capable of handling this," she said.

Gideon's lips were tucked inward. "Yes, I believe you are."

Dawn edged up to the table and ran her fingers over the pages before her. Newspaper articles, handwritten documents, and maps were strewn across the table, not seeming to be in any semblance of order. She picked up a map and squinted at the tiny dots that were scattered across New York, through Massachusetts, down to Connecticut, and into Rhode Island.

"The different locations," he said. "Where his . . . creations have been found."

She slowly lowered the map and picked up a document.

"Police reports. They describe the deaths in detail, of the women found, the limbs that were missing, but every lead has been a dead end."

She nodded and walked around to the other side of the table. She retrieved a book on top of a stack and flipped open the pages.

"Everything I could learn about murderers and their psychological states," he continued. "There has to be a reason he's doing this, and I figured if I could get inside his mind, it would help lead me to him."

Dawn peered closer at the text.

Psychological gratification is the usual motive for killing. Most serial killers instigate sexual contact with the victim. Characteristics can include extreme anger, thrill-seeking tendencies, or an attention-seeking mentality. Victims may have something in common—appearance or gender.

She slammed the book shut.

Gideon lifted a brow. "Any idea where to start?"

"I think we need to start by researching the first victim. Where did it happen, how much time took place before his next victim, how long it takes to piece his creations together. We need to figure out why he's doing this, and why he feels the need to display them. There has to be a connection between these women."

Gideon gave a sharp nod. "I have the paperwork for the first victim here." He dug through a stack until he pulled out a paper from the bottom. He passed it to Dawn and she clutched it in her hands, her eyes scanning the page.

"Mary Jane Josephson," she murmured. "Found just outside of Central Park. Bruises around her neck. She appeared to have died by suffocation." She finished scanning the document and lowered the paper. "An arm missing."

Gideon made a noise in the back of his throat. "Look at the date. February twenty-fifth, nineteen eighteen."

"He's been doing this for *two* years?"

"It took a while before press got ahold of it. It was kept under wraps for a long time."

"Who's the next victim?" Dawn asked.

Gideon rifled through another stack of papers and pulled out a sheet. He really needed to organize this mess. She read the next document.

"A calf amputated. It says here she was seventeen. How old was Mary Jane?"

"I'm not sure. It doesn't say."

Dawn pressed her lips together. "And the next one?"

Gideon handed her page after page, and then her insides went cold. Her vision blurred as she read the words scrawled in front of her.

"Clementine Phillips. Decapitation."

"And the list goes on," he said wryly. "It appears that he attacks women for their limbs first. Hands, feet, torsos, et cetera. And his last victim is always the head. Then his creation is displayed."

A chill shot through Dawn, ending in her toes. "It's begun again then."

Gideon frowned, little lines creasing around his mouth. "Yes."

She squeezed her eyes shut. "I can't let this happen to Rose."

"It may already be too late."

8
Tick Tock

Dawn spent hours in Gideon's apartment poring over paperwork. Her eyes ached as she finally exited onto the street, blinking at the sudden light. She smoothed out her orange skirt and straightened her coat. She needed to get back home and change. She couldn't very well do her patient visits dressed like this. Gideon had insisted on walking her home, but she needed air. She needed to be away from him. His brooding demeanor was starting to have an effect on her.

Gray clouds hung overhead, and a light breeze lifted the little hairs off the back of her neck. The sun had started to descend. She'd probably have only an hour of daylight left. Not nearly enough time to change and do her visits. She peered down at the ruffled dress and inwardly groaned. Perhaps she'd have to wear the dress after all. She groaned again. Why should she be worrying about her dress when Rose was still missing? She still hadn't spoken to Chester. Did he know? She hadn't heard anything from the authorities yet.

The thought of Rose sent another surge of panic through her. What was she experiencing now? Was she scared? Was she conscious? The Dollmaker had great skill with the girls he dismantled, but did he treat them like animals or people before he killed them? She swallowed her panic. She couldn't worry about that now. She was doing what she could with Gideon. She would find her.

She headed down a cobblestone road, twisting through the streets filled with apartment buildings until it opened up into the town square. Only a few people were out, as the day was ending, most of the vendors gone. Shops were closing, except for Nora's—she always kept late hours. Dr. Miller's office sat just across the way, and Dawn squinted, seeing if he was inside. She should go visit Mrs. Smith's baby again, but should also check on Johnny Wilson to make sure his splinter hadn't become infected. Tending to patients would help ground her.

She needed to keep herself distracted. Dawn continued to cut through the large square, past the fountain, which roared in the otherwise silent air.

As she exited the square into another maze of buildings, the sun seemed to have descended faster than she'd expected. She peeked behind her, shivering. She really ought to go home, but she'd already made it this far, and it wouldn't make too much of a difference if she spent another hour out.

Soon all carriages and cars vanished for the night; the people were off the streets. She passed by buildings that were tucked in close to each other, each with stairs that led up to the doorways. Small alleys cut between the buildings every so often, and she kept close to the lampposts, the glowing light illuminating her way.

As she walked, a creeping suspicion began to tingle along her back. An awareness—one that rang like tiny bells zinging in her head. What if the Dollmaker was watching her now? The niggling feeling that someone was watching pressed in on her like heavy bricks. She picked up her pace. Perhaps Mrs. Smith would let her stay the night, or maybe there would be a carriage she could rent to take her home.

As she continued, the feeling wouldn't leave her. Eyes were on her. Her heart started to pound furiously, her pulse thumping through her entire body. Visions of the dead girl in the square jolted her mind, and she picked up her feet, running in a slight jog. Out of the corner of her eye, a figure of a man on a rooftop moved. She skidded to a stop. She didn't know *why* she stopped—it was insane to stop—but if this man was destined to hurt her, he would attack her whether she ran or not, and there was nothing she could do about it.

He was nothing more than a silhouette, crouched on the roof. He froze, staring at her, and then cocked his head to the side, his dark hair wild. His silhouette was lean. Tension emanated between them, an unspoken communication. He would've already hurt her, she thought, if he wanted to kill her. But he just sat there in silence, staring her down, not moving an inch.

"Who are you?" Her voice croaked as it echoed on the empty street.

He tilted his head to the other side, still staring her down.

Dawn edged back further, keeping her arms tight around her.

"I'm going to leave now. Unless you have something to say." Her voice shook. She edged back, afraid to turn from him. She moved to the side, and he followed her with his head, still silent.

Shouting came from down the street and Dawn jerked. The silhouette's head turned toward the sound before he leaped away, disappearing down the backside of the building.

Men emerged from down the street, singing a brazen song, some staggering to the side, bottles in their hands. Her father's face appeared in the lamppost light, and Dawn fixed her face into a scowl.

"What are you doing here?" she snapped.

Her father faltered and the men around him stopped. She recognized their faces, including Johnny Wilson, whom she'd helped earlier that week.

"We're the watchmen," her father slurred. He held up his bottle of spirits. "We're out to protect the streets and make sure young ladies like you aren't murdered."

She eyed the alcohol, wondering how they got it.

"You?" Dawn said, laughing. As if they could take on a psychotic killer. They could hardly stand upright.

Johnny's eyes lit with amusement. "Not that you need protecting. You're a strong girl. I could use a girl like you by my side." He staggered forward and gripped her arm, pulling her up against him forcefully. His breath stank of whiskey and he smiled, revealing a gap-toothed grin.

Dawn placed her hands against his chest and shoved. "You're right. I am strong. You should all go home. Especially you," she said to her father. "I can't remember the last time you were there."

Johnny's face turned red and he threw his own bottle to the ground. It smashed into several pieces and he marched forward once more.

"Your brat has a tongue," he said more to her than her father. "She needs to be punished."

Her father waved his hand. "She's all yours. A disappointment, she is. Running around like she's better than everyone. Killed her own brother, and she doesn't even have remorse. Have your way with her. She'll be married soon enough."

A leer spread over Johnny's face as he stalked her once more. Backing up, Dawn tripped over her feet. She wasn't afraid of Johnny—at least she thought she wasn't—he was inebriated enough, she could probably kick him and run. But his shoulders seemed to grow in size the closer he approached, and she wondered if she *could* fight him off.

He reached forward, grabbing her roughly. Pain bit her arms where he squeezed, and she pounded on his chest, trying to get her foot up to kick him.

"What is this?" Gideon's voice disrupted the night, and Johnny paused.

Gideon marched up and pushed Johnny back, drawing Dawn to his side. Johnny swayed backward, stumbling over his feet. Gideon towered over all the men, his body straight, thrumming with tension.

"I said, what is this? Do I need to report all of you? Send you all to jail? Perhaps one of you is the Dollmaker? Or all of you? Is it a combined effort?"

Dawn knew the thought was absurd, but judging by the way the men's faces paled, it was a good threat.

"Just having sssome fun," Johnny said. "There's no need to overreact."

Gideon's eyes darkened. "Oh, I can assure you, you don't want to see me act, let alone overreact. Now leave or I'll have all of your heads."

Her father glanced from Gideon to his friends, indecision flickering over his face. He clearly didn't care about Dawn, the way he'd let Johnny attack her, but he backed away and the men rushed down the street, leaving Dawn and Gideon alone. The sounds echoed around them, the lampposts lining the street in small orbs of light.

"What are you doing here?" Dawn asked. A part of her softened, and then she realized he must have followed her. Her mind briefly went to the man on the roof before she shook her head. It hadn't been him. "I'm perfectly capable of handling myself."

Gideon twisted his lips, the nearest lamppost light accentuating the grooves of his face. "Oh? It certainly looked like it. And what are you doing out here this time of night? I thought you were going straight home." He raised his brows.

Dawn opened her mouth and closed it. "Nothing of your concern."

She didn't know why she was being snippy with him. Perhaps it was the long day. She'd spent all day with him investigating murders when she could've been helping patients. He had robbed her of that.

"What about you?" she said. "Seems you're also guilty."

Gideon clamped his jaws together tightly. "What do you think I'm doing? I'm walking the streets trying to find that madman and stop him from hurting another innocent woman like you."

"Oh."

"Oh, indeed."

Dawn scrubbed a hand over her forehead. "I wouldn't mind the walk home if you feel so inclined. It's been an . . . interesting night."

"I wouldn't have it another way." He moved ahead of her, and Dawn rushed to catch up. He didn't offer his arm, which somehow hurt her. He'd done the same thing earlier that day. Could he not stand the thought of being close to her? They were pretending to be engaged, after all.

They walked in silence for a long while, just the two of them breathing, white air puffing in and out of her lungs. An awkwardness settled between them, which didn't make sense, as they'd spent the whole day together. But there was a sudden connection—her body hyper-aware of his—as they walked in the dark. Did she really know him? Could she really trust him? What if his intentions toward her were bad?

No. If he'd wanted to take advantage of her, he'd had all afternoon to do so. His grief for his Sophie was real and his intentions were pure, albeit improper.

"Tell me more about Sophie," she said. "What was she like?"

His jaw tightened again at the mention of her name, and she didn't think he'd respond, until he whispered quietly in the night.

"Like I said, she was a ballerina in New York. I was spending the summer at an estate with my great aunt. Sophie was . . . she was walking poetry. Everything about her drew you to her, like a thirsty man to a glass of water. After the first performance I saw her in, I was able to meet with her, and I'd made my intentions quite clear upfront. Though I was only one of many suitors. It only took seeing her once, and I knew I wanted to marry her."

Dawn swallowed, and a new sensation fluttered in her chest. She had never wanted to marry, but suddenly . . . the thought of someone loving her like that stuck in her throat.

"Is that why you bought the ballet theater, then?" she asked. "In memory of her?"

Gideon shook his head. "No. I bought the theater because . . . I thought there might be a connection between her and the murders. Sophie was a ballerina just like some of the other victims. Maybe that's the link."

"He took Rose," Dawn said.

The memory of Rose dancing in the studio—her perfect, ethereal beauty—blossomed to the front of her mind. Perhaps Rose and Sophie had a lot in common.

"Why didn't you tell me this before now?" she asked.

"That I bought a ballet theater as a pretense to hunt for a murderer? No, I need to put on the act. I will act as the director there and gather as many clues as I can. Even if people think it's odd."

"But you don't know anything about dance."

"Don't I? I did spend months watching Sophie, watching her in rehearsals, onstage . . . I analyzed every detail of technique and precision I could. I think I can handle a ballet company. I'll do anything to stop this and . . ." He sucked in a deep breath.

"Get your revenge?"

"Yes."

They fell quiet once more, the night air still around them. The chill had left, and Gideon emanated warmth next to her. They headed through the town square, back to where her house was. The streets were cleaner at this end of town, not as much trash on the ground.

"It's right up here," Dawn said, speeding to her building.

"I'm aware."

"Right."

Gideon stopped in front of the building as Dawn hovered next to him. She really shouldn't be alone with him at this time of night, but there was an unspoken pain between them, and she wanted to fix it. She was a healer, after all.

The night's events caught up to her, and a part of her crumpled inside. She had been followed. She'd almost been attacked. Her father had allowed it. Gideon had once again appeared at the perfect time. Too many thoughts bombarded her at once. Rose. Her own practice. Gideon. The man on the roof. The Dollmaker. She didn't know if she could handle this much longer.

"We'll find him," she whispered.

He gave a firm nod. "I'll hold you to that."

9

The Cold Vein

The next morning, Dawn decided she needed to distract herself from the night before.

She wasn't to meet Gideon until later that day, and so she headed to the clinic early in hopes there would be an early patient she could treat before Dr. Miller arrived. The old man tended to sleep in and wander into the clinic around noon; there must be someone who needed help before then.

She wore a loose blouse tucked into a skirt with a thick belt around her waist. Her nearly-black hair was pinned up on top of her head, with little wisps that would never stay in place. The heavy breeze in the air didn't help her appearance.

As she walked down the front steps of her home, a car pulled to a stop in front of her, its engine running. The valet that had taken her to the Hemsworth manor the other night jumped out and circled the car, taking off his hat in greeting.

"I was sent straightaway for you, miss," he said. "I am to take you to the theater."

Dawn clasped her medical bag closer to her side. "What's happened?"

"It's one of the ballerinas. She's fallen and can't walk. Mr. Hemsworth sent me to you."

Her heart warmed at the thought of Gideon sending for her. He trusted her. He trusted her to help this young woman. She didn't expect that. He didn't seem too keen on her spending her time on something other than searching for Sophie's murderer, but she couldn't help but smile as she helped herself into the car. She was finally going to be useful for once.

"We best get going then," she said.

The valet drove quickly through the streets, Dawn's teeth vibrating from the rumble of the car. She stared out at the city, at the housing and parks. The car stopped outside the theater's courtyard. Without a word, she jumped out of the car and rushed into the grassy area, running across the lawn instead of taking the paved walkways.

The courtyard was empty—no people lounging underneath the large oak trees, just the early-morning light filtering down through the clouds.

Dawn rushed into the rehearsal hall and bolted down the hallway to the studio at the end. She threw open the wooden door and stopped inside. There wasn't anyone there.

"Hello?" she called. "Caldwell? Gideon?"

Silence echoed.

She tentatively moved into the studio, her reflection staring back at her, her dark hair and pale skin sallow in the early light. Maybe they were in the back dressing room. She was crossing the space to the other entrance on the far side when the door creaked open behind her.

Arthur Hemsworth limped into the room, cane in hand, his emaciated form hunched over. Wrinkles folded over his face, and he smacked his lips as he looked Dawn over. The few white hairs on his pockmarked head matched his button-up white shirt.

"Mr. Hemsworth," she said abruptly. "What are you . . ." She glanced around her. "What are you doing here?"

His lips curled upward as he smacked them again. "I came here to see what my nephew was up to. Strange, that he would purchase an entire ballet theater, is it not? Then I heard that you treated the ballerinas, and I thought that was one way to get you here. Alone. Where we could speak."

"So no one needs my help?"

He leered, smacking his lips a third time.

"We don't have anything to talk about," Dawn said.

"Oh, I think we do." He hobbled forward, his knuckles bony on his cane. "My nephew has made known his intentions toward you, and your mother has accepted his offer to court you. Well, I won't have it."

Dawn lifted her chin, staring him down, though her insides shook. "That isn't your decision. If Mr. Hemsworth wants to court me, then he will. And I choose him over you."

He barked out a laugh, before he broke into a fit of coughing. The gargled sounds echoed through the studio. When he cleared his throat, his eyes looked over her body, hungry, and he limped closer.

"I could ruin you," he said. "You think I don't know about your father's debts? One word and I could have you out on the street. Or I could tell everyone that you bedded my nephew. You'd be an outcast. Then there's the fact that people call you a witch. Gertrude has already alerted the authorities and made a complaint about you. You killed her husband. I've stopped the authorities from arresting you, but one word from me and I could have you cast into prison."

Dawn stumbled back a step. "You wouldn't do that."

"Wouldn't I? When I want something, I get it. You *will* marry me."

She shook her head violently. "You wouldn't be that cruel."

"Then you don't know me at all, young one. I'm a man of power. People do what I say. Besides, you would live a comfortable life. And I think you will succumb to my tastes."

Dawn scrunched her face. The thought of being with him was too much. She crossed her arms and continued backward.

"I won't do it," she said. "I don't care if I'm ruined."

He stopped, and his face contorted. "Is that a *challenge*? I'll offer your family more money. Money you could use on your . . . doctoring. Don't you want your own practice? I could give it to you. I'll give you the freedom you want, as long as you warm my bed at night."

She paused. Could she bear being with him if it meant that she'd be able to do what she loved? The money. Her patients. She'd have the freedom to help others. For a moment, she was tempted. It was all she wanted. And Arthur was standing right there, offering it to her.

No.

She clenched her eyes shut, trying to breathe steadily. She wouldn't give herself up like that. She'd find another way.

"I don't want your money," she spat. "And I'll take my chances with your threats." She marched past him, heading for the door, and he shuffled after her, gripping her around the wrist. His fingers pinched her skin and she yanked away, stumbling. The door swung open and Gideon stepped inside, the two nearly colliding. Gideon glanced back and forth from Dawn to his uncle and his face hardened.

"Is there something I should be aware of?" His scowl deepened.

"No, nothing," Dawn said, breathing hard. She pushed past him and rushed down the hall, out into the courtyard once more.

"Dawn, wait!" Gideon's voice echoed after her.

She continued to run.

Gideon caught up with her and gripped her arm, spinning her around. He stared down at her, eyes fixed.

"*What*?"

Gideon slowly released her. "What was that about back there?"

She pressed her lips together tightly, and she crossed her arms. "I saw your face. You think I *want* to be with that sick man? You think I'm playing you?"

Gideon's face softened, and he ran a hand over his sleek hair. "No, of course not. I think I know you well enough now to know you're not after my uncle's money. But why the secret meeting?"

She held silent, their eyes locked, until she said, "He arranged it."

He gave her a curious look, his eyes searching hers, and he exhaled. "I came here to investigate the theater. In New York there were a couple of incidents where girls were found dead in the dressing rooms. As I've looked into it further, more ballerinas than I thought have been murdered—I didn't catch it at first because most of the girls had stopped dancing and were about to be married, so there definitely is a connection to ballerinas. We were right."

Dawn nodded slowly. "So the girl out in the square the other day—" She remembered the bottom half of her leg missing. "Was she—"

"A member of the corps de ballet, yes," he said. "I also didn't piece that together until last night."

Dawn tried to remember her face, but she'd been so focused on the missing leg. "But she wasn't found dead in the theater."

"She could've been abducted there, we don't know. But somehow, I know this madman has a thing for ballerinas and some of his murders surround the theater."

The wind gusted as Dawn peeked up at the ominous structure. Gray stone pillars lined the front of the building, with detailed carvings adorning the outside. Massive steps led to the front doors, where carvings of different creatures hung overhead. The clouds moved fast in the sky above the structure, and there was another surge of wind. She shivered.

"So, what's the plan?" she asked.

"The plan is to let me investigate. It might not be safe. You probably have patients to attend to. I'll have a look and then meet you back at your home later to call on you?"

She peeked over at the towering building again. She didn't want to leave Gideon alone, but she also wanted to get back to Dr. Miller's office.

"Fine," she said. "I'll meet you later."

<hr>

The afternoon was more eventful than she'd expected. A few patients came in, and Dr. Miller hadn't yet surfaced. She'd been able to tend to a sprained wrist, a nail in the foot, and a crushed finger. It wasn't surgery, but at least she was helping people. Who knew where the old doctor was? Perhaps he'd been called on another trip out of town. Dawn couldn't get her mind off Gideon and if he had discovered anything.

After closing up the clinic, she noticed Nora speaking with an officer across the square. The officer was wide around the shoulders, with a barrel chest. Was Nora all right? The two spoke for a moment, and then he tipped his hat and walked away. Nora began sweeping outside her shop, brushing away a few crumpled leaves. She wore a loose dress with a V-neck that plunged down to her bosom, her long black braids hanging down over her shoulders as usual. It wasn't proper for a lady to wear her hair so, but it spoke volumes about Nora and her care for society.

Clutching her medical bag close to her, Dawn headed across the square, past the fountain, and stopped in front of the shop. Nora lifted her head and her eyes twinkled in acknowledgment.

"Dawn, what a surprise. Are you in need of more herbs, then?"

"What? Oh. No." She patted her bag. "I was just wondering how the séance went."

Nora leaned on her broom, her mouth twisting upward. "Why? Interested in coming to the next one?"

Dawn was just being polite, but she bit the inside of her lips, her mind spinning. "Do you *really* speak with the dead?"

"That you'll have to see for yourself." Nora cocked her head for a moment, analyzing Dawn. "I was right, there *is* something different about you." Her forehead pinched. "You *have* met someone . . . but it isn't the someone you're meant to be with. But it is . . . I can see his face . . . but it isn't. That's curious."

All thoughts of believing that a séance could be real fled. Nora wasn't making any sense. As if she could call on the dead when she couldn't even speak coherently.

"You're about to meet the love of your life," Nora continued. "I can see it in your eyes."

Heat surged to Dawn's cheeks. She feigned humor and let out a shaky laugh. "I really doubt that."

Nora leaned back, observing her further. "I'm never wrong, Dawn. I have the gift of sight. When I see something, it happens."

The world seemed to disappear as she took in Nora's deep eyes. Intelligence swam behind them, her black braids dangling in the wind. Maybe there was something to her. An unearthly feeling had settled between them, as if *she* were the one controlling the wind.

Nora couldn't be speaking the truth. She wasn't about to meet the love of her life. The idea was absurd. Though when Nora spoke, it was as if she truly believed her own words. Who would this new person be?

Dawn dusted off her hands and blinked. "It's good to see you, Nora. Good luck at your next . . . séance."

Nora's lips twitched. "The truth makes people uncomfortable, Dawn. Come to me when you realize I'm speaking the truth. I can always help."

Dawn's throat thickened, so she just nodded.

She waved good-bye and headed back across the square. Shoppers bustled back and forth, and she brushed past shoulders and darting kids as she exited onto the street.

It had been a long day. Fatigue settled onto her shoulders, the weight of it pushing her down. She needed a bath and a few moments to close her eyes. But if she went home, she wouldn't get respite. Her mother would pressure her about Gideon and their engagement, and she might make her wear another hideous dress. Maybe she could go to the theater to catch up with Gideon instead of making him come to her house later.

Rose needed to be her priority, after all. Another flux of panic hit, and her feet were rooted to the street. Her breaths came in fast gasps; she was unable to steady them. She set a hand to her heart, willing it to slow. Rose wasn't dead. She couldn't be. Dawn would *never* be okay again if she was.

The memory of sipping tea in Rose's parlor flashed to mind. Painted china and doilies. Sugar cubes and cream. Their dolls would sit at the table, and they'd pretend they were princesses conversing in their castles. She could envision Rose perfectly in her lace dresses with pink bows. They'd laugh for hours, sipping their tea, and Rose would speak about a prince sweeping her off her feet.

There was already buzz around town about Rose's disappearance, but people seemed to think that she'd run off with another man rather than being snatched by the Dollmaker—since her dead body hadn't been found.

Gideon *had* to be right that there was a link between ballet and the girls' murders. It was their only clue.

Setting her chin, Dawn made her way through the streets and back to the theater.

10
Theater of Shadows

The sun descended fast, dipping through the heavy layers of clouds on the horizon. Dawn stood in front of the towering theater, wind whipping her skirt. She imagined Gideon walking in the hallways, searching through the dressing rooms. Was he still there? Or perhaps he had left. He did say he was going to call on her. Maybe she ought to return home.

But she was already here. It wouldn't do too much harm if she were to take a peek inside. If the deaths really were related to ballerinas and the theater, then she needed to know.

Rose's face came to mind—her dark lashes that always swept over her cheeks, her porcelain complexion, her lips flawlessly painted with rouge. She had a kindness about her she had always shown Dawn, regardless of status. She'd always been the beautiful one. Even as a young girl, men seemed to give her attention. Dawn's own mother had ogled her beauty. But Dawn had never felt jealousy. There was a softness and genuineness to Rose that made everyone love her.

She couldn't suffer a horrific death. But as Dawn stared up at the towering structure, a chill rocketed through her. Maybe it wasn't wise to go inside without Gideon. What if the Dollmaker was in there? What if there was another victim waiting to be found? What if the Dollmaker had gotten to Gideon?

She shook the thoughts away. Steeling herself, Dawn pushed out a breath and walked up the front steps. Her hand slid along the cool iron banister, her footsteps soft against the gray stone. When she reached the top, she pushed open the heavy double doors, stepping inside the grand space. It was always open to dancers at this time of day.

She had never been inside the theater space itself—there hadn't been any reason to. She'd always tended to girls inside the rehearsal hall. Because of her father's habits, she'd never been wealthy enough to go to the ballet, though she'd always imagined what it would be like. To see the dancers onstage—their bodies ethereal— or to sit in the audience wearing an evening gown. It was a dream she didn't allow herself to have very often.

A massive chandelier stretched across the ceiling, its legs crawling outward, candles adorning each tip. Jewels dripped from the center, sparkling in the dim light. No lamps burned, the early moonlight shining through the large windows that circled the gigantic room. Velvet carpet stretched beneath her, and gold trim with leaves decorated the walls.

She crept into the room and headed toward the hallways in the back. She ducked inside and ran her fingers along the trim, clean without dust, even though the building smelled of musk, revealing how old it was. Her footsteps creaked on the carpet, her heart steady. There was nothing to fear. She only had to rule out that this place had nothing to do with the murders.

She entered a back hallway. Dressing rooms lined the space, with a costume room full of tutus. The white fluffy material hung on multiple racks, bright in the dark, but she passed by, entering a dressing room on the left. The room was empty, save for a couple of clean mirrors and a few chairs. Another costume rack sat at the far end, a few tutus hanging, and a pair of pointe shoes were on the floor. She stepped into the space to see if there was anything unusual. She didn't know what she was looking for—blood on the walls? A knife on the floor?

It was absurd. The Dollmaker wouldn't leave such evidence around. He'd never been caught for a reason.

She stepped into the next dressing room, and it was more of the same, along with the next one.

Soon she entered the backstage area, stepping through the large dark wings and onto the stage floor. Rafters towered above her, along with ropes and wooden planks. She squinted at the dark auditorium, at the lines of seats that stretched out like a velvet blanket. She wondered what it would be like to dance—to feel the stage lights on her face, to have the audience's applause rolling off her. It must've been why Rose wanted to dance as a career—it must've been thrilling.

She walked to the edge of the stage and peered into the orchestra pit below. Stairs led off to the side and down into the pit, and she slowly descended. Chairs were lined up where the musicians sat, and she ran her hand along each wooden back. She could almost hear the echo of the orchestral music, still hanging on the air, wanting to be played again, living on forever.

Keeping her satchel at her side, she eyed a pair of doors at the back of the pit. Curious, she slowly crept forward and pushed one door open.

A rustling sound came from below the stage, and Dawn paused, suddenly aware of her heart. It beat heavily in her chest, thumping up into her throat.

"Hello?" she called out. She snuck in further and saw a single oil lamp burning on a far table. She moved past piles of boxes and other dark objects. Another rustle sounded, and she paused again. Her heart wouldn't stop beating too fast. She willed it to calm, pushing out deep breaths. Her muscles tightened and her feet glued themselves to the floor. She suddenly cursed herself for coming here.

What was she thinking?

"Gideon?" she whispered.

"I'm *not* Gideon." The voice rang out smooth and clear, cutting straight through Dawn's core.

All reason told her to flee, but what was the point of coming down here if she didn't gather information?

"Who are you, then?" Dawn asked.

In a burst, the figure emerged and rushed toward Dawn before she could blink. A hand gripped her around the throat and pushed her up against the far wall. He stuck his silhouetted face in hers, the scent of lavender emanating off him. It was pleasant in her nose, a contrast to his sudden, violent behavior. Her back was pressed against the cold wall, her palms flat against it.

"What are you doing here?" he barked.

"I'm . . ." She could hardly breathe.

He gripped her harder and she choked.

"P-please . . . stop."

His grip loosened, as if he realized how tight he was holding her. He took a step back, but he was still too close. She had never been so close to a man, even with Gideon, and he crossed boundaries. She couldn't see the stranger's face, only half of it lit by the lamp, highlighting the grooves of his bones. The sharp angles reminded her of Gideon's face, though this man's bones seemed to be sharper, his cheeks extra hollow. His skin nearly glowed in the dark, and she wondered how someone could be so pale.

"I asked you what you were doing here," he repeated.

Dawn's fists clenched together, and the fear suddenly vanished. How *dare* this man address her so? She might not have been as ladylike as Rose, but she was still a lady.

"And what business is that of yours?" she retorted, anger drowning out her lingering fear and igniting the words.

He was quiet for a moment, before he let out a low chuckle. "Because this is my home, and you're invading my home."

Home?

He lived here?

She swallowed, bits of fear creeping back in. What if the Dollmaker lived in the theaters? Maybe it was where he kept his victims. He was obsessed with ballerinas, after all.

"Ah," he said. "I can sense your fear. Well, good. You should be afraid."

She clamped her teeth together, staring at him in the dark. She stepped away from the wall. "I'm not afraid of you. I'm here to expose you."

He was silent again, as if thinking. Finally, he said, "Oh? Expose me for what?"

She blinked. "You know."

"I hardly know what you're talking about. Now, to figure out how to deal with you for finding me here . . ." He circled her like a villain. "I can't very well let you leave—in case you tell people that I live down here—but I also can't very well keep you. The last thing I need is a pet."

A pet?

So now she was a pet. He really didn't think of her as a lady at all.

"Still. We'll have to figure this out."

He began to slowly pace in front of her, his shaded head tilted in thought. His legs were long, though he wasn't much taller than her. Bits of slanted light streamed in through the floorboards above them, highlighting parts of his face. She still couldn't see him clearly.

"I've never had anyone find me before," he said. "And I take pride in the fact that no one does. I lead a quiet life, an uninterrupted life, and now you've interrupted it." He paused, facing her head on. He seemed nothing more than a shadow in front of her.

She held still, silent. If he *was* the Dollmaker, she didn't want to make him upset. He hadn't killed her yet, but maybe he liked to toy with his prey before he slaughtered them.

"I won't tell anyone about you," she choked out. "Just let me go."

He let out a bitter laugh. "And why should I believe you?"

"Why are you trying to stay hidden?"

Both of their questions hung in the air.

He started pacing again. Her heart was hammering its way into her throat; she could barely breathe. She edged to the side. His head snapped up and he sprang forward once more. He gripped her upper arm and began to drag her into the dark, away from the orchestra pit. She struggled against him, trying to rip herself out of his embrace, but his hold was like concrete. He led her through a dark hallway inclining until it stopped at a dead end. A door towered in front of them. She still couldn't see his face.

He moved in close, yanking her up against him until she felt his breath on her cheek. "If you tell anyone about me—anyone at all—I will know, and there will be consequences greater than you can imagine. Death will follow, I can assure you that."

"You're . . . letting me go?" Her eyes stretched wide in the dark, but she still couldn't see him.

They stood facing each other in silence, both of their chests heaving up and down.

"Don't make me regret it," he said, shoving her forward. He opened the door and thrust her into the cool night air. The door slammed closed. She stared at the wood, breathing hard. A tangle of bushes surrounded her, and the smell of decaying roses wafted on the air. She breathed in the scent, edging back and bumping into a thorny rosebush. She twirled around, the moonlight illuminating a pathway through the dead gardens, the courtyard in the distance.

She stood trembling for a moment, before she took off into the night, trying to shake his touch off her.

⚬⚬⚬ ⚬⚬⚬ ⚬⚬⚬

She didn't know how she made it home, but she did. Having escaped her mother's clutches, Dawn found herself in bed. She lay fully clothed, pulling her blanket up to her chin. The chill wouldn't leave her bones. She didn't know if Gideon had ended up calling on her, but it didn't matter. The investigation needed to stop.

That man *had* to be the Dollmaker. And now she was marked. He had seen her face, hadn't he? He knew who she was. If she continued with this investigation, he would come after her. Unless he hadn't seen her face. She hadn't seen his. But if he was the Dollmaker, why did he let her go? Shouldn't she be part of a Frankenstein-esque doll by now?

Then it occurred to her. She wasn't a ballerina.

She wrapped the blanket closer around her. She never wanted to leave this bed again. But as her heart settled, she decided he hadn't seen her. She was safe.

But what of his threats? If she told anyone about him—even Gideon—death would follow.

She thought of Rose. What if he had her? Was that the death he was talking about? Her breathing sped up and she hiccuped. No. She would keep his secret.

But she would also keep investigating.

Soon Dawn fell asleep, but fitful dreams overtook her. They were filled with dark shadows stalking her on the rooftops, and no matter how hard she ran, the shadows followed. Finally, when one shadow caught her, she felt as if she were suffocating, she couldn't breathe, and just before darkness engulfed her, Gideon's face appeared, his mouth open in a silent scream.

Dawn was jolted awake when her mother burst into the room waving her hands frantically, her skirt swishing.

"Get up, you lazy child!" She reached over and threw the covers off of Dawn. "A messenger came this morning! You're meeting Gideon tonight at the ballet. A car is coming at seven to escort you. We must find you something to wear, so you don't look so . . . drab. Perhaps that silk gown I wore at Mrs. Thompson's party last summer—the one with the bows? But no, maybe it's too outdated. Yes, we must see what pennies we can find and purchase you a new dress today. It will be worth it when you land Gideon as a husband, and you will have more dresses than you can count!" Her face twisted wistfully. "And so will I."

Her mother's eyes zeroed in on her, glaring.

"Why aren't you moving? Get up! You look horrid. It will take all day to get you ready! I'll have Mrs. Cook take you into town. She can sacrifice her pay for the month to find you a dress. Yes, that will work. Move, you imbecile! You must get presentable!"

Her mother stomped out in a flurry, and Dawn clenched her eyes shut, leaning back into her pillow. The last thing she wanted to do was go inside that theater again. Her nightmares still lingered with her, floating in the forefront of her mind, and the thought of Gideon being that shadow had been all too real. She knew he wasn't, but she couldn't shake the feeling.

She wanted a day in the clinic, but she expected the authorities to question her at any moment. She *was* the one who first alerted them to Rose's disappearance. She wanted a break from Gideon and their fake courting, and their investigation. But she knew she had to go to the ballet that night. She couldn't very well keep spending time with him unless they made it known to the world that he was courting her.

But the thought of seeing the ballet . . .

She sat up in a rush and swung her feet to the floor.

Her blouse and skirt were rumpled, her belt digging into her side. She stretched her back, the bones in her spine popping one by one, easing the tension some. She sat down at her vanity and began to repin her hair, taming the wild curls that had escaped during her escapade last night.

She exited, started down the stairs, and then paused. Chester stood in the entryway, pacing, his hands clutching his bowler hat. Suspenders stretched over his silk shirt, a handkerchief in his pocket. She gripped the banister tightly. Anger flooded through her, and she clenched her jaws together.

Mrs. Cook was trying to get him into the parlor.

"I really don't have time to stay," he said. "I just need to speak with Miss Hildegard for a moment."

Chester's eyes darted up to the top of the stairwell and he made a small bow, relief spreading over his face. "Miss Hildegard."

Mrs. Cook hovered by the parlor door, hesitating.

"It's okay, Mrs. Cook. I'll walk Mr. Doxey out," said Dawn.

A sheen of sweat shone on his face. He kept his gaze glued to her as she descended the stairs. Mrs. Cook left the foyer, leaving the two alone. Dawn stepped up in front of him, her chin lifted.

"Can I help you, Mr. Doxey?"

Chester wrung his hat in his hands, his weight shifting from side to side. "I heard it was you that entered the party the other night, screaming that Rose had been kidnapped. I was . . . gone. I didn't see it happen. I'm so sorry no one believed you."

Dawn tried to swallow, but her throat was too swollen. "Have you heard anything?"

His mouth flicked downward. "No."

She kept her chin lifted. "What have the authorities said?"

"It's either she ran off with another man or . . ."

Dawn nodded. Or she was being hacked to pieces. She tried to steady her breaths. "So what are you doing here?"

"You saw something, didn't you? That night?"

"I . . ." She squinted up at him. "Not much. It was dark." Why did he care now?

His shoulders slumped. "At least you're all right."

"And why would you care about that? Why would you care about Rose?"

He continued to wring his hat. "I feel as if . . . as if it's my fault. It's punishment for my actions. If I hadn't"—he lowered his voice—"behaved the way I had, then Rose wouldn't have been taken from me. I feel responsible for her disappearance. And if I ever saw her again, I would never take her for granted. If anything happened to her . . ."

Dawn eyed him, her mouth pinched. She wasn't the superstitious sort, but he clearly was. "Well then, you'd better start cleaning up your act now," she said. "Maybe if you do, Rose will be returned to us. Now, if you'll excuse me, I have some business in town."

Chester nodded his thanks, giving a shaky bow. "If you discover anything about Rose's whereabouts, please let me know. I know I won't stop looking."

Dawn clicked the door shut behind them, and he hurried down the front steps. She pressed her back against the front door, watching him depart. Chester wasn't okay. And neither was she. If she didn't find Rose, she would never be whole again.

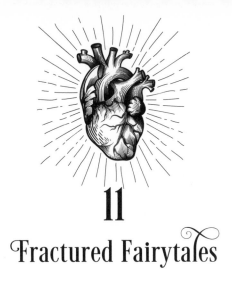

11

Fractured Fairytales

Dawn spent the day walking around town gathering material with Mrs. Cook, finding jewelry, and picking out a new evening shawl and gloves. She apologized profusely to Mrs. Cook that she was taking her month's pay, but Mrs. Cook assured her that nothing would make her happier, though the lines around her eyes seemed extra deep.

The dressmaker in town had assured Dawn that he could make the dress by evening and that she would be the most stunning lady at the ballet. She doubted that, but as long as she didn't stick out like an infected thumb, she would be satisfied.

She knew she needed to meet Gideon that afternoon, but the thought of spending all afternoon *and* evening with him made her insides squirm. The dream she'd had about him the night before still hovered over her shoulder: his mouth contorting into a silent scream; he being the shadow that stalked her. But she knew that couldn't be the case. If anyone was the shadow that had stalked her that evening, it was the man she'd met underneath the theater. He did fit the silhouette. Lean build, ruffled hair. He seemed like the type of individual who would leap from rooftop to rooftop.

After shopping, Mrs. Cook dragged Dawn back home, saying her mother would throw a fit if she didn't start preparing for that night. But Dawn knew that if she didn't show up at Gideon's place, he'd be livid they hadn't worked the afternoon together. He half expected her to give up her life to help him get his revenge on the Dollmaker, and if he knew she was playing princess by getting ready for their fake evening, he probably wouldn't have asked her to go in the first place. But she decided to return home, hoping Gideon would be just fine without her.

The afternoon faded away as Mrs. Cook spent an hour on Dawn's hair, pinning tight curls into perfection. The hairstyle showed off her neck, with little pearls adorning her ears. The dress arrived, its fabric light and airy, with just enough weight to drape in straight lines. It was black and sleeveless, with metal sequins. She wore a black headband that matched the dark material.

Mrs. Cook took another half hour to gently apply Dawn's make-up, lining her eyes and smearing rouge on her cheeks and mouth. By the time they had finished, Dawn didn't recognize herself in the mirror. A lady stood before her, older, more seductive, more daring. She had never seen herself as appealing before, nor did she think she could pull off such a look.

Her mother screamed from downstairs, yelling at her to hurry. A sleek car waited out front, and Dawn quickly wrapped her new jade green shawl around her shoulders. Cool air bit her cheeks as the usual valet opened her door and she silently glared, remembering how he'd deceived her by bringing her to Arthur.

She let the valet help her into the vehicle but kept her chin up and her mouth set tight the entire car ride, staring out into the dark night.

Lampposts lined the sidewalks, moonlight shining down from above. Stars filled the clear sky, like splatters of glowing paint on a black canvas. The car came to a stop outside the theater, and Dawn exited before the valet could open her door. Gideon waited next to the wrought-iron gates that surrounded the courtyard. Her heart pounded at the sight of him. The more she looked at him, the more he reminded her of the man underneath the theater. He wore a black fitted jacket with swallowtails in the back along with a white vest, silk striped pants, and a white tie. He gave a formal bow, half of his mouth crooked up.

"Miss Hildegard."

Dawn fumbled a greeting, suddenly awkward at the formality. He offered her his elbow. She stared at it. She peered at his pressed coat, and gently slid her arm through his. He turned his profile, looking her over, and it was as if he finally took her in. His gaze roamed over her face to her hair to her gown, his eyes trying not to linger on her neckline.

He cleared his throat. "You clean up well."

Her mouth flicked up. "Thank you, Mr. Hemsworth."

They walked along the winding walkways to the theater, passing by the large oak trees, and she shivered at the thought of poor Frederick being crushed by one of its limbs. She stared at the spot where the event had taken place, before glancing away. She needed to clear her mind. Focus on the present.

"Thank you for going along with this pretense," Gideon said. "The other day Mr. Thomas saw us walking together and he asked what I was doing with you. I thought it was time I formally announced us being together by taking you out here tonight. For your reputation, of course."

"I'm doing it for Rose," she said. "That's what is important." She had almost allowed herself to be captured by the moment.

"You do look beautiful, by the way. A real lady." His mouth quirked upward for a moment, then relaxed.

She kept her lips sealed together. They walked up the front steps of the theater, where music from a string quartet drifted out from the open doors. Her black sparkly dress swished below her knees, and her hand tightened around Gideon's arm. Gideon and Dawn stepped past the theater's large cracked and worn columns. Light from a grand chandelier glowed from the inside, and soft chatter whirled through the air.

Everything seemed to sparkle and spin in the main entryway, from the dripping diamonds of the chandelier to the jewels around exposed necks. Soft laughter tinkled through the room. Dawn paused on the red velvet carpet, taking it all in. Life emanated from all corners of the space, opposite from the last time she had been there. Her breath caught in her throat.

Gideon led her through the crowd, not saying a word to anyone, though a few people paused their conversations and stared at the two of them. More people noticed, with more hushed conversations as Gideon led Dawn up and around to the side foyer, where stairs took them to the second tier.

"We have a suite," Gideon murmured. "I think you'll be quite impressed." He led her down the hall toward a burgundy side curtain. He parted the curtain, motioning her inside, and she stepped into the dark suite, where a few velvet seats awaited her. The suite overlooked the entire auditorium, including the stage, where a large, tasseled curtain hung top to bottom. A pristine chandelier extended across the vaulted ceiling, golden legs shooting out from a circle of dazzling crystals. Massive tapestries hung on the walls—woven pictures of dancers in tutus, surrounded by forests and flowers.

"It's marvelous," Dawn said.

Gideon made a noise in the back of his throat. "Wait until the curtain rises."

People filtered into the room, and soon everyone was seated. Ladies used fans to cool themselves in the stuffy space, but the heat didn't affect Dawn, as she sat above everyone. The orchestra tuned their instruments as the conductor walked out. The audience applauded at his arrival, and he took several bows before he raised his baton. In a downbeat, the orchestra began, the sweet and lively melody drifting through the auditorium. Dawn sat on the edge of her seat, her hands neatly in her lap. The violins' music soared through the auditorium as the brass mingled with the woodwinds. The music filled her soul, swirling around her.

Her mind completely floated away, forgetting all the hardships and hurt she had felt in the last week, as the curtain rose and the stage came to life. Bright colors lit the scene as the dancers entered, the scenery mimicking a town square. She had never seen *Coppelia*—or any ballet, for that matter—but she had seen the girls rehearsing it during her time in the studio. The villagers were celebrating the new town bell that was going to arrive in a few days, and dancers flittered around the stage, telling the story. The characters, Swanhilde and Franz, were celebrating their engagement when Franz noticed a girl named Coppelia, who sat motionless at the top of the balcony. He was mesmerized by her beauty; Swanhilde ran away, heartbroken.

The orchestra continued to play, and Dawn allowed her gaze to scan the audience. Everyone seemed to blend together in a sea of wealth, heads glued to the stage. Below, on the mezzanine, a man in a dark suit was staring right at her. He kept his eyes locked on her, his head turned upward, when the rest of the audience focused forward. His dark hair was strewn in all directions, and his angled bones were prominent in the dim light.

Dawn jerked back, ripping her gaze away. It was *him*. His ruffled hair, his lean build. His body matched the silhouette of the man she met underneath the theater. The man who had been following her from the roof.

Was he really staring at her? Or was it a trick of the light? She slowly peeked again, and sure enough, his black eyes were staring her down, a stern expression on his face. The shadows in the theater cut his strong features, hollowing out his eyes and cheeks. A heavy feeling settled in the air between them, and she couldn't find the strength to tear her eyes away. She couldn't for the life of her think of *why* he was staring at her.

The story continued onstage, but she could hardly pay attention. His gaze attacked her to the core, filling her with a sharp, cold feeling, extending out to her fingertips.

Dawn finally ripped her gaze away, not able to take it anymore. Swanhilde had snuck into Dr. Coppelius's workshop and discovered that Coppelia was a life-sized mechanical doll. Swanhilde hid herself and started dressing up as the doll, before pretending that the doll had come to life. Dawn's eyes drifted down to the audience again and her heart rate picked up once more. The strange man was still staring up at her intently, not watching the scene before him. The stage lights highlighted half of his face. She yanked her gaze away again. When her gaze darted down once more, the man was gone. His seat was empty next to the sea of viewers, and her gaze shot around the room, her heart picking up speed. Where was he?

Gideon noticed her attention and leaned in, touching her arm. "Are you all right?"

Dawn flinched and zeroed in on his face. "I'm fine . . . I'm . . . good."

Her gaze returned to the audience, adrenaline spiking. She glanced around the large room, frantic, until she noticed the man slipping out a side door. She straightened against the edge of her seat, then peeked over at Gideon.

"I need some air," she whispered. "I'll be right back."

Gideon scowled. "I'll come with you." He started to rise from his chair.

"No," she said quickly. "I'll be just a minute. You stay." She gently pushed him back down into his chair and swept past the suite's curtain with Gideon's confused face staring back at her.

Dawn rushed out into the hallway, finding the steps that led down to the foyer. Red velvet carpet lined the floor and gold trim adorned the walls. She brushed past the décor, a swirl of color in the edges of her vision, and her chest heaved as she turned the last corner. She skidded to a stop.

The man stood in the middle of the foyer, his necktie up close to his throat, his mouth set tightly. He was long and dark, no color on him, just his pale skin against his black slacks and coat.

"What is wrong with you?" Dawn whispered.

He continued to stare her down with his severe eyes. "What is wrong with me? What is wrong with you?"

Dawn blinked back. "Excuse me?"

He tsked, clicking his tongue. "You know, I actually admired you. It's why I let you go that night. You seemed . . . different. You seemed strong. A female healer, not too common in these parts."

"And what's wrong with that?"

He let out a short laugh. "What's wrong? What's *wrong*? What's wrong is that you are here with that imbecile of a man. Consorting with someone like him. I thought better of you. I thought you were different. But you are the same as all the young ladies here. Starry-eyed and swooning over any man with money, thinking you can secure yourself a comfortable life. Well, I can assure you, *that* man is nothing more than a liar and a cheat, and you would be better off on the streets than be with him."

"Gideon?" Dawn asked. "I mean . . . Mr. Hemsworth? How dare you? What do you know about him?"

His face darkened as he took one long step forward. "I know that he hurts everyone he comes into contact with. I know that he's only out for himself and his twisted proclivities. And I know that he's a murderer."

Her hand flew to her mouth and she held her breath. What he was saying was absurd. Gideon wasn't a murderer. He'd dedicated his life to finding the Dollmaker. If he was a killer himself, then why would he spend so much time finding another?

"I think you're jealous of him," Dawn spat. "It's clear by your mad rantings that you have it in for him and that you'd say anything to discredit him."

The man stepped toward her on his long legs, his gait smooth. Dawn held her ground, she didn't want to give him the satisfaction of backing away. He stopped in front of her, too close, only a breath away. Lavender emanated off him, settling in her nose. His lean form shifted and his jawbones flexed.

"I don't know why you hide in the shadows," she said. "And I don't know why you let me go the other night, but it's clear you're mentally deranged. You need help."

An unreadable emotion crossed over his face. A tic jumped in his jaw before he composed himself. He leaned down so his eyes were level with hers. "Stay away from him. If you care for your life at all, stay away from him."

He straightened and departed out the front doors of the theater into the night. Dawn stood there a long while, long enough for her heart to slow so she could return to Gideon and the dance concert, though her mind wouldn't stop spinning.

What if this man was right? What if Gideon was a threat?

And now she'd put herself on a path she wasn't sure she could get off.

12
Mystery Hole

Dawn walked in a daze, going through her daily routine, visiting a few patients and checking in at the office. But nothing would appease her thoughts of Rose and the strange man. Each of their faces floated in the forefront of her mind, mingling together, sharing space.

Rose, with her dark lashes and pouty lips. And the man, with his sharp bones and hollow cheeks.

Dr. Miller finally made an appearance at the clinic—he bustled around, straightening vials of medicines and herbs, mumbling underneath his breath. His gray hair was wispy behind his ears, his wrinkles extra deep in his face. He had on his leather apron, as if he had already tended to a patient that day.

He spun around as Dawn stepped inside, the bags under his eyes extra deep. Her forehead wrinkled at his appearance.

"Dr. Miller. Are you all right?"

He waved his hand, then continued his bustling. "Fine. Fine. Just another patient out of town is all. Had a hernia to fix. It was a long procedure and a long ride back."

Dawn bit her lip. "I wish you would've asked me to help."

Dr. Miller's shoulders sagged as he paused. "It isn't proper, Dawn. I appreciate your help around here, but there are only so many things you can do."

"You let me help with the tonsillectomy."

"Yes, quite different from a man's hernia. It wouldn't be appropriate." He continued his rifling. "It seems we're missing some opium."

"Is that what you're looking for?"

"Yes. No. That, and I've seemed to have misplaced my cutting scissors. I brought them along with me when I was to amputate Mr. Roper's foot, but they're missing."

"Missing? That's strange." Her brows pressed downward. "I haven't seen them. Or the opium."

He let out a long sigh. "The scissors are probably just in my home. I'll look there later."

"You really should go home and get some rest," Dawn said. "I can stay here and wait on any patients that may arrive." She needed something to distract her from thoughts about Rose's kidnapping.

The circles underneath Dr. Miller's eyes seemed to darken. Hesitation crossed his face, but he conceded. "Perhaps you're right. I can hardly see straight." He walked over to the coat rack and retrieved his coat and hat. "You're sure you'll be all right?"

Dawn started to respond, when shouting came from outside. Footsteps pounded, and in a heartbeat, a sea of officers barged into the clinic. The door banged open, hitting the wall. The men all wore wool coats with brass buttons along the front and flat hats. The men fell on Dr. Miller, grabbing him on both sides and pulling him toward the door.

"*What* is going on?" Dawn asked, heart spiking. Her gaze darted around the room.

One of the officers tipped his hat. He was the officer who had been speaking with Nora outside her shop the other day. "Are you all right, miss?"

She blinked, forehead creased. "Me?"

Dr. Miller struggled against the men. "What is this madness?"

"You're under arrest for the murder of multiple women," the officer said. He turned back to Dawn. "I'm Officer MacLarin. Are you sure you're all right? He hasn't tried to harm you?"

"Dr. Miller? Of course not! Why on earth do you think he's murdered anyone?"

"He was spotted just outside of town last night where another body was found. He's also been identified by witnesses in other locations murders have occurred. And who else knows the art of amputation?"

"You're not saying . . . that he . . . another body?" Dawn couldn't wrap her mind around this. Her hands trembled and she clasped them together, trying to steady them. The Dollmaker had struck again.

MacLarin nodded. "Dead. A young woman by the name of Margaret Fairfield. She had part of her arm missing."

"This is absurd! Dr. Miller hasn't killed anyone!"

"Tell that to multiple witnesses. It seems that the streets may finally be free of this . . . Dollmaker."

She shook her head quickly. "No. Dr. Miller, no."

He continued to fight against the men, but they were bricks against his frail body. "He's a doctor. He heals for a living. He would never hurt anyone!"

The officers pulled him outside of the shop, where a crowd had gathered.

"You should feel lucky, miss," MacLarin said. "You very well could've been his next victim." He tipped his hat again and followed the other officers outside.

Dawn rushed to the door, following after them, and nearly ran into Gideon's chest. He wore a dress shirt and black vest, a fedora over his sleek hair.

"What's going on?" His mouth turned down in a frown.

"It's Dr. Miller. They think he's the Dollmaker. It's ridiculous, right?"

Gideon stared into the crowd, where more people had gathered, sun shining down through the town square. The line of his jaw was tight, his eyes narrowed.

"I'm partial to agree with you, Dawn. I don't see how the doctor could've done this."

"Then we have to do something!"

He turned to her and took her by the shoulders. "His fate is already sealed, Dawn. Once a man goes to prison for such a crime, he hardly ever comes out."

Her stomach lurched and she placed her hands over her abdomen, trying to breathe. "We can't let that happen."

"Then let's get to the bottom of this," Gideon said. He took her arm and looped it through his. "Let's go to my place."

Dawn quietly entered Gideon's house. The table was, as always, full of papers and stacks of books loomed in the corners. Papers were piled on top of the chaise and scattered on the floor. Gideon strode inside, lighting a few oil lamps. He scrubbed a hand over his face, leaned against the table, and set his palms over his eyes. Dawn took in the mess. It was worse than the last time she had been in here.

"You said you believe me that Dr. Miller isn't the killer," she said tentatively. "Why is that?" Her voice echoed through the room.

Gideon froze for a few moments, finally lifting his head.

"After the ballet last night, I couldn't sleep. I went into town again to walk the streets. I felt like I was being followed, which is exactly what I had wanted. I've been stalking the Dollmaker for a while, and he's clearly a knowledgeable man and would have to be aware of his surroundings. I've been hoping he would recognize my face and know what I was doing—which I then wanted him to confront me about. I figured I might not be able to find him, but maybe he'd find me."

The image of the man on the rooftop surged into Dawn's head, along with the mysterious man at the theater. Was he the one who was following Gideon last night?

He did have it in for him.

But she still didn't want to bring up the man. Gideon would only press her for more information—which she didn't have. And what if the man was right and Gideon was dangerous?

Then she remembered the threat. If she told anyone about him, death would follow.

"Who was this man following you?" she choked out.

Gideon pushed off the desk and strode away. "I don't know. I tried to confront him, but he got away. And he never showed his face. But what I do know is that if this was the Dollmaker, then he was in town last night. And Dr. Miller was out of town. It couldn't be him."

"But the latest body was found outside of town."

He spun around, lifting a brow. "And do we know how long the body was there? No, you know as well as I that Dr. Miller is not the culprit."

She nodded, though she could see why the authorities thought otherwise. Who else knew the art of amputation? It was a rare skill, one that she didn't have.

"So we should look at other doctors," Dawn said.

Gideon's jaw tightened. "I've already thought of that. I've looked up every doctor from here to New York. None of them have been near any of the murders that have taken place. And none of them seem to have any cause to be involved in such things. But I suppose you never know."

"Maybe we need to get back to the basics," Dawn said. "You knew Sophie well. And I know Rose well. They were both ballerinas. We need to find another connection between them. Find someone who would've been . . . fascinated with them . . . determined to kill them for whatever reason."

She furiously thought, ideas whirling around inside her head. Then the world stopped dead around her. "I know who it is."

Gideon went still, his entire body thrumming with tension. He looked as if he were about to burst. "Well?"

"Caldwell," Dawn whispered. "The ballet director. He's from New York. His accent is clear. It's where the murders started. He hasn't been in the company for too long. I'd bet with some digging we'll discover he could've worked with the ballerinas there."

Gideon's dark brows pushed together.

"He was obsessed with Rose," she continued. "Always speaking with her after class. I caught them in an alleyway the other day. His fixation with her seemed unhealthy."

Gideon's expression tightened. "I think I would've heard of Caldwell with how much I went to the ballet when Sophie performed, but it's possible he was there."

"It's worth looking into," Dawn said. "I get . . . this horrible feeling around him. Something's off."

Gideon gave a sharp nod. "Then it's a good thing I'm his employer. I'll ask to speak with him at once."

<hr />

Dawn stood outside the studio waiting while Gideon spoke with Caldwell in his office. The girls in the studio sat huddled on the floor, chatting, tying up their pointe shoes. Their faces were painted to perfection. Pale skin. Rosy cheeks. Red lips. Long lashes. None of them were as exquisite as Rose, but they all put on a perfect facade.

It must've been difficult to always exude beauty. Dawn could disappear in the shadows, be unseen, but these ballerinas had to live up to their supreme images. Ballerinas were meant to be perfect, to be flawless, to be angelic on the stage. The same was expected in the classroom.

They sat with stiff backs, waiting for Caldwell to return. The room was quieter than usual. A solemn feeling hung in the air, the events of late left unspoken.

If Caldwell was the Dollmaker, it was no wonder he would choose to spend his time here. These women were as close to porcelain dolls as they could come. The thought only reminded Dawn of the performance the previous night, and how Swanhilde had pretended to be a doll to win Franz's love back. As if she couldn't be herself to regain that love.

A woman should be able to be herself and be loved.

"Do you think she's dead?" one girl whispered.

The room went silent.

"You mean Rose?" another girl whispered.

"Of course she's dead," someone said. "All the girls who are taken wind up dead."

"But we don't know if the Dollmaker took her," someone else said. "She could've run off. She didn't want to get married, after all."

"So she leaves her status and newfound fortune behind to run off with some nobody? That's highly unlikely."

"If she *were* to have run off with anyone, it would've been Caldwell," one girl said, giggling. "You've seen the way they are together."

"Maybe she's with child," another said, snickering. "With Caldwell's baby. Can you imagine the scandal? Perhaps she was sent away to have the child."

Dawn pumped her fists as she spun from the doorway. "Don't be ridiculous!" Her chest rose and fell. "Rose would never do such a thing. And she hated Caldwell. He made her uncomfortable. You were her friends. If she heard the way you were talking about her..."

The girls sealed their lips, glancing at one another. Silence stretched between them, until shouting came from down the hall.

Dawn jerked to attention, then rushed into the hallway to find Gideon pressing Caldwell up against the wall. He had his elbow across Caldwell's throat, his face stuck up right into his.

"Tell me where she is!" Gideon growled.

Caldwell was turning purple, his eyes bulging from their sockets. He writhed and wriggled underneath Gideon's hold, struggling to breathe.

"Gideon!" Dawn yelled.

Gideon didn't pay any mind. He pressed his elbow tighter into his throat. "Tell me where Rose is, or your last breath will be right here and now."

Caldwell continued to struggle, his eyes wide, mouth gaping, but Gideon's hold was relentless. Caldwell sagged against the wall, his head lolling to the side.

"Gideon! Stop!" She rushed forward and tried to pry Gideon's hold away. But Gideon seemed to be in some sort of trance, his eyes fixed on Caldwell, his jaws tightly clamped together. Tendons strained in his neck and sweat ran down his forehead.

"Gideon, please! Think of Sophie! She wouldn't want this!"

His face faltered, and Gideon suddenly stepped back. He blinked as if waking up from a dream. Caldwell collapsed to the floor, his body crumpled on the battered carpet. Dawn fell to her knees, rolling Caldwell onto his back. She placed her hand over his mouth, waiting.

"He's not breathing!"

She placed two fingers against his throat. No pulse.

Her hands frantically hovered over Caldwell's body. Her mind went blank, fear screaming through her, until she forced herself to think. She recalled a German surgeon she had read about who saved two young patients by administering chest compressions to restart the heart. It wasn't standard, but it could work. The world started to fade away as she zeroed in on Caldwell's lifeless body. He was a patient, nothing more. Not a murderer, just a human being. Flesh and blood in front of her, needing to be healed.

The world disappeared further as she placed her palms over Caldwell's heart. She rose on her knees and pressed down as far as her weight would take her. She found a rhythm, pumping up and down, her hands digging into his sternum. The body caved in to her weight, nothing but dead flesh needing to be restored, and she continued her compressions, focusing solely on Caldwell's face.

She didn't know how long she pumped her hands into his chest, but it was long enough that Caldwell sputtered, his eyes shooting open. She collapsed back, falling onto her backside, her arms and chest aching. Caldwell slowly sat up, rubbing his chest and wincing.

"You're going to be all right," Dawn said, scrambling back over to him. "Lie back down. You need to rest."

Caldwell stared at her blankly before his gaze shot up to Gideon standing over him. Gideon backed away, clearly pale, shock written all over his face. Dawn kept her hands on Caldwell, keeping him down, even though his face showed that he wanted to murder Gideon, just as Gideon had him.

The girls had exited out into the hall, clasping each other, eyes wide.

Gideon was the first to leave the building.

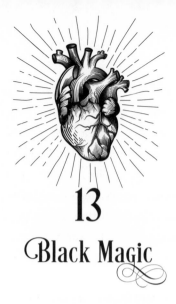

13

Black Magic

With every day that passed, Dawn became more dejected. The Dollmaker was winning, and it was getting more and more unlikely that Rose was still alive—her body still hadn't turned up.

Dawn hadn't seen Gideon for two days, though it felt more like an eternity. They'd been working together nonstop for the better part of the week, and now at his sudden disappearance, she felt at a loss. She'd checked his building, ringing the doorbell multiple times. She'd waited at home for him to call on her. She hadn't gone to the Hemsworth manor in fear that she would run into Arthur, but she'd considered it a dozen times. A sick feeling stirred in her stomach. What if the Dollmaker had gotten to Gideon? Was that why she hadn't seen him?

Without Gideon, her search for Rose ceased. She went through her days, fingers itching, blindly helping her patients, unable to focus. Rose was still out there, and with every second that ticked by, Dawn's heart sank deeper. She needed to find Gideon or continue the investigation herself. But she didn't know how to do it alone. What chance did a woman have against a man? A man like the Dollmaker?

She paced inside the clinic, organizing and reorganizing the shelves. She'd dusted them twice, and even though everything was pristine, she cleaned them a third time. She tried to find the missing opium, but Dr. Miller was right. It was gone. The thought of Dr. Miller sent a pang through her chest but working alone also excited her. There might be some big injuries or surgeries she'd have to attend to, and there wouldn't be anyone to help but her. But she shot the thought down immediately. Dr. Miller wasn't okay.

She needed help. She needed advice. She needed someone to turn to.

She peeked outside the front window and squinted across the town square to Nora's shop. She did have Nora, *and* Mrs. Cook. But Mrs. Cook was too close to her mother. She couldn't go home. Nora it was.

She grabbed her coat and set out across the street. Shoppers brushed past her shoulders and a few cars rumbled by. The late-morning sun blasted down on her head, and a trickle of sweat ran down the middle of her back, itching. She dipped inside Nora's shop, where the air was slightly cooler. Candles lit the space, the light from the flames flickering on the walls. A few taxidermy animals were hung, along with animals in jars and bones that lined the shelves.

Nora looked as if she were anticipating Dawn's arrival, her hair out of braids today, hanging over her loose white blouse. The blouse was far too low for a lady; her milky white skin shone brightly in the dim light.

"I thought I might be seeing you today," Nora said, humor in her eyes.

A crease lined Dawn's brow.

"Your friend came to visit me last night," she said.

"My friend?"

Nora's full lips lifted upward. "Mr. Hemsworth. The younger one—that is."

"Gideon?" Relief swept through her, and then she pressed her lips together. He'd come to visit Nora, but had been ignoring her? Why hadn't he come to see her? She crossed her arms. "Oh yeah? And what did Gideon have to say to you?"

Nora walked deeper into the space, running her hands along the shelves, her feet bare on the wooden floor. Her long fingers stopped on a small skull. "He wanted to know if I could communicate with the dead." She turned and raised a brow.

Dawn blinked, lowering her arms. "The dead?"

"Yes. One dead person in particular. Sophia Gustafferson. He wanted me to reach out to her. I told him I couldn't, not unless he came to a séance. He'll be there tonight, if you'd like to come."

Dawn clamped her teeth down tight. So Gideon was continuing the investigation without her? She should've felt relieved. She shouldn't have cared that he'd given up the pretense of them being together, but she felt betrayed.

Was she not good enough for him now? She was the one trying to find Rose. Was communicating with his dead fiancée more important?

"What time is the séance?" Dawn's voice was terse.

"It's just out of town in the Aurora Graveyard. Midnight. You'll be there?"

She gave a tight nod. "I'll be there."

⊰ ⊱

Dawn spent the afternoon pacing in her bedroom. The hours couldn't tick by fast enough. She couldn't believe Gideon had been ignoring her this whole time. She'd been worried about him, been searching for him, and he was simply ignoring her? Her thoughts wouldn't slow down. Images jumped in her head from Rose, to the dead girls, to Gideon, to Dr. Miller, and to the strange man.

Mrs. Cook tried to get her to eat a platter of biscuits and jam before she left, telling her it was a special recipe she'd fed soldiers in the war, but Dawn's stomach was in knots, anticipation fluttering through her. She couldn't eat. Her mother would be furious that she'd left, but Mrs. Cook assured her that she'd keep her secret.

Dawn had never believed in the supernatural. She believed in the present—in flesh and blood before her—not apparitions from the other side. But if Gideon was desperate enough to try to contact Sophie, she wanted to be there. Morbid curiosity. Either that, or she wanted to ream him out.

Finally the time came, and Dawn headed out of town on foot, not having enough money to rent a carriage. She walked through the streets, sticking to the shadows along the houses and shops until the land began to open up. Thin clouds stretched across the moon, a slight breeze in the air. Dirt roads wove through thick green forest, tall trees, and grassy land. Shadows seemed to extend from the trees, making the deep pockets of the forest feel extra dark. Moonlight shone down from above, lighting her path, and she wrapped her arms around herself, trying to keep out the chill.

Firelight was glowing in the distance as Dawn entered the graveyard, smoke billowing up into the sky. Her heart pounded, because this was where her brother was buried. Her feet itched to take her to his tombstone, but she forced herself forward. She meandered around the dead grass and gravestones, trying not to step on the tombs. Even though she didn't believe in waking the dead, she still wanted to be respectful. Her feet crunched softly as she approached the circle of men and women huddled around the fire. Laughter tinkled through the air, while men with wandering hands played with the hair of the women sitting on their laps. Dawn cringed, searching for Gideon. He stood alone in front of the fire, the flickering light hollowing out his cheeks and eyes. His body was stiff and dark, as black as the night behind him. Nora hovered off to the other side, piling up a tower of rocks, matching the other two towers that made a triangle around the fire.

Gideon's gaze flew up to Dawn as she approached, and his eyes widened before curiosity overtook his face. She stood opposite from him on the other side of the fire, and his gaze skated away. He swallowed.

When Nora had finished placing the last rock, she lifted up her hands, and bracelets rattled along her wrists. The chatting and laughing ceased, and the men and women rose from their positions around the fire, circling it.

Nora looked over them, the firelight casting shadows on her face. Her charcoal hair was completely unpinned, hanging around her shoulders and loose blouse. The smoke stung Dawn's eyes, but she didn't dare move, as a solemn feeling had settled over the group. A heady scent hovered in the air, like incense, thick in the back of her throat. It seemed familiar, though she couldn't pinpoint it.

Nora looked at each face individually, welcoming them with her eyes, and when her gaze stopped on Dawn, her lips lifted up into a smile.

"The spirits will be grateful we are here," Nora said, her voice ringing out into the night. "They each long for a chance to be alive again, to communicate with us again, for it is their only way to feel warmth in their cold, dead bodies." Her eyes darkened as her gaze continued to circle the group. "We need the spirits to be comfortable. They need to feel this is a safe place. If any of you are a skeptic, it will weaken our energy. Only join hands if you are a true believer." Her eyes flicked to Dawn again, and this time, Dawn stepped back, though not far enough to escape the scent. Her head began to spin, and her vision wavered.

The group joined hands, save for Dawn and Gideon. Gideon stood tall and straight inside the group, keeping his gaze fixed out in front of him.

"I will act as the medium," Nora said. "And the rest of you will be the sitters. We have gathered tonight for one purpose only: to find Sophia Gustafferson."

A muscle ticked in Gideon's cheek and he swallowed again, his body still thrumming with tension. Dawn's vision blurred at the edges, and it felt as if her head were floating above her. She struggled to keep upright.

"By holding hands," Nora continued, "it allows our energy to be transferred from person to person. No matter what happens, keep the connection until our business is finished."

The fire continued to crackle as silence settled around them. The heat burned Dawn's face, though a chill pierced her bones. Gideon's eyes connected with hers again, and she didn't look away. She gave him a questioning look, but his expression was unreadable.

"Let us begin." Nora took a deep, shuddering breath and murmured, "*Sanctus spiritus mortuus nahm.*" A few heartbeats passed before she repeated, "*Sanctus spiritus mortuus nahm.*"

The group tightened their hands and began to chant with her. "*Sanctus spiritus mortuus nahm.*" The words were repeated over and over, sailing in the air, settling onto Dawn's shoulders. Gideon's gaze returned to the fire, every line in his face tight.

It was as if the air became thickened with the words swirling around her, making Dawn dizzy. The ground shifted underneath her feet, and she swayed to the side. The fire roared higher, Gideon's face hollowing out further.

The chanting heightened and Nora began to lift her arms, the group following suit. She stepped sideways, slowly circling, and the group followed until they circled counterclockwise around the fire. They continued to chant, but Nora's voice rang low and clear through the din.

"It's time to give your offering," she said to Gideon. "Something that will connect Sophia to her old life."

Gideon slowly stepped closer to the fire and dipped his hand inside his coat. He pulled out a pointe shoe from his front pocket and turned it over in his hands. His knuckles turned white as he gripped it, before his hands relaxed. With his jaw set, he tossed the shoe into the fire and flames spat upward.

Sanctus spiritus mortuus nahm.

The circling intensified, and Dawn's heart began to pound in time with the chanting. A myriad of emotions flashed over Gideon's face. Hope. Fear. Determination. Anticipation. She wondered if her face was doing the same. The firelight glowed in his eyes, the flames dancing, and Dawn couldn't rip her gaze away. What if it worked? Was he about to communicate with his Sophie? No. She wouldn't believe it. She didn't believe in the supernatural. But the energy that surrounded the group made her feel like she was breathing through slush, like something unearthly was stirring.

The firelight began to brighten, the flames glowing, no longer a deep orange but a translucent white. Dawn stood paralyzed, eyes burning, unable to blink. A figure began to materialize in the fire before them, slowly at first—just a flicker of an outline. The outline began to solidify, eyes and a mouth shaping inside the flames: the curve of a face, the tracings of a body. Red hair cascaded down her back. Gideon stumbled back, hand over his heart.

"Sophie?"

Sophie reached a hand forward, slowly raising her arm, her fingertips still inside the white flames. "My Gideon."

The sound of his name coming from Sophie's lips jolted Dawn. She couldn't believe what she was seeing—what she was hearing.

"Tell me what happened to you," Gideon choked out. Sweat shone on his face, and his knees were locked so tight, Dawn was sure he was going to pass out. "Tell me where you are."

Sophie's eyes widened, the flames licking over her face. She seemed to glow inside, bright light shooting up to the moon.

"Please," Gideon said. "I need to know what happened. Who did this to you?" His body sagged, and it was as if he had finally accepted that she was gone. The fact that she was here meant she was dead. Perhaps he had hoped that she was still out there alive.

Sophie kept her arm outstretched toward him. Her face was blank, save for her wide eyes.

"My Gideon . . ."

"Stop!"

A voice rang through the night, cutting through the spell. Gideon's gaze shot upward, and Sophie vanished in an instant. The flames roared orange again, and Gideon's face turned murderous.

"No!" he yelled. "Sophie! Come back!" He leaped toward the fire, but flames shot outward, and he fell onto his backside. He sat panting on the ground, before scrambling to his feet. "Who's there?"

The group parted as a figure stepped forward. The wind blew, clearing the smoke and scent from around Dawn's face.

The figure before them was lean and dark, wild hair out to the side. Her heart pounded triple time. She knew who this was. It was *him*.

"We have a guest," Nora said. "Welcome."

But the man didn't move forward. He remained silent, the fire crackling. Dawn could hardly breathe.

Gideon and the man stared at each other past the fire, their eyes locked between the flames. Another gust of wind blew the flames outward, and the firelight highlighted the stranger's face. Cut bones. Hollow cheeks and eyes. He looked so much like Gideon, only paler, thinner, a bit more emaciated.

"Sebastian." Gideon's voice rang deep.

Sebastian? He knew the psychopath's name? It felt odd that he should have a name.

"You've gone too far," Sebastian said. "You can't bring her back. I didn't take you for the type to reach out to such dark measures."

"If you were in my position, you would do the same," Gideon spat. "But you don't know what it is to love."

Sebastian's face tightened. "Well, I know what it is like to have an idiotic brother. To watch him throw his life away."

Brother? *They were brothers?*

Gideon scoffed. "Throw his life away? Who's the one lurking in the shadows? I'm the one fighting for something. You're just a coward."

A muscle ticked in Sebastian's cheek.

"What are you doing here, anyway?" Gideon asked. "Besides ruining my chance to find any answers."

"I'm here to warn you," he said simply.

Chills erupted down Dawn's back as another gust of wind blew. The gravestones sat cold and silent around them, the stars frozen in the night sky.

"If you continue down this path, you will die," Sebastian said. "I've seen it. I've seen others like you. You can't beat him." His gaze skated away from his brother and he looked at Dawn directly. "It's time you accept the loss of Rose and move on."

Another breeze skimmed Dawn's shoulders and she wrapped her arms around herself. Nothing sounded, just the flames snapping between them.

"Go back to your hiding," Gideon finally answered. "I don't want you here. No one does."

Sebastian's jaw tightened, the shadows playing off his defined bones. "I gave you a warning. I won't help you anymore."

Gideon continued to stare him down.

Sebastian stepped back into the shadows, his silhouette a paler black against the night. He lingered for a moment, as if deciding whether to leave, but his footsteps slowly disappeared, his form vanishing from sight.

Gideon crumpled to his knees.

His hands dug into the dirt and his shoulders were wracked with sobs. He let out a loud cry, the sound cutting straight to Dawn's core. She watched Gideon weep, his body curled over, and a new strength took root inside her gut.

She would help Gideon. She would prove Sebastian wrong. He clearly wanted them to cease the investigation. She wasn't going to let that happen. If she could do something to give Gideon peace, she would.

14

Lightning Crack

Dawn returned to the theater.

Ballerinas were clearly a target, and it wasn't reaching to think that one of them might be next. She knew Sebastian was probably lurking underneath the theater, but that wouldn't stop her from getting answers. She'd already searched the dressing rooms and other locations for clues, but nothing had come up. There had to be more that she hadn't seen. She needed to speak with the girls.

Pulling her gloves up tighter against her wrists, she set out into the fall air and marched toward the rehearsal hall, hoping to find the girls inside.

She was to visit Dr. Miller later that day. She'd made a call to Officer MacLarin, who had reluctantly agreed to let her see Dr. Miller, who'd been transferred to the local jail, though he'd warned her that it wouldn't be pretty. He said the accusations of her murdering Frederick were starting to circulate, and that it'd be best if she stayed away for her own protection. But Dawn tried to push thoughts of her fate out of her head. For now, she needed to be a step ahead of the Dollmaker. She passed the large oaks that left piles of leaves on the ground in orange, red, and yellow. A gardener was raking them up, clearly chilled with his chafed cheeks below his gray cap. The air cleared Dawn's head from the darkness she'd experienced the night before, and part of her wondered if she had imagined the whole thing. She *surely* hadn't seen Sophie in the fire. It was probably a trick of the light. Nora was a professional, after all, and Gideon had probably paid her a pretty penny. She had known how to deceive and give the customer what they wanted.

Music drifted from outside the rehearsal hall as Dawn stepped inside, keeping her coat on. She headed down the hall to the open studio door and peeked inside. A swirl of white tutus filled the space. Caldwell stood at the front of the class, tapping his stick, the girls dancing in time with his beat. As soon as he saw Dawn, he paled and motioned for the music to stop.

The pianist ceased and the girls spun around, a sea of questioning faces staring back at her.

"Can I help you?" Caldwell asked, his voice catching in his throat.

"I was wondering . . ." Dawn stepped deeper into the room. "If I might speak with a few of your dancers. I have some questions."

Indecision flickered in Caldwell's expression, but then the planes of his face relaxed, and sorrow settled in his eyes. "Yes, of course. Anything. I owe you my life. Whatever you need."

Dawn kept her chin up, but a lump swelled in her throat. No one had ever thanked her for saving their life before.

Caldwell waved a hand and motioned for the girls to disperse. "If Miss Hildegard wishes to speak with you, then give her your full attention."

Dawn had thought to speak with the girls one on one but realized she might save time by speaking to the group as a whole. She held up her hand. "If I might address them all?"

Caldwell rubbed a hand over his furry chest, his white shirt cut low. His brow quirked, but he gave her a bow. "I'll be in my office if you need anything. And girls, there's a staging rehearsal tonight.

Don't forget." He touched Dawn's shoulder gently as he strode from the room, leaving her alone with a room full of ballerinas.

Dawn cleared her throat and quietly stepped up to the front of the classroom. She unbuttoned her coat and placed it over the nearest chair. She rested her hands over her stomach, the low-waisted dress hanging off her frame. The girls stared back at her blankly, a group of perfectly painted faces reminding her too much of Rose.

"I . . ." Dawn looked them over. "I need to know if any of you have experienced anything . . . unusual lately." The girls blinked their long lashes at her. She steeled herself, straightening her shoulders. "Felt as if you were being followed? Noticed any strange behavior from strangers? Felt uncomfortable in any way?"

The girls peeked over at one another. Some pressed their mouths tightly together as they exchanged glances.

"What?" Dawn asked. "What is it?"

A blonde in the front tucked a loose strand of hair into the scarf around her head, smoothing it until it was perfect. Her long lashes lowered before she looked up at Dawn.

"It's Caldwell," she whispered. "Ever since Rose disappeared, he's started to give the rest of us more attention—inappropriately so. The other day he offered to take me home, and when I refused, he became angry. I still have bruises." She pulled down her sleeve and revealed purple marks that looked like fingers around her upper arm. "I'm not the only one." Her gaze skated over to the girl next to her.

"I know it's miraculous that you brought him back from the dead and all," the next girl said. "But . . ." Her eyes narrowed to slits. "We wish you hadn't."

Dawn blinked back. "What?"

"He kissed me," another girl said. "I almost didn't come today. But I don't want to lose my spot in the corps. If I ever said anything, he'd tell everyone it was my fault. I'd be ruined."

The girls quieted, and Dawn wondered how many more stories existed between them. Had she brought a monster back to life? What had she done? She'd taken an oath to help any man or woman in need—she didn't have a choice. But she could see the fear in each of these young ladies' eyes. Caldwell's existence threatened them.

But could he be the Dollmaker? If so, she had put him back on the streets. Caldwell did have a thing for ballerinas and had violent tendencies. He had been obsessed with Rose. Had it driven him to take her? Because she'd rejected him?

"Don't tell anyone," Dawn whispered. "Not yet. See if you can avoid him. I'm going to . . . I'm going to fix this." She grabbed her coat off her chair.

"No!" the first blonde said. "You can't say a word! You would ruin us all! Don't you know how the world works? We women don't have any power against a man. The only thing we can hope for is to stay pure for marriage. If we're ruined, then we have no hope for a future. You can't destroy our futures."

Dawn shook her head. "Caldwell can't get away with treating you like this. I'm *going* to stop this."

"Please, no!" a few more of them cried.

But Dawn marched from the room, fury in her eyes. She had done this to them. This was *her* fault. And now she was going to fix it.

<hr>

Officer MacLarin stepped into the waiting room, where Dawn was pacing back and forth. She had gone straight to the jail where Dr. Miller was being held. The small front office held a desk that swallowed the room. Several bookshelves surrounded the desk, running along the walls. The books were stacked, clean and precise, labeled alphabetically. Most looked like journals, probably a roster of names of men and women who went in and out of the facility.

MacLarin locked the door behind him and gave her a quizzical look, arching one of his eyebrows. He wore his gray wool uniform with his flat gray cap. He was a bit heavyset around the middle but with strong, broad shoulders.

"Your appointment isn't for another two hours. Is everything all right?"

Dawn wrung her hands. Her fury hadn't settled. With each step she had taken there, her anger for Caldwell grew. She paused, gripping her fingers.

"No, everything is not all right. Caldwell is a beast, and I need you to arrest him at once."

MacLarin sat down behind the desk, linking his fingers on top.

"Why do you say such things?"

"He's . . . you have no idea what he is doing to those women over at the theater. He's an animal, taking what he wants. I . . . I believe him to be the Dollmaker. I need you to apprehend him now before he hurts anyone else."

MacLarin sat back in his chair. He observed her with one eye squinted. "Those are serious accusations, Miss Hildegard. Especially coming from someone who's rumored to have killed a man. Have you any proof?"

She opened and closed her mouth. The accusations about Frederick didn't matter now. "He took Rose. He was obsessed with her. He's been attacking these other women. They're ballerinas. The Dollmaker is obsessed with them."

"And you think Caldwell has the skills to amputate?" He let out a huff. "I'm sorry, Miss Hildegard, but no more murders have occurred since we apprehended Dr. Miller. I'm afraid Caldwell is innocent. The date for the doctor's trial has been set."

The world screeched to a halt. Sights and sounds stopped around Dawn; MacLarin's face blurred in and out of her vision.

"Let me see him," she choked out. "I want to see him."

MacLarin heaved out a breath, his shoulders sagging. "Are you sure, miss? It isn't a pretty sight."

"Now."

"If you must." MacLarin rose from the desk and pulled out the keys jangling from his coat pocket. He separated one brass key from the cluster and unlocked the door behind him. He swung it open and motioned her into the hall.

The jail had been used as a gaol back in the eighteen hundreds. Through the years, they had renovated a few parts of the building, but they had kept the actual cells the same. It was the only penitentiary in town. Dr. Miller would probably be transferred to a more updated prison if he was convicted fully.

The two walked down a hallway with stone pavers and gas lamps every few feet, making their shadows long out in front of them. The floor went downward at a slight incline, and the air chilled a few degrees, goose bumps rippling along the back of Dawn's neck. Their footsteps clacked softly, and the cop's keys jingled. The hallway turned, slowly descending until they faced a steel door. MacLarin pulled out his keys again and the door clicked open.

The immediate scent of unwashed bodies and chamber pots filled the air, and Dawn covered her nose and mouth with her hand. It was as if she really were back in the eighteen hundreds with the poor living conditions. She tried to take even breaths. MacLarin led her past several cells where the crumpled forms of human beings lay in their own filth on the floor, looking like sacks of bones.

She frantically scanned each cell. Dr. Miller didn't deserve this fate. He had dedicated his life to helping people, to healing people, and now he was left alone to rot until his death. She swallowed back the bile that rose in her throat and slowly lowered her hand, trying to breathe through her mouth. Finally, MacLarin stopped and pulled out his keys once more. They clanked together as he unlocked a barred cell, and the door's hinges squeaked as it swung open.

"You have five minutes," MacLarin said. "And you're lucky you get that."

A form was huddled in the corner, unmoving. Dawn squinted into the dark and stepped inside the cell, something sticking to the bottom of her lace-up boots.

Her eyes adjusted, and Dr. Miller's crumpled form solidified in her vision. He wore a thin shift that was stained brown and yellow. A threadbare blanket was spread out next to him, vomit sticking to the edges. She lowered herself next to him. His mustache was untrimmed.

Dr. Miller groaned and his head lolled to the side.

"Dr. Miller!" Her heart pounded. "It's me. Dawn." Her hands hovered in front of him. She wanted to comfort him—heal him—something, but she slowly lowered her hands back into her lap. "What can I do?"

His eyes fluttered open and Dawn jerked back. They were a filmy white, glazed over and dead-looking. Another moan escaped his lips, bits of vomit on his chin.

"What is this?" Dawn whirled around, attacking MacLarin with a glare. "He's drugged. Why?"

MacLarin straightened his hat. "There's nothing I can do about it, miss. They give experimental drugs to the prisoners. I expect he won't be coherent for a few hours."

Dawn surged to her feet and stuck her finger in his face. "I demand to speak with the person in charge at once."

MacLarin reached out and lowered her hand.

"I'm afraid that isn't possible, Miss Hildegard. Come, you've already been here long enough. Say your good-byes to the doctor and accept his fate."

"No!"

MacLarin gripped her upper arm and began to drag her out of the cell.

"No!" She dug her feet into the dirty floor, but the officer was too strong. She strained to peek at Dr. Miller. "I will get you out of here! I swear it!"

Before Dawn knew it, she was thrust outside, the crisp afternoon air on her face. MacLarin slammed the prison door in her face without a word. Gray clouds moved quickly across the sky, thick and heavy, threatening rain.

15
Black Velvet

Dawn pounded on Gideon's door, her knuckles aching. Cold bit her skin, and each knock jolted pain into her hand, but she kept pounding. The sun had descended, trapped behind the tall buildings, and a chill cut the air, the streets quiet, her knocking echoing.

Gideon creaked open the door. His eyes roamed over her, his face dead, until he sighed. "What are you doing here?"

"What am I . . .? Have you lost your *mind*?" She pushed herself past him, barging inside. She marched down the hall to his study. Papers had been completely cleared off the table, scattered on the floor. Furniture was turned over, including chairs and a bookshelf, with torn and bent books piled on the floor.

"What happened in here?"

Gideon slowly entered the room after her, swiping a hand over his face.

"I'm not in the mood, Dawn. If you came to say something, just say it and leave."

She blinked back at him, before her eyes narrowed. "What is wrong with you?"

He walked by and lowered himself to the chaise. "What is wrong with me?" His head fell back over the edge of the couch, his long legs out in front of him. "I can't believe you have to ask that. I *killed* someone, Dawn. As in murdered. How can you think I'd be all right?"

Dawn went still, as she took in the tight planes of his face. A line was permanently etched into the middle of his brow.

"Caldwell's not dead," she whispered. "He's all right."

He shook his head. "He *was* dead. I was willing to kill someone. *Kill*. And then what do I do? I convince Nora to do a séance for me. Only to have my brother . . ." He shut his eyes, agony painted on his face.

Dawn tentatively went to him, her footsteps soft on the carpet. Her anger had faded. She hadn't thought about how he was feeling. "Who is your brother? And why is he here? I mean . . ."

"My brother is a nuisance. A cheat. A liar. He only cares about himself and will do whatever it takes to get what he wants."

A series of questions were bombarding her brain, but she settled with, "What happened between you two?"

Gideon made a noise in the back of his throat. "How to tell a hundred-page saga in a few short words?"

"You can try."

He shook his head again. "He isn't worth the energy."

"Then at least tell me why you think he's here. He . . ." She swallowed. She knew she shouldn't say anything, but now that she knew he was Gideon's brother . . . "He lives underneath the theater. Why?"

Gideon's eyes popped open, and he slowly sat up. His usual sleek hair was ruffled in the back. "He's shown himself to you? Other than last night?"

Her brows pinched. "Yes. Why?"

"Because"—he sat up further—"he hasn't shown himself to anyone since . . . well, he disappeared after an argument we had about my Sophie. He hasn't been seen since. I've asked about him . . .

inquired as to his whereabouts, but no one has heard a word from him since that night, two years ago. Why would he show himself to you?" Then he let out a dry laugh. "Of course. I should've suspected."

"What?"

"He thinks we're engaged. That's why. He couldn't help himself." He rose from the chair and started to pace in front of her. "I ought to wring his neck."

"You're not making any sense."

"It doesn't matter," he said. "Forget it." He bit down hard, a muscle flexing in his jaw.

The mention of his brother seemed to have brought new life into him. When he'd first answered the door, his eyes were dead; now there was fire in them.

Dawn cleared her throat. "I'm here because Caldwell needs to be stopped, and Dr. Miller—"

"It's not Caldwell," he interrupted. "He's not the Dollmaker. I could see it in his eyes right before . . ." He pushed out a shuddering breath. "I could see fear. There was no challenge in his eyes before death. No satisfaction. Caldwell was only afraid."

She shook her head. "No, you don't know what the girls have told me. He's evil, Gideon. They're living in fear. He needs to be stopped."

He held up a hand. "My business doesn't involve anyone who doesn't lead me to the Dollmaker. Besides, I can't show my face around him again. I'm sure you can understand that."

Dawn hovered on the balls of her feet, biting her lips. She wouldn't abandon those girls. She'd have to do this part on her own.

"I can see your face," Gideon said. "You're still going to go after him, aren't you?"

"I have no choice."

"Think of Dr. Miller. His only chance is for us to draw the Dollmaker out. Another attack is the only thing that will save your doctor now."

She shifted her weight from side to side. He was right. If there was another attack while Dr. Miller was still in custody, he'd be proven innocent. "Fine. What do we need to do?"

Gideon slowly turned to her. "It depends on how far you're willing to go."

"I'll do anything." She lifted her chin. "I'm not afraid."

He nodded once. "Then you'll need to be our bait. If we're to find that psychopath, we need to dress you up as one of those perfect ballerinas and lure him out."

<hr />

Gideon and Dawn headed straight for the theater. There was a late rehearsal that night—if they hurried, Dawn would be able to get inside, find a way to dress the part, and leave with the other girls.

Gideon led Dawn inside the theater and down the back hallway, past the gold-trimmed walls and velvet carpet to the back dressing rooms. Music drifted down the hall, echoing out from the theater, so she knew Caldwell was rehearsing with the girls onstage.

"Back here," Gideon murmured, leading her into the costume room. Tutus filled the racks, white fluffy netting attacking her from all angles. White corsets also hung on the racks, their smooth ribbons dangling from the bodices. The white netting glowed in the dark until Gideon lit a lamp on the far table, where a mirror was placed upright, a scatter of makeup and pins strewn on top of a table.

She paused in the middle of the constricted space, wringing her fingers. "You really think we can pull this off?"

Gideon reached over and removed a tutu and bodice from one of the racks. He snatched a pair of stockings off a neighboring rack. He held them out to her. "Put these on."

She eyed the garments, hoping they would fit. She grabbed them and headed to a dressing shield in the back corner. She dipped behind it and began to pull off her clothes, acutely aware that Gideon was only a few feet away. She peeled off her dress, leaving it in a heap on the floor. Standing in her thin chemise, she pulled the bodice tight around her, but couldn't lace it up correctly. She pulled on the classical tutu and slid her stockings up her legs. She stood behind the shield, trying to take even breaths. She'd never been so indecently dressed in front of a man before, and the lack of clothing made goose bumps tingle along her arms.

"I'm . . . I'm coming out," she said. "I need help with my bodice."

She emerged from behind the shield, her arms wrapped over her chest. The cut of her chemise against the corset was low, and in the mirror, her milky skin glowed in the dim light. Gideon's eyes lit up for a moment. He cleared his throat.

"Come here."

She spun around quickly, keeping her arms crossed around her chest, and Gideon's long form loomed up behind her. He tugged the ribbons in the bodice tight, cinching inward. Visions of what it would be like to dance with him flashed to her mind, but it was Sebastian's face that stuck inside her head, floating out in front of her, his eyes dark, welcoming.

She blinked, shivering. Gideon finished cinching up the bodice and guided her to sit in front of the mirror.

He waved his hand forward. "All right. Do . . . er . . . what you need to do. Make yourself presentable."

Her mouth fell open. "As if I know what to do!"

His brows pushed downward. "You're a lady. You know how to pin up your hair, do makeup and stuff."

"Makeup and stuff?" She let out a dry laugh. "You don't know what you're asking."

"You've . . . fluffed yourself up before. I've seen you dolled up. You're actually quite lovely when you're put together."

She pressed her lips together.

Footsteps clicked from down the hall, and a voice said, "I'll be right back!"

The blonde Dawn had spoken to earlier that day stepped into the costume room and paused in her tracks. Her gaze slid from Gideon to Dawn, stopping on Dawn's appearance.

"What . . . what is this?"

Dawn fumbled up from her chair and knocked it to the floor. "Please don't say a word. There's a good reason for this. I'm here to help you. You have to believe that."

The girl creased her thin brows together. "Of course I believe that. After what you did for us today . . . listening like you did. I trust you." She went silent for a moment before she said, "I'm Angelica, by the way."

"Angelica," Gideon said, and her eyes flew over to him again. "Can you help us? We need Miss Hildegard to look like you. Can you . . ." He waved his hand. "Make her presentable?"

Humor teased Angelica's lips. "You mean make her look like a ballerina?"

"Please, can you help us?" Dawn asked.

Angelica glanced behind her before she ducked into the room. "I'll have to hurry."

Dawn set the chair upright again and placed herself in front of the mirror.

"I'm not sure why you need this," Angelica said. "But like I said, I trust you." Her long fingertips reached for the pins on the table, and she began to tuck Dawn's hair up against her head, looping the hair into tight curls. She rummaged through the makeup on the counter, applying black to Dawn's eyelashes and rouge to her cheeks and lips. She drew liner around her eyes, making them look extra big and her cheeks more angular.

"The color is beautiful against your pale skin," she murmured. "All right, have a look." She spun Dawn around so she could see herself in the mirror, and Dawn blinked. She hardly recognized herself. Even though she had been done up for the ballet the other night, this was different. She looked like a porcelain doll. She looked . . . flawless.

Gideon stared at her in the mirror from behind, wonder on his face. "You look perfect."

There was that word.

Perfect.

Was she perfect though? What was perfection? Who was to say that having her hair precise and her face painted made her a thing of beauty? Wasn't she beautiful enough by herself?

Gideon turned to Angelica and took her hand. He placed his lips on top. "You are a true lifesaver. Thank you."

Angelica blushed and headed for the door. She spun back around, her golden locks shimmering in the dim light. "Good luck with whatever it is you're doing." She gave a small smile and disappeared down the hallway.

"What now?" Dawn asked softly, though it seemed loud in the small room.

"Now we wait."

Dawn and Gideon stayed in the dark dressing room for some time, listening to the music continue down the hall. At moments, Caldwell's voice would reverberate outward, yelling at the girls to stay in line and move together. The sound of his voice made her insides crawl, and it took everything in her not to barge into the theater and slap him in the face.

She felt helpless sitting inside the small costume room, and she suddenly wished she were a man. As a woman, she found that no one took her seriously. If she were a man, Officer MacLarin would've believed her that Caldwell was a threat. He would've arrested Caldwell on the spot. But because her voice was small, she had no validation.

Soon, girls began to pass by the doorway, headed to the dressing rooms, not taking notice of Dawn and Gideon hiding inside. They chatted with one another about different sections of *Coppelia*'s choreography. When the halls quieted, Gideon turned to Dawn.

"It's time. The girls should be exiting the theater now. You need to linger behind. Separate yourself from them. We need to draw him out. If I'm right, he'll be watching, trying to find his next victim."

Dawn swallowed a hard knot in her throat. She wanted Gideon to be right, but she also hoped he was wrong at the same time.

"And you think that me walking out in my tutu isn't going to look suspicious?"

"I've seen other girls do the same. Their carriages and cars pick them up and they return home to change. It should be fine."

Dawn nodded, though she did have her doubts.

"I'll be waiting in the shadows," Gideon said. "I'll meet you around front." He disappeared out the hallway, heading in the opposite direction.

Dawn stole a breath, her ribs crushed tight in her bodice. All she needed to do was walk out the front doors. Gideon would be there waiting. No harm was going to come to her. But she couldn't help the blood that pounded heavily through her veins, the flutters that flapped in her stomach.

She slowly exited the costume room and made her way down the hall. The air hovered thick around her, as if she were walking through mud, but she pushed forward through the silent halls. Most of the lights were burned out for the evening. She entered the large and silent foyer, the massive chandelier above her dead in the dark.

Moonlight trickled in from the front windows as she crept forward, pushing open the heavy double doors. Fresh air stung her face. Chills rippled along her chest and bare shoulders. Her white tutu was stark against the dark night before her. She slowly walked down the front steps, the air wrapping around her, guiding her forward. Lampposts glowed throughout the empty courtyard, the last of the cars pulling away.

She wandered through the walkways that cut through the grass and fall leaves, around the large oaks that stood tall and silent. The moonlight filtered down through their silhouetted branches, extending long shadows from the trees. She placed her hands over her abdomen, her eyes wide, peering into the dark. She kept her chin forward, but her gaze stretched from side to side, little bugs crawling underneath her skin.

She felt someone's presence out there in the dark, like two invisible eyes watching her every step. It could be Gideon—but this felt different. It was like the gaze was eating her up, taking in every bit of her, following her every move. She peeked behind her at the ominous theater building, itching to run back inside, but she forced herself forward. She only needed the Dollmaker to show himself. Then Gideon would come. Everything could end tonight.

A light rustle came from the nearest tree as a breeze tickled the fall leaves. Moonlight lit her path; her skin was white in the dark, her footsteps soft. Her breathing sped up, and a shadow shifted in the corner of her vision. It seemed to be following along with her, matching her pace. She changed directions, heading back toward the middle of the courtyard, and the shadow shifted closer, closing the distance between them.

"Come on, Gideon," she whispered under her breath. "Where are you?"

She picked up her pace, heading for the wrought-iron gates in the fence that surrounded the courtyard. What should she do when she reached the end? Exit onto the street? Turn around and go back? What if this shadow had already taken Gideon down? What if Gideon wasn't there to save her?

She continued to pick up the pace, and then a shadow emerged in front of her. She halted abruptly. She hadn't seen a shadow in front of her. The figure was portly, round in the middle. Its feet were planted firmly on the ground.

She stood facing the silhouette for a moment before she breathed, "Who are you?"

The shadow didn't move. Its broad shoulders were stiff as it stood, unmoving.

"I asked who you were," Dawn repeated. "Step into the light."

It took one step toward her, and Dawn edged back. With another smooth step, Dawn fumbled back further, her tutu ruffling. Her mind was screaming, but she couldn't formulate any words.

At its next step, a shadow darted in her peripheral vision. A strong hand gripped her own, yanking her away from the figure. She was pulled backward, tripping over her feet, and she had to run to keep up.

"You fool," the person said. "Are you trying to get yourself *killed*?"

At first she thought it was Gideon, but the voice was different—smoother. He continued to drag her back toward the theater. She zeroed in on his lean form and wild hair and her heart picked up again.

"No!" she said. "Sebastian, let me go!"

A low chuckle came from him as he continued to drag her. "You should be thanking me."

He drew her along the building, into the tangled gardens that lined the side, and the thick scent of roses filled her nose. Thorns brushed past her bare shoulders, scraping her skin, and she winced.

A cry echoed out from behind, and Dawn dug her feet into the ground, stopping.

Was that Gideon? "Gideon!" she yelled.

"His fate is his own," Sebastian said and yanked her forward once more. He pulled open a stone-paneled door on the side of the theater and pushed her inside, darkness stretching out before her. "In. Before I change my mind."

He shoved her forward, and she blinked. A single oil lamp lit a descending stairwell.

"Follow the stairs," Sebastian said, gripping her upper arm. "We'll wait out the night below."

16

Black Gold

They descended several flights of stairs downward as Dawn gripped the iron railing. They wound around and around, the stairs making her head spin as her stomach sank deeper and deeper. She didn't know where Sebastian was taking her, and she didn't know if she felt relief or dread.

Soon the stairs stopped, and Sebastian led her through a pitch-black space, her eyes wide and blinking. She could hardly see Sebastian in front of her. The dark hallway opened up to reveal a large cave deep underneath the theater. Water trickled down the stone walls, the drips echoing in the space, and rock jutted out from the surface.

Four large basins of fire roared in the massive space, their flames licking upward, casting shadows on the towering rock walls. The ground turned to a smooth stone beneath her, where carpet had been spread, revealing tables full of trinkets—dolls, pointe shoes, knives, tools, books, small figurines. Several divans were spaced out on the carpet. Was this where he lived?

"What is this place?" Dawn asked.

Sebastian let out a small noise. "Isn't it obvious?"

Her eyes roamed over the dolls on the tables. They each wore different intricate costumes—tutus—adorned with lace and ruffles, bright colors. Their hair was curled in tight ringlets, their faces painted in fine detail. They were miniature ballerinas. Her gaze flew up to Sebastian and her mouth dropped open.

"*You*?" She edged backward in the dark.

Sebastian quirked his head to the side. "If you're insinuating something, just say it."

Dawn paused and lifted her chin, but her heart pounded furiously. "You're . . . you're the Dollmaker."

Sebastian barked out a laugh, and the sound rumbled off the high ceiling.

Her brows creased together. "You're mad. You really are a psychopath."

His mouth twisted upward. "Are you quite finished?

She continued to hold her ground. "Where's Rose? I need to see Rose! Why have you brought me here? Am I your next victim?" Her heart wouldn't slow.

His gaze slid from her bodice down to her ankles. "And if you were?"

She kept her chin up. "Then I'd say to trade me for Rose. Let her go. You can have me."

He barked out another laugh, this time dry with humor. "You'd trade your life for hers? I believe *you're* the crazy one."

The adrenaline was starting to fade as Dawn noticed he was prolonging his attack.

"I've brought you here because there's a real madman on the loose and I was *trying* to help you," he said. "I was aware of your little scheme with my brother, and I want to murder him for putting you in danger."

"So you *are* a murderer, then."

He lifted a dark brow. "That is to be determined."

He was playing her—teasing her. How could he joke at a time like this? She eyed the dolls and tools on the tables again.

Sebastian peered back at the tables. "I'm a dollmaker, yes. I craft dolls and sell them. Though business hasn't been good as of late. I'm sure you can imagine why."

She didn't believe him. He *could* be the Dollmaker, and he just wasn't attacking her because she . . . because she wasn't a real ballerina. Her hands ran over her tutu, and his eyes followed.

"You look ridiculous, by the way," he said.

Her gaze snapped up to his. "Excuse me?" Gideon had said the same words to her when she'd worn her mother's gown.

He waved his hand at her. "You're not a frilly girl. It doesn't suit you."

She peered at him closer. "And how would you know? You don't know me."

His mouth twitched and he linked his hands behind his back. He began to pace in front of her. He wasn't as tall as his brother, he was smaller in height and in stature, but he had the same lean build, the same long legs, the same hollowed-out features, though he needed more sun.

"Oh, I've watched you, Dawn Hildegard. You're not afraid to get your hands dirty. You care more about others than yourself. You have no need for decorum and you definitely won't let a man tell you what to do. You're smart, very smart, and . . ." He stopped pacing, facing her. "And you have a compassion I've never seen in anyone before. Compassion is the greatest gift any of us could ever hope for."

His voice cut off, and the echo of his kind words hung in the air between them. No one had ever spoken to her like that. How could a serial killer be so kind?

No, she wouldn't fall into his trap.

"Well, you're wrong," she said, though she couldn't tell him why.

His mouth twitched again as he resumed his pacing.

Silence settled between them before Dawn asked, "Why do you hide down here?"

He paused, his jaws clenched tight. "Why does anyone hide? We hide when we have shame. And I have great cause for shame."

She blinked. He gave such an honest answer. Sebastian was beginning to be . . . surprising. She didn't expect him to have this much depth. If she could believe him. But even a murderer could have depth—especially a psychotic one.

"You mean shame with Gideon?" she asked.

He spun on her, attacking her with a glare. "I won't talk about him."

She held up her hands. "Fine."

He stared her down for a moment before he said, "Find a seat. Get yourself comfortable. I'm not letting you leave until daylight."

She couldn't move. What if he *was* the Dollmaker? And she would be spending the night with him? Her heart began to speed again.

Sebastian sat down at one of the tables and picked up a porcelain doll that didn't have a face. He retrieved a fine paint brush, dipped it into a palette of black paint and began to outline eyebrows. His hair fell over his forehead, his face set in concentration, his jawline tight.

She tentatively peeled her feet from the floor and crossed the carpet that covered the smooth stone. She would never be able to rest. How was she supposed to spend the night with a man who might be a murderer?

Think of Rose, she told herself. She couldn't let anything distract her from Rose. She sat on the edge of a divan, her body stiff. She wouldn't let sleep take her. She couldn't let her guard down. Sebastian's movements were fluid, his face filled with concentration. He could pounce at any moment. But fatigue from the long evening settled on her shoulders, making her feel as if she weighed an extra twenty pounds. Her eyelids burned, but she forced them open.

Yet still, Sebastian showed no sign of threat.

She watched him for a long while.

Shivering in the cold cave, she retrieved a knitted blanket that hung over the sofa. She willed her eyes to stay open, but eventually sleep overtook her.

When she woke, she sat up in a rush. How could she have let herself fall asleep? She patted along her body. She was fine. She was here. She still had all her limbs.

The fire still crackled around her, heating her face. She searched for Sebastian, her eyes taking in the tables, but he was gone. She threw off the blanket, standing. He was nowhere to be found.

Next to her on the couch, her loose dress was laid out along with her boots. He must've retrieved them from the costume room. How he knew they were there, she didn't know. Maybe he had been watching her more than she thought.

Thoughts of Gideon surged to her mind, and she recalled the cry she'd heard in the dark.

What if he was hurt?

She quickly dressed, peeling off her tutu and pulling her dress over her head. She faced the dark tunnel she had entered the night before. She knew she was free to go, Sebastian wasn't there to stop her, but she couldn't help but feel at a loss leaving the cave, which didn't make any sense. She felt like she needed to learn more about Sebastian and his conflict with Gideon.

So much had happened in the past week, from Dr. Miller being apprehended, to the séance, to another victim being found. Thoughts of Sebastian still made her insides crawl, but there was something about him. A darkness hovered around him like a cloud, but there was also a light in his demeanor that drew her to him.

Rose. Focus on Rose. She couldn't be down here any longer. She could still be in danger.

Shaking her head, Dawn left the cave and went up the spiral staircase.

She exited into the gardens, the early-morning light cascading down through the gray clouds. Frozen breath puffed from her mouth as she made her way back home, hoping to slip inside unnoticed. Her mother would be beside herself if she knew Dawn had been out all night.

She knew she ought to go straight to Gideon's house to make sure he was safe, but she couldn't be seen like this. Out this early in the morning with her hair unruly and makeup probably smudged on her face. She couldn't risk being the talk of the town.

She slipped through the streets, everything silent, the town not having risen yet. She was relieved when she entered her neighborhood. A light fog crawled along the ground over the cobblestones, and the smell of fresh bread wafted out from one of the apartments. She stayed close to the buildings, making one last turn, and then stopped dead.

A car sat in front of her house, its engine silent. She knew that car. It belonged to Arthur. She edged closer to her house, staring at the front steps and then planting herself on the ground. She couldn't go in. Not now. She peeked up at her bedroom window on the second story. The front door swung open and Mrs. Cook stuck her head outside. Her eyes lit up in surprise before her brow furrowed.

"You best come in, miss. Before you make things worse."

Dawn peeked to either side of her, her feet shuffling. "I . . ." She swallowed. "I can't."

Mrs. Cook bustled down the front steps, her heavy chest heaving. She gripped Dawn around the wrist with a strong hand. "You're already in enough trouble as it is." She tugged Dawn forward but gave her a sympathetic look.

A fire crackled inside the parlor, its waves of warmth melting her chilled skin. She took in the room, her gaze stopping on each person. Her mother. Her father. And . . . Arthur Hemsworth. She'd been right.

"What is this?" she asked, her heart speeding.

"What is this?" her mother screeched. "What is *this*?" She marched up to her and yanked her farther into the room. "Sit. Now." She shoved her into a chair by the fire.

Her father stared her down, a clarity in his gaze she hadn't seen in a long while. He must not have been drinking last night. His hair was combed back smoothly, and he held an untouched glass of amber liquid. Arthur Hemsworth's eyes traveled over her and a sudden chill rippled down her body despite the fire. He licked his lips, hands clenched on his cane.

"You want to tell us where you've been?" her mother ranted. "*Who* you've been with? You've been out all night! A disgrace! Unseemly!" She ran a hand over the scarf tied around her head.

Her father continued to stare her down, swirling his amber liquid. Why hadn't he drunk it? Usually he couldn't keep it outside of his gullet for more than five seconds.

"You will marry Arthur Hemsworth *today*," he announced.

Dawn froze. She blinked at her father, feeling as if her lungs had turned to ice. "What?" It barely came out in a whisper.

Her mother set a hand on her forehead, falling into a chair across from her. "Imagine the horror when the young Mr. Hemsworth came to our doorstep early this morning," she said. "Asking your whereabouts. I told him you were in bed, but to my dismay, you weren't. He told us you had been together and that you'd disappeared. A scandal, it is. Out last night with that man . . . We told him that he needed to marry you at once—that you would be ruined because of this. But he refused. We ought to toss you out on the streets, if it weren't for Arthur here."

Arthur smacked his lips again, leering.

Her father wouldn't look away. There was a darkness in his eyes—an alertness that pierced her soul. He continued to swirl his glass.

"I won't have it," Dawn choked out.

"You *will*," her father bit out. He slammed his glass down on the side table and rose from his chair. He moved so he was towering over her. "The ceremony will take place today. Arthur is the only one who will take you at this point, and you're lucky he will still have you."

Her gaze shot over to the old man. Bags hung underneath his eyes and gray wisps of hair stuck out from behind his ears. His back was curled over, his spine sticking out through his silk shirt.

"I won't have it," Dawn repeated.

Arthur's bony fingers tightened on his cane and he licked his lips again. "I assure you your daughter will be very well taken care of. We can have the ceremony at my estate this afternoon and you can send over her things later."

"I've already called the minister," her father said.

Dawn sprung up from her chair. "I said I won't have it!"

The room silenced. Every pair of eyes slid to her.

"I don't care if I'm ruined," she said. "I don't care about my reputation or about being married. The only thing I care about is my practice. I'm a healer. That's all I want out of life." *And to find Rose.*

Everyone continued to look at one another, silent, until Arthur burst into a fit of laughter. The sound was hoarse, scratchy; he broke out into a series of coughs.

"As if anyone will take you seriously," the old man said. "Do you think you will actually get patients when they're all whispering behind your back? Don't forget, one word from me and the whole town will know you're a witch. I stopped the rumors once, but I could start them again." His lips curled up wickedly. "Besides, my offer still stands. Marry me, and you will have your practice."

Dawn blinked, heat coursing through her. Her mind raced. Once again, she wondered if it was worth it. Arthur could give her what she wanted. She'd be out from under her parents' roof. She could have her own patients. Freedom to treat whomever she wanted. She'd have money and wouldn't have to worry about making ends meet.

Marriage had always been her worst nightmare, but was it really the worst thing that could happen? Maybe she was lucky. Rose was to be married, but she had to give up the one thing she loved. Dawn was being offered her dream on a platter.

But could she do it?

She zoomed in on Arthur's pockmarked face. Sacrifices always needed to be made to achieve goals. Maybe this was her sacrifice.

She opened her mouth, but she didn't know her answer. Mrs. Cook stepped in so she didn't have to.

"Come, child," she said, linking her arm through hers. "It's best to give them some space to get things arranged. We ought to go get you ready."

Dawn allowed herself to be pulled from the room, thinking furiously. There *had* to be a way out of this—but maybe she didn't want a way out. As Mrs. Cook dragged her upstairs, the notion that she was going to be married that day planted itself in her head. Perhaps she was sealed to this new fate. Perhaps there was nothing she could do.

17

White Satin

Dawn sat in front of her mirror, staring at the picture Mrs. Cook had created. She looked nothing like she had last night—no extravagant hair and makeup, no tutu. Just a simple blue silk dress that hung loosely from her thin frame. Her hair was pinned tight against her skull under a constricting headband. The rouge on her cheeks did nothing to improve her pale complexion.

When she'd woken in the lair that morning, she didn't imagine it would be her wedding day.

She placed her hands over her cheeks and stared into her own dark eyes, fear and doubt staring back at her. Dawn had always prided herself on being strong. Sometimes she even felt invincible, but in this moment, she felt smaller than the dust mites wafting on the air. She couldn't go through with this, but she didn't see how she had a choice.

Before she knew it, she was whisked into Mr. Hemsworth's car alongside her parents. Mrs. Cook stood on the front porch watching them depart, her chubby face squished in concern. Dawn kept her gaze on her home as long as she could. Would this be the last time she saw it? What if Mr. Hemsworth was lying, and he stole her away and made her live in the countryside? What if she never saw her town again? Had she healed her last patient? Her future was uncertain; the further the car drove, the colder she became.

The ride was silent, her mother gazing wistfully out the window, her father with a fixed frown on his face. She could feel his stare on her every few moments or so but didn't dare look back at him. He had no right to come into her life now and demand such things of her. He had been absent for so long—hadn't cared a wit about her life and how she lived it until he saw her as a walking paycheck. Securing her future with Arthur Hemsworth would set him up for life: It'd pay off his debts and give him more money to gamble away. He didn't care what it cost her.

The car pulled to a stop in front of the Hemsworth manor, the late-afternoon sun high in the sky. Light filtered down through the scattered clouds. A slight breeze rustled the silk scarf flowing around her neck, the beautiful stitchwork the only thing that could give Dawn any joy in this moment. She wondered what Rose would think of her now, walking silently to her demise. Would she try and stop it? Would she say she was doing the right thing? Was Rose even alive?

She set a hand on her racing heart.

Dawn glided up the front steps. She willingly walked, deciding she needed to face her fate head on. She wouldn't go kicking and screaming and give her parents any more power.

Percival answered the door. Dawn kept her eyes fixed on the bow tie at his neck. She couldn't look at his face—she didn't want to absorb any detail about today. She hoped to put it in the back of her mind as soon as possible.

She stepped into the marble foyer and her mother clapped with glee, chattering about the entryway and the marble staircase that cascaded down from above. The world blurred as she followed the butler down the hall, focused on his straight form, passing the pictures and green plants without notice. She entered a study on the right, opposite from the study she had been in with Gideon earlier that week. She recalled those early days with him and how she'd believed him to be a thoughtful, caring person. Now he was feeding her to the wolves—to the alpha wolf—uncaring about her plight with his uncle.

Arthur and Gideon were standing in front of a large mahogany desk when she entered, and her gaze immediately shot to Gideon. He kept his gaze glued to her as she approached, a solemnness in his expression. He kept his jaw shut tight, his teeth clearly clamped together. She gave him a pleading look—suddenly she was desperate—but he kept his face blank and continued to stare her down. She narrowed her eyes and lifted her chin.

So that was how it was going to be.

Dawn paused in front of Arthur Hemsworth, keeping her chin up. "Shall we get on with it, then?" She felt Gideon's presence next to her but forced herself not to look at him.

Her parents followed in after her, accompanied by the man she assumed was the minister. He rushed in, a cap on his head, black robes draping from his shoulders. He held the Holy Bible, a book Dawn had tried to read only once. It was filled with too many miracles. She didn't believe in miracles—she believed in science, in making things happen for herself. But she suddenly *wished* she believed in miracles. She could certainly use one.

The man dusted off his robes, settling himself between Dawn and Gideon. He clutched the Bible to his chest and glanced from Dawn to Gideon.

His furry eyebrows rose. "Are you two the lucky ones, then?"

"No," Gideon said sharply. "She . . ." His gaze skated to Dawn.

"I'm marrying the man just to your left," she interrupted.

Arthur shifted his weight, half of his mouth curved up. He gripped his cane, beads of sweat running down his face. His pallor had a sickly light green color to it.

The minister's eyebrows shot up further. "Him?" He did a double take.

Dawn straightened her shoulders. "Yes."

Her mother and father stood off to the side against a polished side table, a decanter on top. Her father eyed the liquid but kept his hands clasped in front of him.

"Let's get on with it, then." She said it with brevity, but her voice shook.

The minister kept his gaze on Gideon. "Are you married then, sir?"

The lines in Gideon's face hardened. "No, I'm not. I don't see how that's relevant."

Heat rose on the minister's cheeks, and he coughed. He glanced at both Dawn and Arthur again before straightening his cap. "If you're sure then."

"She's sure," her father said.

Dawn kept her gaze fixed above Arthur's head during the proceedings. The minister droned on, talking about the seasons and change and how life cycled through the seasons. Her mind drifted and she began to wonder if the minister was stalling, as his gibberish continued. She jerked to attention when he said her name.

"Hmm?" She snapped her head over to him.

"Do you have rings to exchange?" The minister's robes flowed as he leaned back.

"Oh. Umm."

Arthur snapped his fingers and Percival, who had been lingering in the back of the room, brought forth a velvet box. He presented the box and revealed a wedding ring. A diamond sat fixed on six prongs of white gold, the facets of the gem sparkling in the dim light. Next to it sat another ring with diamonds embedded into the gold. Dawn cringed at the sight, her heart rate suddenly picking up. The rings made everything feel real, and her pulse sped quicker and quicker. Her breathing became labored. She placed her hands over her stomach. She dared to glance at Gideon again, but he kept his gaze fixed forward, lips sealed together. She wanted to scream at him, to tell him to stop the ceremony, but he wouldn't give her the time of day. Heat bubbled at the surface of her skin and she gritted her teeth. She reached into the velvet box, grabbed the gold ring, yanked off her gloves, and stuffed the ring onto her finger.

"There. I have a ring. Shall we continue then?"

She was internally screaming at herself. She didn't want this. But she felt abandoned by everyone around her, and Gideon's betrayal felt the worst. She would rather accept her fate with her head held high than be treated like a wounded animal.

Arthur took his ring and slid it onto his own gnarled finger. His eyes were lit with hunger, his gray hair fluffing outward. His wrinkles pulled tight when he gave a half smile.

"Do you have any vows?" The minister peered down between the two, red brushing his cheeks. He tugged his collar, peering over at Gideon again. She wanted to scream that he wouldn't do anything. Gideon clearly had no intention of helping her.

"No vows," Dawn said. "Continue, if you please."

The minister coughed, his eyes darting from side to side. He sighed. Arthur peered over at her with heat in his eyes, excitement in their depths. She forced herself to look above his head again, swallowing down the bile that was suddenly rising in her throat.

The minister continued, his voice extra slow, enunciating each syllable. Dawn wanted to yell at him to speed up. The sooner she got this over with, the sooner she could accept her fate and move on. Every part of her itched to be out of Gideon's presence.

When the minister asked her if she would take Arthur's hand in marriage, she opened her mouth, and choked out, "Yes."

When he turned to Arthur and asked him the same question, a voice yelled, "Stop!"

Dawn nearly fell over. The voice jolted right through her, cutting through the stiff layers she had built up around herself. An immediate calm came over her, smoothing out her frayed nerves.

"She won't be marrying my uncle this day."

For a moment, Dawn thought that Gideon had stopped the proceedings, but the attention was toward the back of the room. Gideon paled and his face hardened. Dawn slowly turned around.

Sebastian stood in the doorway, his dark hair wild, his hollow features severe in the dim light. His black coat was tailored perfectly against his lean frame.

"Stop this at once," Sebastian said.

The room blinked back at him and relief swept over the minister's face. He set the Bible down on the table behind him. Gideon glared at his brother, every line of his body tight.

Arthur gripped his cane, smacking his lips, his gaze slithering from person to person. "Speak, boy. What is this?"

"Yes, what are you doing here?" Gideon asked.

Sebastian kept his gaze locked with Dawn's. He stared down at her with an unreadable expression, his body as tight as Gideon's.

"Do you want this?" Sebastian asked Dawn. "Is this what you want?"

"What . . .?" She shifted her stance. "I don't know what you mean."

"Do you mean to marry my uncle?" he said. "Is it what you want?"

Her gaze darted over to her parents, both of whom were glaring at her.

"I . . ."

"It's a simple question, Dawn."

Arthur gripped her arm in a flash, his knuckles bony against his grip. "Yes, it *is* a simple question. And one I would be very careful answering."

She jerked at the touch, wrenching out of his hold. She looked back at Sebastian's face. His dark eyes were hollowed out, the shadows underneath his jaw heavy.

"Of course not," she whispered. "Of course I don't wish to marry your uncle."

Arthur let out a howl, shaking his cane in front of her. "Be careful with what you say. I have power in ways you'll never know about. You're about to make yourself a very dangerous enemy."

"But you feel you have to," Sebastian continued. "You feel as if your reputation has been compromised."

Her gaze skated around the room again before Dawn nodded.

Arthur stuck his face in hers, his breath foul. "It's not too late to take back your words."

Sebastian glided forward, putting himself between Dawn and his uncle. He removed the ring from her finger and handed it back to the minister.

"She won't be needing this," Sebastian said curtly.

Dawn didn't know what to say. Even though she felt the entire room's gaze on her, she couldn't take her eyes off Sebastian. His long fingers dipped into his coat pocket and he pulled out a ring of his own. It wasn't extravagant, just a simple gold band. The kerosene lamps glowed around them as Dawn stared down at the ring, her heart picking up again. Sebastian gently took her hand, placed the ring at the end of her fourth finger, and slid it on. He kept his eyes locked with hers, an unspoken communication between them. Even though she didn't know anything about him, a feeling of comfort and peace was there. She couldn't take her eyes off him.

"If you need to save your reputation, if your family needs money, and if you wish to have freedom, marry me instead. I will give it to you."

The room went still. Dawn could barely breathe. It took a few moments for her brain to catch up with what he was saying.

"You?" It was all she could muster.

"No!" Arthur howled. But he didn't move to stop his nephew. He stood with his weight over his cane, glaring at the proceedings.

Sebastian lifted her hand and placed his lips on top of her skin. The warmth of his mouth sent a shudder through her, making her arm tingle.

"Or would you rather I leave you here to my uncle?" Sebastian asked. He quirked up a brow.

Dawn clenched her eyes shut, her head spinning. The sense of relief that flooded through her was overwhelming, but could she marry Sebastian? She didn't know a thing about him. And there was a possibility that he could be the Dollmaker.

What if she was about to marry a murderer?

Her pulse skipped and skidded, and she tried to slow her breaths. Was being married to a serial killer worse than being married to Arthur? She peered over at Arthur's gnarled face, then to Sebastian, who stared at her intently.

What would Rose say? She wished Rose were here. She had never intended to marry. She didn't want to marry. The thought of a man owning her was appalling. But Sebastian had mentioned freedom.

She peeked at Gideon, who was still glaring at his brother.

"You just can't help it, can you?" Gideon bit out.

Sebastian kept his gaze locked on Dawn. "I don't know what you mean."

"First Sophia, now Dawn. You just have to take whatever is mine."

"Last I checked, you weren't engaged to Dawn, so I don't know what you mean. You were about to let her suffer a fate worse than death and weren't doing anything about it. I, however, will not let that happen."

Gideon faltered, stepping back. Sweat shone on his brow. "I couldn't." His eyes caught Dawn's. "I just couldn't. My Sophie . . ."

Dawn realized that to Gideon, marrying her would seem like a betrayal, even though Sophie was dead.

Dawn kept her gaze locked on Sebastian. "I'll do it," she said. "I'll marry you."

Something shifted behind Sebastian's gaze. Relief? Satisfaction? Excitement?

Her father burst forward. "I won't have this!"

"Neither will I!" Arthur limped around to the front of them.

"If it's money you're worried about," Sebastian snapped at her father, "I'll make sure you're taken care of. I may be the younger brother, but I'm independently wealthy. Though you don't deserve it."

Her mother's hand fluttered to her throat and a smile played on her lips. She set a hand on Dawn's father's arm. "Let them be, dear. After all, should we stop true love?" Greed shone in her eyes.

Arthur's face turned bright red.

Dawn tried to block the room out. All that mattered was that she didn't marry Arthur Hemsworth. But would Sebastian give her the freedom she needed to find Rose? To have her practice?

"As long as the proceedings take place right *now*," her father demanded.

Sebastian continued to stare down at Dawn, unmoving, and for a moment he looked like a statue, with his perfectly chiseled face and frozen expression.

The minister picked up his Bible again readily, a large grin on his puffy face. "Let's get to it, then!"

Arthur started to back away, muttering to himself. "Filthy nephew. You will regret this."

The minister began to speak and the next few moments felt like a dream. Dawn hardly noticed the minister's words as Sebastian continued to stare at her. She could barely focus on anything other than his angular face and dark eyes. His gaze held her upright, as if there were an invisible force between them and his eyes were the only thing keeping her on her feet. This should've been the most terrifying moment of her life—she had *never* wanted this—but somehow his presence made it all right.

After they had exchanged the proper words, the minister announced their marriage and said it was time to kiss the bride. Sebastian, as stiff as a rod, didn't move. He slid his gaze away, turned, and started to head out of the room.

"I'll come for you later," he said. "Pack your things. I won't have you living here, nor will I have you living down . . . elsewhere."

She knew that he meant the cave below the theater.

She wanted to call out after him, feeling a sudden loss at his departure, but he left her standing alone.

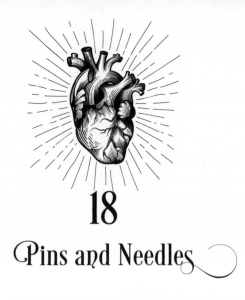

18

Pins and Needles

It didn't take long for Dawn to pack her things. She didn't have many things to pack.

When she returned, Mrs. Cook had set to the task, folding her dresses neatly in her luggage, including all her chemises and undergarments. Dawn would miss Mrs. Cook. Even though she had only known her a short while, she had shown Dawn a kindness no one else had. Dawn would've loved to have had her as a nanny. She had a tenderness toward Dawn like a mother would a daughter. She didn't want to leave her alone with her parents. But as Dawn watched her pack, a horrid feeling settled in.

Sebastian didn't . . .

Did he expect for them to have a *real* marriage? A real, physical, intimate marriage? Her breaths came out in gasps and she tried to take a full breath, but her lungs felt shrunk.

She couldn't do it.

She wasn't ready.

The thought of being with a man in that way . . .

Sebastian clearly hadn't wanted to kiss her, she reminded herself. Perhaps he wasn't interested in a physical marriage.

But did that bother her?

No, of course not.

Sebastian had spoken about her freedom. Maybe that's what he meant. She'd be free from the physical bonds of marriage.

Her lungs seemed to expand; she gulped in a fresh breath of air.

Mrs. Cook shut her luggage and Dawn grabbed her medical pouch from her bed. Before exiting, she took a moment to look around her room. The dusty desk and mirror in the corner. The small lumpy mattress. The chair by the hearth. The window that opened onto the street. She would not miss this place for a heartbeat.

The car arrived, and as soon as Dawn was settled inside, the vehicle took off. There wasn't so much as a word from her parents. No good-bye, no heartfelt words of encouragement. They were probably already spending their money—either on fine dresses or drinking it away.

The car didn't turn down the streets she'd expected it to. She imagined Sebastian would either find her a home near the outskirts of town or whisk her away to the countryside, where she would never be seen again.

Instead, the car drove through the wealthy part of town. They passed by Rose's home, with its tall pillars and clean walkways, the streets swept clean. The car took one last turn, then pulled over to the curb and stopped.

An extravagant building sat before her, with pillars similar to Rose's adorning the outside. Clean stone steps led up to a carved wooden door with a golden knocker. Lace curtains framed the windows. A butler stood on the stoop, waiting.

The valet exited the car and opened her door for her. She stepped outside, a light breeze whisking her hair across her face. The valet began to retrieve her luggage and she slowly went up the walkway to the butler.

"I am Graham," the man said. He was young, probably only a decade older than she was, with sandy hair swept neatly across his forehead.

"Surely this can't be the right place," she said aloud, before she could stop herself.

Graham laughed, and a twinkle sparked in his eyes. "I have known Sebastian for a long time, miss, and I can assure you, he would only provide the best for someone he chose to spend his life with. He only purchased it a few days ago. He must've planned on your arrival."

Planned?

The constricted feeling settled over her again, and she tried to breathe evenly. Before she could regain her composure, Graham opened the door and motioned her inside.

The interior of the house opened into a decent-sized foyer with a dazzling chandelier hanging over her head. Stairs with smooth blue carpet led upward. Golden-handled doors lined the room. The ceiling bore crown molding, the corners free of cobwebs. She couldn't remember if her own home had ever been this clean.

"Is Sebastian here?" Dawn asked. Her voice echoed off the ceiling.

"No, miss. I don't expect him to be here for some time. He has business."

Her brows pinched together. "What kind of business?"

Graham's mouth twitched. "I can't say. He is a very private person."

She gently nodded. Private indeed. He'd been living underneath the theater, crafting dolls.

The thought sent a shiver through her. Had Rose stood in that same spot? How many people had he murdered down there?

But she'd felt oddly comfortable with him during the wedding. It was a new feeling, one that had settled in the air between them.

Would a murderer really do something as kind as saving her from marrying a creep like Arthur?

"I'll escort you to your room."

Dawn followed Graham up the stairs to a door on the left. Inside, sun shone through an open window, the lace curtains fluttering in the breeze. A large four-poster bed sat in the middle of the nicely-sized space—not too extravagant but nicer than she'd ever had. A finely carved wardrobe adorned the corner, its open doors displaying a myriad of hanging dresses.

"The master wanted you to have new clothes," Graham said. "He wants you to look like a lady, if you so desire. He wants you to have the best." The valet walked into the room and set her luggage on the floor.

"What I have is sufficient," Dawn said, though she glanced to the wardrobe once more. This was ridiculous. Rose was out there being tortured while she was being pampered with new dresses. She didn't have time for this. She needed out.

"I'll let you get settled. Our housekeeper, Mrs. Hampshire, already has tea on the kettle. Come down when you're ready."

Graham left the room and Dawn stood alone in the middle of the space, peering at the fluffy white pillows on her bed. She longed to lie down and shut her eyes—it had been a long day—but her mind was spinning furiously. She took in the room in greater detail. China lined the mantel and a chaise sat in the corner. A soft Persian rug covered the shiny wooden floor. She eyed the bed again. Frilly white lace adorned the comforter. She could hardly picture Sebastian lying in that bed. He must have a separate bedroom.

Another sense of relief swept through her and she set her medical bag on the corner of the bed.

What had her life become?

She'd never pictured herself married so young. Twenty-one was a normal age for girls to get married—some were married even younger—but she could've never predicted that she'd be in this predicament. Rose must've been terrified to be married to Chester. All she'd wanted to do was dance, and now she didn't even have that. She squeezed her eyes shut, her throat thickening. Each day that passed, the more likely it was that she was dead. But her body *still* hadn't turned up. Which meant she *had* to still be alive. Right?

The thought of Chester sent a wave of sickness through her. Maybe Rose's fate was better than being married to him. Would it be worse to live a life with a man who was unfaithful to you? Would it be worse to be tied down and not be able to do what you loved? Perhaps it was better to die a swift death than to be tortured for the remainder of your days.

She pinched the bridge of her nose and began to pace the room. Too much time had passed. If Rose was alive—and that was a strong if—who knew what permanent damage had been done to her? If she returned home, would she still be bound to the same fate she had been before?

And what of Sebastian? Was he the same type of man as Chester? Perhaps that's where he was now. Visiting a brothel, getting drunk, and lying with women. He couldn't have wanted this marriage. For some reason he felt a sense of duty, and she didn't know why.

Dawn stopped pacing. The realization of what had happened to her finally took root. She didn't want to believe it before—she'd gone through the motions, but so much had happened too fast, she hadn't been able to truly process her new predicament. Emotion swelled in her eyes and before she knew it, tears spilled out onto her cheeks. She couldn't remember the last time she'd cried. She hadn't even cried when she delivered Mrs. Creswell's stillborn baby last spring.

Her knees hit the floor and she gripped the rug beneath her. Tears fell from her cheeks, staining it. Sobs wracked her shoulders;

she was unable to contain the emotion flowing through her. This couldn't be her life. This couldn't be her fate. What would've happened if the Dollmaker had gotten to her last night instead of Sebastian pulling her to safety? Perhaps that fate would've been better than this. She continued to sob, knowing she wasn't thinking rationally.

Dawn lay curled up for a long time, until her tears expired. She finally wiped her eyes, her vision slowly clearing.

She wouldn't be weak. She wouldn't live her life as a victim. She wouldn't be owned by a man.

No.

She would take her fate into her own hands.

Dawn needed to regroup.

Just because she was married, just because her life had taken a downhill turn, didn't mean she couldn't still find Rose. In fact, bearing Sebastian's name might give her more freedom. The Dollmaker was still out there; she needed to find him before anyone else turned up dead. Dr. Miller was still in prison and the only thing that could release him would be another murder.

Caldwell was still a suspect, and she needed to do what she could for those girls, but one thing at a time. First, she needed to continue the investigation by herself. Gideon had abandoned her, and now she couldn't trust him. He could continue his investigation on his own. Though perhaps Gideon was right: The Dollmaker had to have learned the art of amputation somewhere. Maybe he was a doctor in the surrounding areas. Dr. Miller had a list of contacts in his office. She would start there.

Sebastian didn't show up. She spent the night and all the next morning waiting to see if he'd surface—though she wasn't sure if she wanted him to. A part of her wanted to speak with him, get inside his head, but she mostly wanted him to stay as far away from her bed as possible.

She quickly drank tea and scarfed down a platter of scones and raspberry jam. She donned her usual blouse and skirt, eyeing her new wardrobe again before shaking her head. She snatched up her medical satchel and wrapped her silk scarf around her neck.

She was outside before Graham or Mrs. Hampshire had anything to say about it.

The crisp morning air cleared her head somewhat, though her eyes were still puffy from crying. There was a car at her disposal but she wouldn't resort to using it. She had legs. She could walk.

She headed through the nice part of town: Ladies were taking strolls on the street; a few gentlemen tipped their hats. She held her satchel tight to her side, trying to keep her gaze forward. The breeze chilled her skin even though she began to sweat at the back of her collar. The sun warmed her in the chilly air.

She entered the town square, feeling much more at home in the crowd. She looked around the area. It was strange that people could be living a normal life when hers had turned upside down. Shoppers bustled around, chatting in groups. She eyed the clinic across the way and continued to trudge toward it. The list of names had to be inside.

When she reached the clinic, she unlocked the doors and stepped inside the musty space. It seemed like forever since she'd been there. She lit the few lamps in the room and ran her fingers along the shelves of medicines. The vision of Dr. Miller's glazed expression—his milky eyes and sickly appearance—floated in the front of her mind. He must have been drugged with some sort of opiate. But it had to be in its purest form. MacLarin had said they experimented on the prisoners. Perhaps they wanted him to appear more crazed and delusional. They *wanted* to pin him with these murders.

She searched through the bookshelves before heading to the desk. She opened a drawer, rifling through paperwork, looking for anything with a list of names on it. Dr. Miller was good friends with all the doctors in the surrounding areas. He must have kept their contact information somewhere. Where they lived. Where their practices were located.

She closed the drawer and opened another but became distracted as images from the day prior filled her mind. Gideon, standing next to the minister, unmoving. It was as if he hadn't even cared she was about to be married to his uncle. She had actually thought Gideon charming at one point. But the way he had abandoned her . . .

Sebastian's face came to mind, his dark eyes staring her down, and her insides shook at the memory. She'd never had anyone look at her like that—it made her feel as if she were about to be eaten alive, as if he . . . *owned* her. From memory, she analyzed the grooves of his face from his hollow cheeks to his defined jawline.

Suddenly a scream pierced the air. Dawn jerked upright, dropping the papers back into the drawer. Several men rushed up to the clinic door and threw it open, carrying a young woman inside. Dawn recognized her as Angelica, the ballerina who had helped turn her into a porcelain doll. Her blond hair was down around her shoulders, tousled, as if she'd been in a fight. Blood was seeping from her puff sleeve, half of it ripped, a gaping wound in her skin.

"What happened?" Dawn surged to her feet, clearing off the operating bed. "Set her down."

Officer MacLarin and a couple other men laid her on the bed as tears streamed down Angelica's pale face, her lips and nose red.

"She was attacked," MacLarin said. "She says it was the Dollmaker."

"*What?*" Dawn examined the wound. Bits of dirt and rocks were trapped inside the open flesh. The cut was deep enough that she'd need stitches.

"Give me some space," Dawn ordered. "The wound needs to be cleaned out." She rushed over to the shelf and retrieved the carbolic acid. She looked Angelica in the eye and tried to give her a reassuring look. "This is going to hurt, but it's going to be okay."

Angelica nodded, tears in her eyes.

"Officers, if you'll hold her down?" Dawn asked.

They nodded, eyes wary, but did as she said.

Dawn poured the liquid over the wound, and Angelica screamed. The men pressed her writhing shoulders down into the bed as Dawn poured more of the antiseptic over her skin. Angelica whimpered, her eyes squeezed shut.

"Tell me more about what happened," Dawn ordered. She moved over to the side of the room and opened a drawer, retrieving a needle and thread.

Angelica continued to cry, tears streaming down her face.

"It's all right," Dawn said, pausing. "It'll help you if you talk about it. It'll also distract you from what I'm about to do. Can you be brave?"

Angelica nodded, sniffling. The men hovered around her, continuing to hold her down. MacLarin stood back.

"Keep a firm grip on her," Dawn said. "Now, tell me what happened," she said to Angelica.

"I was walking to an appointment with Mrs. Wadsworth. I got engaged last night—we were going to start planning the wedding today." She hissed as Dawn stuck the needle into her skin. "It all happened so fast. One moment I was on the road, and the next I was in a back alleyway. He was large—a heavy man—and his hands were immediately around my throat. I didn't even see his face."

She winced as Dawn dug the needle into her skin again, pulling the thread tight.

"He choked me until I passed out," Angelica continued. "I think he thought I was dead, because when I awoke, he was pressing a blade into my flesh. I screamed for him to stop, but he continued to saw down on my arm. It was—" She broke off into another fit of sobs. "He wouldn't listen to me. But these men out on the street must have heard me. They rushed into the alley, and the Dollmaker disappeared. I told them to bring me straight to you."

Dawn finished cinching up the wound, tying off the thread. She retrieved some sterilized bandaging.

"You're lucky to be alive," MacLarin said.

Dawn finished wrapping the wound and leaned back on her heels, a fine line between her brows. "It doesn't make sense. It doesn't seem like the Dollmaker to be so careless. He's getting sloppy."

The men helped Angelica sit up, tears still staining her cheeks. "But he's still out there."

Dawn spun on MacLarin, her heart speeding in her chest. "This will clear Dr. Miller's name. He needs to be released at once."

MacLarin shook his head. "No one died, miss. For all we know, she was just attacked."

"He was trying to saw off her arm!"

His lips turned down. "Again, just a wound. She didn't lose her arm now, did she? We can't prove it was the Dollmaker."

Dawn gripped her skirt. "You can't be serious."

MacLarin turned to Angelica. "We should get you home straightaway. We will escort you."

Angelica was still sobbing, and the sight only reminded Dawn how she had been so weak the night before. She wondered if her eyes were still puffy.

Before MacLarin left, he turned to Dawn and said, "If you want to free the doctor, you better hope that a real murder turns up soon." He tipped his hat and exited.

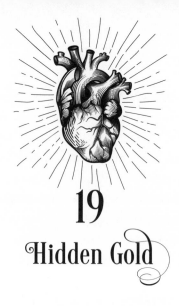

19
Hidden Gold

Dawn returned to her new home in a daze. She had spent the rest of the afternoon tearing the clinic apart, looking for a list of other doctors she could investigate, but there was nothing. She'd wanted to run to Gideon's house and tell him about the new developments, but things were severed between them now. She couldn't go to him for help. He'd abandoned her—he'd only had any interest in her when she was helping him with Sophie. He didn't care about Dr. Miller. He didn't care about Rose. He probably didn't even care about any of the other girls.

The other girls.

Who would be his next target?

Angelica had said she'd just gotten engaged. How terrible to have her life almost ripped from her. Thank goodness those men found her in the alley, and that MacLarin had been nearby to help. She couldn't imagine how frightened Angelica must have been.

The man who'd almost attacked Dawn that night in the theater's courtyard had *also* been heavyset. But Dawn couldn't think of a suspect of that size. MacLarin was a big man, but he seemed as determined to find the Dollmaker as she was. He was an officer of the law and wanted this man off the streets. There was no way it was him.

She entered the kitchen, where Mrs. Hampshire was pulling a plate of scones out of the oven. She was a wire of a woman, the opposite of Mrs. Cook, with a narrow face and no extra flesh. A platter of curd and cream was already set out on the table, and Mrs. Hampshire turned as Dawn approached, eyeing her warily.

"I've just pulled out some scones," she said. "You'll need to wait a minute for them to cool." Her voice was flat and stern.

Dawn's brows crept together. "You don't like me very much, do you?" she asked.

The old woman pinched her lips together. "I don't know you. I have yet to make a judgment about you."

Dawn sat in a chair, itching to stick her finger into the cream and taste it.

"Have you known Sebastian long? Graham said he's known him for years."

Mrs. Hampshire waited a few moments before she answered, as if debating whether to trust her. "I've known Sebastian since he was born. I raised him in part. I worked at the Hemsworth manor."

Dawn's eyes widened. "You knew Sebastian as a boy? What was he like?" The question just came out.

Mrs. Hampshire placed a few scones on a platter and set them in front of Dawn.

"He was a quiet child, always reserved, whereas Gideon loved to get into mischief. Sebastian always, even though he was the younger brother, seemed much older than Gideon. He was the one who took care of his mother before she died. And then his father, after that." She cocked her head to the side as she continued. "Gideon handled his grief in other ways. He ran wild, having unseemly relationships with women, while Sebastian retreated. He'd spend hours in his study, doing who knows what. But I've always loved him like my own son, so you can understand if I'm wary about his marrying a stranger."

Dawn nodded. She had a hard time imagining Sebastian as a child. Gideon, on the other hand, was easy to picture.

"Something happened between Gideon and Sebastian," Dawn said. "What was it?"

Mrs. Hampshire linked her long fingers in front of her, shoulders stiff. "It isn't my business to tell but as his wife, you should know." She sighed, sitting down next to Dawn at the table.

"Sebastian was found alone with Sophia on the night of her engagement party. She was indecently dressed. Supposedly, Gideon walked in on them and he couldn't handle it. He was beside himself with rage. He beat his brother to a pulp and told him he never wanted to see him again. So Sebastian disappeared."

Dawn's mouth fell open. "That can't be true."

"Believe what you must, but there was hardly anything that went on in that house that I didn't know about."

Dawn nodded again, taking it in. She was married to someone who had seduced his brother's fiancée? A wave of sickness washed through her. Who was Sebastian, really?

"I'm sharing this information with you because you should know all the facts," Mrs. Hampshire said. "Though perhaps you shouldn't believe Gideon's story. I believe something else happened that night."

Dawn's mind raced. She *wanted* to believe that Sebastian was a good person, but could she really? She didn't know him. Whom did she trust more: Sebastian or Gideon?

She stood up abruptly from the table. Even though the heady smell of scones wafted deliciously on the air, her stomach turned. "I think I'll need to eat later. Thank you, Mrs. Hampshire."

She headed up to her room, hoping to clear her head, but thoughts of Sebastian had taken root. Her doubts were only growing.

Sebastian didn't come that night. Dawn waited in her room, listening for the entryway door to open, but it never did. The house stayed silent as a still night, disturbed not even by sounds from Graham and Mrs. Hampshire below. They must've known Sebastian wouldn't turn up, otherwise they would've been preparing for his arrival.

Dawn's thoughts jumped back and forth between Rose and Sebastian. She worried about how Rose was doing; she feared when Sebastian would return. The hours ticked by while Dawn sat by the window or paced the floor. Wind whipped along the windowpanes; splatters of raindrops beat against the glass. The wind howled, and Dawn lingered by the fire in her room, trying to stay warm against the chill. She rubbed her hands together and paced in front of the hearth, her short skirt swishing. The longer Sebastian took to arrive, the more unsettled she felt. Where was he? She was his bride, was she not important enough to attend to? Not that she cared, but she couldn't help the disquieting feeling that had wrapped itself around her gut and the irritation that bubbled under her skin.

How *dare* he plop her into a house and not return? He had promised her freedom, but she didn't feel free. Even though she was free to go and work at the clinic, to investigate Rose, he seemed to have an invisible hold on her, as if her thoughts weren't her own anymore. Her mind always returned to him. She couldn't focus. She needed to speak with him. She needed to see him. She wanted to know where he was.

She paused.

His lair underneath the theater.

He had to be there.

She peered out the window at the whipping trees and icy rain and eyed her coat, hanging over the chair. She couldn't use the car at this time of night—she wasn't about to wake the valet to help her—but she also couldn't wait until morning to see Sebastian. She *needed* to know what he was doing. Why he was avoiding her. Otherwise, she couldn't help Rose. She needed to get her head straight.

She snatched her coat from the chair, quickly threw it on, and pulled on her gloves. She dipped out into the hallway, descended the stairs, and exited the front door without so much as a movement from Graham or Mrs. Hampshire.

The wind stung her cheeks and needles of rain plopped down on her head as she raced down the front steps. Each raindrop felt like a cold, miniature knife slicing into her skin; she headed down the street as quickly as possible.

The wind loosened her hair until it fell over her shoulders. Puddles soaked the hem of her dress and her boots. Moonlight reflected in the pools of water; half of the lampposts were burned out in the dark night.

A part of her feared it wasn't wise to be out at this time of night, but she reassured herself that even the Dollmaker wouldn't subject himself to such weather—even though she might be heading right to his lair.

By the time she reached the theater, her clothes were completely soaked, clinging to her skin and weighing her down. Her teeth chattered violently as she entered the gardens at the side of the theater. The foliage was overgrown and dead. Thorns stuck to her side as she pushed through the rosebushes to reach the side door. She had no idea if it was unlocked, but she had to try.

She turned the brass knob and the door opened with a creak, heavy against the wind. She hurried inside, the sudden silence echoing in her ears. She stood for a moment in the dark, staring at the stairwell in front of her. She squinted, eyes slowly adjusting, and moved forward, wringing out her skirt.

She took the stairs down, her heart beating faster the further she descended. What would she see when she found Sebastian? Did he have a secret life he was keeping from her? Would she find him torturing a victim? But no, Sebastian didn't fit the heavy physique of the Dollmaker. He was too lithe, too thin. It couldn't be him. Dawn's shoulders relaxed as she entered the dark space before the cave.

Bits of light glowed in front of her, growing in size as she approached. Dawn stepped inside the large cavern and took in the scene before her. The long tables stretched out in the middle of the space, four large basins of fire surrounding them. Trinkets lay on top of the tables—weapons and dolls and material and paintbrushes.

She slowly crept into the space, a trail of water following her. As she passed by one of the large basins, she longed to peel off her clothes and warm herself in front of the fire. Instead, she walked over to the nearest table. She noticed a porcelain doll displayed in the middle of the mess.

The doll wasn't a ballerina like the others—she wore a silky red dress instead of a tutu, beads finely stitched into the fabric, bits of lace layered on the outside. It was the most exquisite dress she had ever seen—and it was on a miniature doll. How Sebastian was able to create such beauty in something so small.

The doll's hair was black as midnight and done in curls that cascaded around her pale face, which had large, dark eyes. A satchel hung on the doll's shoulder. Dawn's hands flew up to her mouth. If she didn't know any better, she'd think the doll was . . .

Her.

She dropped the doll on the table, shaken.

"What are you doing here?" The voice was commanding, terse. Sebastian stepped out in front of her. Every line of his body was tight. "You shouldn't be here."

The harshness of his voice shook her. No longer was he the warm, comforting presence that had saved her from Arthur Hemsworth. He stared her down as if she were the last person he wanted to see on earth.

She swallowed, finding her voice. "And what are *you* doing here? You think you can plop me into a home without so much as a word? After . . . after tying me to you? Don't you think you owe me an explanation?"

"I don't owe you anything." His voice was clipped.

She fixed him with a glare. "Oh? So is it your habit to marry women and lock them up in your apartment? Then run off to a dark lair and . . ." She peered at the doll again. "You really are a psycho-path." She instantly regretted the words. She knew he wasn't. She knew she *hadn't* been locked up, but she wanted to hurt him. She wanted him to know how she felt.

Sebastian looked as tight as a string ready to be plucked.

"Go home and leave me be."

"No," Dawn said, tightly. "Not without an explanation."

He stood frozen for a few more moments before his shoulders sagged. He tugged a hand through his unruly hair. "I don't know what you expect from me, Dawn."

"Tell me why you're here. Why you feel the need to hide."

The anger had faded from his features, and his gaze focused on her appearance, roaming over her entire body. "You look a mess."

She lifted her chin. "I'm fine."

"You're going to catch your death."

"I said I'm fine," Dawn repeated, though shivers rocketed through her whole body. Her jaw was chattering again.

Sebastian frowned, shadows flickering over his face. He marched over to her and pressed a hand into the middle of her back. He led her over to a basin of fire and faced her head on. His hands went up to her throat, where they lingered over her top button. He tilted his head, his dark eyes boring into hers. His mouth twitched.

"I'm going to remove your coat," he said softly.

His fingers trembled; every part of Dawn stilled. His face was only a breath away from hers and he kept his gaze locked on her as his fingers gently unfastened the top button. His hands lowered to the second button, his eyes still locked on hers. Her breath caught and tingles erupted down her body, but not in cold—it was a sudden surge of warmth.

He lowered his fingers and smoothly unbuttoned the third button. Her heart was hammering now, and he wouldn't let go of her gaze. She felt trapped in him—swallowed by his presence—and she didn't even hate herself for it. She had vowed to never be affected by a man, and suddenly, just the mere act of Sebastian unbuttoning her coat was undoing her.

He unbuttoned the fourth button, hands pausing at the bottom of the coat. She held still, absolutely paralyzed, unable to look away. His fingers trailed up the length of her arms and stopped at her neck. He touched her delicate skin and his eyes flicked to her lips. For a moment, Dawn thought he was going to kiss her. She realized, ashamed, that she *wanted* him to. She wanted to know what it would be like to have his lips on hers. Would they be warm? Soft? How would it make her feel? Would he *ever* kiss her?

She squeezed her eyes shut. Rose. How could she think such a thing when Rose was out there suffering? She opened her eyes, and her thoughts seemed to have broken the spell. He gently tugged on her collar and lowered the coat off her shoulders, drawing her closer to the fire.

"Stand here," he said. "I'm going to get you a blanket."

He set her coat down on the table and retrieved a blanket from one of the divans. He wrapped the blanket around her shoulders and she drew it closer around her. The fire warmed her skin, sending ripples down her body.

He moved over to a divan and sat down, leaning back with his legs stretched out in front of him, eyeing her quizzically.

"You really are different, aren't you?" he asked. There was no more anger in his voice, just pure curiosity.

She kept her profile to him, facing the fire. "I don't know what you mean."

"I don't know many girls who would run out in the middle of the night into a deadly storm just to seek answers."

"Many? You mean you know other girls who would do such a thing?"

His mouth twisted wryly. "One, I only knew one."

"Past tense?"

He nodded solemnly. "A sister."

The phrase hung between them for a moment before Dawn said, "Mrs. Hampshire didn't tell me about a sister. She told me your parents died."

"I should've known the old woman would rat me out." His lips twisted up in humor for a moment.

"What happened to her?"

"Scarlet fever. It took her young, but my mother later died of the same thing. And my father died of a broken heart."

Dawn swallowed, her throat suddenly thick. "My brother died of scarlet fever too. He . . ." She paused. "My parents blame me for his death. I caught the fever. I transmitted it to him. I survived and he didn't. They never got over it."

Sebastian cocked his head, peering at her more closely. "Is that why you're a healer then? You feel guilty for his death?"

Dawn blinked. How could he have guessed that? The guilt had eaten at her for years. If only there had been proper medical treatment all those years ago. Perhaps if *she* had been his healer, she would've been able to save him.

Sebastian nodded to himself. His thoughts traveled over his face. "Mrs. Hampshire knows not to talk about my sister. I'm not surprised she didn't mention her."

It was Dawn's turn to nod.

Silence stretched between them.

It was a comfortable silence, both of them trapped in their own thoughts.

"Why were you so angry before?" Dawn asked.

Sebastian snapped his head up, focusing in on her face.

"Is it because you're hiding something from me?" she continued. Her eyes darted to the table full of dolls. "Is it because . . ."

His face darkened and he stood up abruptly from his seat. "I hope, Mrs. *Hemsworth*, that someday you will not insult me. I assure you, my motives of keeping you distant are of a generous nature. I could've locked you away in the countryside to keep you safe, but I knew there would be nothing more torturous for you than that. I will give you your freedom to work if you will give me my freedom to attend to my own business. Now, is there anything else you want from me?"

His voice had risen; it boomed off the cave walls. The fire shifted around them, shadows dancing on the rocky surface.

"No," Dawn said quickly. "No, I don't want anything else from you."

She should've felt relieved. He was giving her what she wanted. He'd saved her from Arthur Hemsworth. He clearly didn't want to have a physical relationship with her, which pleased her, but why did she suddenly feel a void?

And he had called her Mrs. *Hemsworth*.

He stayed staring her down, his fists clenching and unclenching until he spun around, turning his back to her. "Stay as long as you want. But I have things to attend to."

He marched away on his long legs until he disappeared on the other side of the cave.

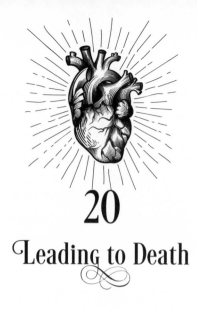

20

Leading to Death

T he next day, Dawn forced herself to go about her normal routine. She got dressed, eyeing the new apparel in her armoire,
before heading downstairs. She ate breakfast in the kitchen,
sternly telling Mrs. Hampshire that she didn't want to eat in the fine
dining room. There was no need for her to have such needless and
gaudy attention, and she was perfectly capable of dining in the small
kitchen.

While eating breakfast, her thoughts were focused on her investigation. From the flawless amputations, it seemed likely that
the Dollmaker was a doctor. Since she couldn't find the names of
the doctors in surrounding towns at the clinic, she'd have to get the
names from Dr. Miller himself. But she needed his head to be clear.
She couldn't speak with him when he was drugged.

If only she could figure out *what* drugs they were using on
him. If she could prove what the authorities were doing to him was
illegal, if he could get his head clear enough for her to speak with
him. But what she really needed, she realized darkly, was another
murder to take place. Perhaps if she staged one.

She shook her head. No. That'd be impossible.

Her smartest bet was to speak with Dr. Miller and concoct a plan for his escape, unless she could catch the Dollmaker herself. That option wasn't off the table. She'd already tried to fish him out, and that plan would have worked if Sebastian hadn't stepped in and saved her. She headed across the town square, where the early-morning shoppers were already out and about, buying bread and vegetables. There was an uneasy feeling in the air. People kept their eyes low and their voices quiet, as if rushing to get back indoors. The Dollmaker's attacks were now in their home. No one was safe.

Dawn passed Nora's shop and headed straight toward the clinic. If she was lucky, she'd discover the opiate Dr. Miller was on and be able to make a complaint by midmorning.

She stepped inside the clinic and gently shut the door. Morning light streamed in through the windows, sunbeams dancing in the air. Dawn went straight to the books. They were clean and lined up precisely—the way she liked to keep them—and she ran her fingers along the titles until she paused on a book she'd once read about opiates and their different uses.

She pulled the book out and started flipping through the pages. Opium. Laudanum. Morphine was experimental, as the hypodermic needle was in use. She'd heard of men crushing opiates and inhaling them for pleasure. Addiction was common, as there were opium dens supplying their needs. And with Prohibition, more men were turning to drugs because of the lack of alcohol. But where was the prison getting their supply? And what drug were they pumping Dr. Miller with? Like she had supposed, it was most likely opium in its pure form, which could lead to Dr. Miller's death. Perhaps that's what they were intending, wanting to kill him before his execution took place and they could pin him with the murders.

Dawn snapped the book shut. She needed air. She couldn't be confined to the office all day. The thought of even waiting for patients seemed exhausting.

She stepped outside the clinic and locked the door behind her. She pulled in a deep breath, the crisp morning air slightly clearing her head. Thoughts of Sebastian wafted in again—his cold demeanor in contrast to the way he'd changed abruptly, making her feel so warm, only to revert to his darkness. She couldn't figure him out. He'd saved her, yet it felt as if he wanted nothing to do with her.

Some ladies were huddled together across the street, and one of them pointed at her. Their eyes were wide, heads dipped, voices soft. They looked at her again before they parted ways, heading down the street. Dawn furrowed her brow, eyeing them as they walked away.

Did they know she was a Hemsworth? Had gossip spread already? Had Sebastian's name surfaced?

She hadn't thought of what people might think of her. She *was* a Hemsworth now, having married an elusive catch, and for the first time, she realized she had money. If she wanted, she could walk down the streets in fine clothes and shop for imported fabrics and ribbons. She could live a refined life, carefree, instead of staying elbow deep in patients' blood. She tried to picture herself wearing the latest fashions, being respected by other women, attending balls and parties, having friends.

She wouldn't be shunned because of her father's gambling habits. Perhaps she could have more respect. Perhaps she would get more patients if people trusted her.

A ruckus came from down the square, and Dawn snapped her head around to see Chester waving a bottle of spirits over his head. His shirt was open and torn, his hair mussed out to the sides. His slacks were wrinkled and his coat was in a sorry state. He staggered from side to side, yelling at the top of his lungs.

"You're all doomed!" he said. "He's coming for you, one by one! Just like my Rose. She was only the beginning. He won't stop until you're all dead!"

He continued to shout, and ladies dispersed around him, squealing. He stumbled forward, ramming into the fountain and plopping down onto its ledge.

"Doomed, I tell you! All of you!" He tipped his head back and took a sip of liquor. He wiped his mouth with his sleeve and continued to rant.

Dawn rushed over and snatched his bottle away.

"Chester," she hissed. "Get ahold of yourself. You're scaring everyone! And you can't be drinking out in public!"

Chester grinned lopsidedly and reached for the bottle. When Dawn pulled it away, he frowned.

"You're not safe either," he said. "No young woman is." He reached for his bottle again. "I never even got to have a life with her. Taken from me just before we were married."

Dawn paused, and it was as if the world stilled. A myriad of thoughts rushed to her brain, until a single thought took shape, floating, before it solidified.

"You were engaged," she said. "Of course." The world seemed to swirl around her as she thought furiously. "Angelica had just gotten engaged too. And Sophie had been engaged to Gideon. I'll bet the other girls . . ." She focused on Chester's face with a jolt. "I need to go."

Chester continued to frown at her.

"You, go home," she said. "Clean yourself up. It's not too late for Rose. We're going to find her."

Dawn tightened her coat and quickly rushed out of the square, feeling as if two eyes were on her back. Her sudden realization at the fountain made her feel as if she'd struck gold, but that the enemy somehow knew.

She raced down the streets, pushing onward despite the cool air burning her lungs. Instead of turning toward her new home she went the opposite direction, winding down the streets that led to

Gideon's house. She knew things weren't good between them—she was still furious over how he had abandoned her—but he had to be told this latest information. She pounded on his door, the sound echoing down the street. She kept knocking until the door creaked open. Gideon stood before her, wearing a loose white shirt and slacks, his face unshaven, his usual sleek hair mussed.

"It isn't ballerinas," she said quickly. "The girls. It's because they're engaged. It's not because they're ballerinas."

His mouth dropped open slightly, and then he pressed his lips together. "Why do you say that?"

"Let me in and we'll talk about it."

His dark brows crunched together, but he swung the door open, motioning her inside. As she walked past him, she was hyperaware of how similar he looked to Sebastian, and tingles spread down her arms at his close proximity. She sped up her pace, keeping her head high until she entered his study. She immediately bent to the floor where the papers were still scattered. She picked up as many documents as she could hold and spread them out on the table before her.

"We need to check the other victims," she said. "We have to find out whether or not these other girls were engaged."

Gideon slowly walked in after her, tugging a hand through his unkempt hair. "Why are you doing this?"

She paused. "Are you serious? You have to ask me?"

"There's nothing we can do, Dawn. It's too late. Whoever this madman is, he's won. Sophie is dead. There's nothing else I can do for her. We might as well stop now, before any more of us get hurt."

"But we won't," she said. "He's targeting girls who are engaged. Look!" She pointed to a piece of paper. "It says here that Madeline Fankhouser was engaged to Benjamin Carlson. She was murdered two days before their wedding." She turned to another page. "And here! Sarah Winstrom was engaged to Johnathon Pearce! Gideon, this is the connection! If we could only figure out why the Dollmaker has it in for engaged women!"

He stepped deeper into the room. "Be that as it may, it doesn't matter anymore. I'm tired, Dawn, and I'm sick of fighting. Maybe it's time for me to let my Sophie go."

"You can't be serious. What about Rose? What about his future victims? We need to figure out where he's hiding!"

Gideon stumbled over to a chaise and collapsed on the squishy cushions. He set his hands on his head, rubbing his temples. He stared up at the ceiling and Dawn crept forward a step. She peered closer at him. Aside from his ruffled appearance, his pupils were dilated, his face a sickly pallor. His usual sweet smell wafted off him, but stronger than usual. She knew that smell. She should've recognized it before.

Opiates.

"Gideon, are you . . . are you on medication?" She crept closer.

He sighed, leaning his head back. "And if I am?"

"Why? Are you ill?" She lowered herself next to him and placed her hands on his face. "You're warm."

He grabbed her hands and threw them away. "I'm fine."

"Have you been sleeping?"

He didn't answer.

"Gideon, have you been sleeping?"

He waved a hand, motioning her away.

"Gideon!"

He whirled on her. "What do you want me to say? That I rarely sleep? And that when I do, it's filled with nightmares?" He groaned, leaning his head back again.

"How long have you been using?" she asked quietly.

His jaw tightened and he shut his eyes. "It doesn't matter."

"Gideon." She put her hands on the sides of his face. "It *does* matter. I don't want you to throw your life away because of addiction.

I've seen men die from it. I need to know how long this has been going on."

He sighed, his eyes fluttering open. "Since New York. Since Sophie died. I needed something to take the pain away. I needed to forget."

"Forget what?"

"Everything. Sophie. Everything."

She kept her hands on his face, her thumbs stroking over his chiseled bones. "Everything is going to be all right. I'm going to help you."

The door banged open at the far side of the room. Sebastian stood in the doorway, energy thrumming through his lean frame. His eyes were narrowed, the hollows in his face extra dark, his chest heaving. Dawn flinched and removed her hands from Gideon's face. His gaze darted between Gideon and Dawn, his eyes darkening.

"We're leaving. Now," Sebastian ordered.

Dawn blinked back at him, her brow furrowed. "Excuse me?"

He marched forward and gripped her by the upper arm, yanking her up from the couch. "I said we're leaving."

Dawn jerked away. "No, I'm not. Gideon needs help. I'm a doctor. I'm not leaving him."

"You know nothing of my brother and what he needs."

"And you do?" Dawn retorted. "You betrayed him. And you left. How could you possibly know what he needs? He needs help!"

"You know nothing about Sophia!" Sebastian edged up next to her, his face inches from her own. "I *never* touched her. And Gideon knows that." His voice was soft, menacing.

Dawn snapped her head over to Gideon. "Is that true?"

Gideon slowly rose to his feet, sweat running down the sides of his face. "Of course not. I know what I saw. Sebastian was obsessed with my Sophie. He tried to take her for his own. She was terrified when I walked in on them."

Sebastian locked his lips tightly together.

"Liar," he said between his teeth. His body thrummed again, looking as if he were about to pounce.

She put her hands on his chest and gripped his shirt in her hands. "Please, Sebastian. Let me help him."

Sebastian's eyes flicked from his brother back to Dawn. He kept his face blank, but the chords tightened in his neck.

"Fine," he ground out. "But I'm not leaving."

Gideon narrowed his dilated eyes, swaying to the side. "I don't need medical attention. I want you both to leave. Aren't you supposed to be on your honeymoon? Or is that already over with? Done with her already, are you, Sebastian?"

Sebastian leaped forward, but Dawn pushed him back. "Stop!"

Gideon stumbled to the side again. He reached for the table to catch himself, but he missed it and fell onto the floor. His head hit the ground with a smack, and he groaned, rolling onto his back. His eyes fluttered closed.

"Gideon!" Dawn rushed over, checking for his pulse. It was slower than normal, but steady. She held his face, trying to wake him. "Gideon, open your eyes." He stayed unresponsive. "Gideon, can you hear me?" She leaned down over his face, feeling his breaths going in and out. "He needs help. He could have a concussion. We need to transport him to somewhere more comfortable where I can take care of him. Sebastian, can you help me?"

Sebastian glared down at his brother but nodded. "There isn't another bed in your new home yet, so we'll have to take him to my uncle's. He'll be most comfortable there."

Dawn paused, her hands hovering over Gideon's unconscious body. "I can't go back there."

"Do you have a better idea? Perhaps under the theater would be more comfortable?" Humor laced his voice.

Dawn set her hands on Gideon's chest. "Fine. Get the car. We'll take him to the Hemsworth manor."

21

Cuts Like a Knife

Sebastian drove Dawn and an unconscious Gideon to the large house, each bump of the road jarring Gideon's head. She kept his head in her lap to protect it from any more injury. Sebastian glared out the front of the car the entire ride, his gaze fixed. The hardened Sebastian was back—she was beginning to realize he was like two different people. He was either unnecessarily cold or so warm he melted her insides. She wondered if there was any middle ground with him, or if it was either one way or the other.

The Hemsworth manor stood tall and oppressive against the gloomy sky, dark clouds moving fast behind the structure. Sebastian helped carry Gideon to a room upstairs with a window overlooking the backyard. A maze of gardens took up the acres outside. Most of the flowers were dead at this time of year, except for a few splashes of color through the area.

Dawn helped Gideon settle into the four-poster bed and propped several pillows up behind his head. She made sure his head was angled to the side so he didn't choke in case he was to vomit unconsciously. Serious head injuries could cause nausea, though she was more worried about how many opiates he had consumed.

Sebastian stood in the doorway, watching her situate him, until she stepped back. The silence hung heavy between them.

"Do you think he'll be all right?" Sebastian asked.

Dawn nodded. "I do. He'll wake soon. I'll just have to keep a close eye on him."

"I'll make sure the staff knows to be at your beck and call," he answered.

She nodded again and silence fell once more. They waited together for a few moments.

He coughed, clearing his throat. "I'll leave you be, then."

He started to turn and leave when she said, "Will you stay? I don't . . . I don't want to be alone in this house. Not with your uncle. Will you stay?"

He peered at her with a questioning gaze, and for a moment there was something innocent in his expression. His guard had dropped and he looked like a young boy. There was such vulnerability in his expression, like he truly cared what she thought of him. But just as quickly, his walls came back up and he was the hardened man once more.

"I wouldn't leave you here alone if my life depended on it," he said. "I'll be right down the hall. Call out if you need anything."

He disappeared out the door and Dawn stared into the empty space after him. She felt a sudden loss with his departure, as if he had taken a piece of her with him when he left.

She shook her head and peered back down at Gideon again. She studied the lines of his face, relaxed in slumber. The weariness around his eyes had left; the lines around his mouth were smoothed out. She hadn't thought about how tortured he'd been all this time. Of course she knew he was hurting, that he would do anything to find the Dollmaker, but she didn't know about his addiction—that he was seeking alternate ways to deal with his pain. She'd seen opiates destroy men's lives. It was why she hardly ever prescribed them, preferring to use natural herbs to cure ailments. Her heart ached that he'd been suffering in silence. She could've helped him. She knew it was in her nature to want to heal, but she felt an extra responsibility for him.

Gideon was her friend. And as with Rose, she would do anything to help her friends.

A maid entered the room, carrying a stack of wood. She knelt down by the hearth and started to pile the wood in the fireplace. She took out her flint, ready to ignite a fire.

"Oh, that isn't necessary," Dawn said. "It's quite warm enough in here. In fact, I think some fresh air will do us some good." She moved over to the window and pushed it open with a creak.

The maid left the wood untouched and stood. "Is there anything else you need, then, miss?"

"Get me a cold washcloth. He's too warm."

She gave Dawn a quick curtsy before she hurried from the room.

Dawn turned to Gideon again, dragging up a chair and setting it next to his bed. She lowered herself to the chair and watched his chest rise and fall. She felt for his pulse again. It was still lower than normal, but that was usual with opiate intake.

The maid quickly returned with a moist rag and Dawn placed the cloth over his forehead. Drips of water slid down the sides of his face, but he didn't stir.

Time passed and the color started to return to Gideon's cheeks. A light pink pigment filled his face over the sickly white. She felt his forehead. It was cooler than the last time she had checked.

She saw Sebastian walk by the open door a few times from the corner of her eye and got the impression he was watching her. She didn't know why. A part of her wished he would come in and help the time speed by with conversation, but he moved so quietly, his form a shadow in the hallway. The next time he appeared, he stepped inside. He was extra pale, his skin white against his dark collar. He stood with his shoulders straight and his feet planted, a slight sheen of sweat on his forehead. Maybe he needed to be in bed too.

"What is it?" Something was clearly wrong.

"I just got word," he said. "There's another one."

"Another one of what?"

"A body. Found just outside the park in town. She's . . ."

Dawn rose from her spot by the bed. "Tell me."

"I think you need to see. I can take you there now."

Dawn lifted her brows, her mouth dropping open slightly. "You'll let me come with you? Most men don't want a lady to accompany them to such unladylike things."

His brows pushed together, and he cocked his head to the side. "You're a healer," he said. "I want your opinion. You have an eye no one else does."

Dawn stood still for a moment. Nobody had ever had this much confidence in her. Her entire career, she'd had men push against what she wanted to be. And now Sebastian willingly told her how much he believed in her. She pressed her hands into her stomach and peered down at Gideon again.

"I want someone watching him the whole time I'm gone, but he should be fine. I feel safe leaving him."

Sebastian's face twisted for a moment, before he relaxed. "I'll tell the maid. Let's go."

⁘ ⁘ ⁘

The late afternoon sun slipped behind the clouds, descending fast. Bits of orange glowed on the horizon as they pulled up to the park, where a circle of officers stood around the body. It was tucked in between two sections of bushes, a space about two body lengths apart. The body would've been hidden from viewers in the park unless someone had come up and peered inside the foliage. Dawn walked through the small group, her eyes immediately going to the young woman. Her skin had a blue tinge to it, already puffy from death. Her eyes were wide open and glassy, staring up at the sky. Her body was splayed at an awkward angle, arms and legs twisted.

But that wasn't what caught Dawn's attention.

Her body had been sliced completely in half, her torso stopping at the edge of her ribs, white bone sticking out from her sawed-off dress. The rest of her body was missing—her naval to her hips—the tops of her legs positioned beneath her as if she hadn't been mutilated. Blood stained the ground, but not enough blood that this would've been where he'd worked.

No, the body had definitely been placed in this position, waiting to be found.

A few police officers stood off to the side and as Dawn approached, one of them stopped her.

"You should back away, miss," he said. "This isn't a sight for a young lady like you."

She opened her mouth to retort, but Sebastian cut in.

"Let her look," he said. "I want her opinion."

The officer started to object, but Sebastian threw him a glare, and he coughed, backing away.

Dawn moved forward without a word and knelt next to the body. Her eyes scanned the woman, taking in every detail from her face to her absent abdomen to her toes. The world faded away—she was looking at a specimen, nothing more.

"She was definitely strangled," she said, "like the other women before her. Look at the marks on her neck."

Sebastian stood tall behind her, staring down at her with intensity in his eyes. "Go on."

"It has to be him. The cuts are clean and precise. He knows what he's doing, not that I've ever seen a torso amputated before." She swallowed on her last words. "And she appears to have been dead for at least a day. Do we know who she is?"

"Lady Catherine Cordova," the officer next to her said. "Everyone knows who she is."

Dawn made a face. Clearly, she didn't. "Let me guess, she was engaged?"

The officer's brows shot up. "Yes, to Lord Huntington. How did you know that?"

Dawn sat back on her heels. "Instinct." She observed the body for another moment before she said, "The Dollmaker still hasn't taken a head. It's usually the last thing he takes before his 'masterpiece' is displayed. So there's going to be at least one more murder."

The thought of Rose filtered in again. Her body still hadn't been found. Perhaps the Dollmaker was saving her.

She clenched her eyes shut. No, she couldn't think like that. At least her body hadn't been found. She could still be alive.

"Come on." Sebastian helped her stand and she brushed off her skirt. "We should let the officers take her away. A crowd is beginning to gather."

A few passersby had stopped on the walk, necks craning to see what the commotion was. There was already an unsettled feeling through town. If the townspeople found out another murder had taken place, mayhem would break loose.

"What do we do now?"

Sebastian pressed his lips together. "If I asked you to stop your investigation, would you?" He quirked a brow, staring down at her with humor in his eyes.

Dawn tucked her own lips in. "No, definitely not."

"That's what I thought." He straightened his coat. "Then what do *you* propose?"

Dawn sighed, gazing out over the park. The leaves rustled in the breeze, a few falling to the ground. "We need to communicate with future victims somehow. Stop any more deaths from happening. Perhaps we could go to the dress shop in town and ask for the names of all the girls who are to be married soon—I think the Dollmaker is targeting engaged women. But that might not be the best way to reach them. Not everyone has a new dress made for their wedding."

"Then what are you thinking?" He stayed still, silent, waiting.

"We need to go to the papers," she said. "Make it difficult for the Dollmaker to obtain his victims. If everyone knew his motive, then the girls could be more protected."

"And you think people would listen?"

"It's a step."

Sebastian nodded. "I'll make a call. The paper will listen to someone of my status." He ducked his head, pulling his collar up closer around his face. "Let's head back to the manor then. I don't like to be out."

Dawn tilted her head slightly at him, her brows slanting together. He didn't like the spotlight. The idea of his going to the papers for her must be hard for him.

She reached out and gently squeezed his hand. It was warm in her own.

He glanced down at the touch, his jaw clenching tight.

"Thank you," she said.

By the time they returned, Gideon was out of bed, pacing the room. Sebastian lingered in the doorway while Dawn rushed inside. Gideon glared at her, his face dour.

"Gideon! Get back in bed! You could have a concussion."

He rubbed the back of his head, frowning. "I *don't* have a concussion, and those blasted maids won't let me leave the room. And what am I doing here?"

Dawn pressed her hands onto his shoulders, forcing him to sit down. He swayed to the side, the mattress bouncing underneath him. She caught him, holding him upright.

"See? You're not all right."

She tried to push him back into bed but he shook his head.

"The maids told me there was another murder," he said. "Is it true?" His face paled and he swallowed, scrubbing a hand through his hair.

"Yes, it's true. We've already gone down to check it out. It was Lady Catherine Cordova. I can only imagine what her family is going through."

Gideon's frown stayed plastered to his face. "We?"

Sebastian stepped into the room. "Hello, brother."

Gideon groaned and lay back down on the bed. "And how's the happy couple?"

Dawn and Sebastian exchanged glances, and she cleared her throat. "You don't remember much of last night, do you?"

Gideon peeked one eye open. "You saw me in a sorry state."

She nodded and slowly sat on the edge of the bed next to him. "Gideon, I need you to be honest with me. How many opiates are you taking? You said you've been taking them since Sophie died. Where are you getting your supply?" She thought of Dr. Miller and how supplies were being stolen from their clinic.

"There are opium dens everywhere. It isn't difficult to obtain it with the money I have. And I'm not taking too much. Just enough to breathe. I promise."

She doubted that. "You said you were having nightmares. What kind of nightmares?"

He breathed in heavily through his nose. "Sophie. They're all about Sophie dying. Now are you through with questions?"

Sebastian moved and the floor squeaked. Gideon jerked, as if suddenly realizing he was still there.

His gaze slid to his brother before returning to Dawn.

"I don't know what you want with me," Gideon said. "I already told you, I'm done searching for Sophie's murderer. He's won."

Sebastian took another step forward. "Then let us take care of it. Dawn and I will figure it out. For you."

Gideon sat up in a rush, and his face contorted. "I wasn't speaking to you."

"Without us, you wouldn't be speaking at all," Sebastian said. "You could've killed yourself last night."

"And why didn't you let me? It's all part of your master plan to take over my life."

A tic jumped in Sebastian's jaw, but he didn't answer. The brothers stared each other down, silence pounding.

Finally, Gideon snorted and addressed Dawn. "If I were you, I'd get as far away from him as possible. He has a habit of stealing other men's women. If you have any hope for the marriage—don't."

Sebastian ground his teeth, his jaw flexing. "I'll be waiting out here," he said, and disappeared out the door.

22

Ghost Dance

D awn sat in the parlor downstairs in a chair next to the fire, watching the flames crackle. The sound usually calmed her nerves, but as she stared into the fire, all she could see was that poor girl's mutilated body. She hoped she hadn't suffered too much. Did the Dollmaker suffocate his victims first? He'd tried to strangle Angelica. Or did he torture them before they died?

Candles lit the small room along with a gas lamp in the corner. The heat burned one side of her face and she knew she should step away from the fire for a moment, but she couldn't move. The images in her mind were stuck to the sides of her brain.

A movement from the corner of her vision caught her attention. She turned. Sebastian stepped into the dark doorway, lurking in the shadows. The light next to him highlighted part of his frame, half of his face still in the dark. The light played off his sharp grooves, and for a moment, she couldn't believe he was hers—that they belonged to each other. He moved into the room, his finely stitched coat gliding along his lean frame, and he sat in a chair across from her. The fire crackled between them and he kept his gaze fixed on her, cocking his head to the side.

"You were impressive today," he said, voice low. "The way you could assess a dead body with such calm. I've never seen anything like it."

She twisted her fingers in her lap. She wasn't impressive. She was just doing her job. "I just wish I knew how to stop it."

He gave a thoughtful nod. "Why is it that you care so much about these women? Aside from the fact that you're a healer?"

She shifted in her chair, rolling her shoulders. "These women, they're perfect. Like ballerinas, they dance and look just like porcelain dolls. And the others . . . so much perfection is expected of them. And men expect them to be as such. To be a wife. To be a mother. To give up what they love just to—" She broke off. "I know I never will be like them. I could never put on that facade."

"Do you think I expect that of you?"

She peered at him curiously. "No, I suppose not. A man shouldn't tell a woman how to live her life," she continued. "I saw the way Chester treated Rose. I saw the way those women were fearful of Caldwell. He's a bad man, Sebastian. The ballerinas at the studio are afraid of him."

Caldwell. Another thing she had yet to fix. Sebastian remained silent.

She closed her eyes and leaned her head back against the chair. "I just don't know how to fix all this."

Sebastian let out a soft laugh. "I don't know why you've taken it all on yourself. Most girls would leave it up to the authorities."

She shook her head. "I'm not sure we can trust them. MacLarin . . . he wouldn't believe me about Dr. Miller and Caldwell. No, I can't trust him."

"Which is why you teamed up with my brother," he said plainly.

She nodded, silence hovering for a moment.

"Well, I'm glad," he said.

Her eyes snapped open. "You are?"

He held his gaze with hers. "It brought me to you."

Heat rushed to her cheeks and she placed her palms over her face. "You can't possibly mean that."

"I told you that I knew you, Dawn. As soon as you started working with my brother, I couldn't help but watch you. It was me on the rooftop that night. You fascinated me, and I knew if I were to link myself to someone in this life it would be someone like you. And I, for one, believe you are one of a kind."

He lifted his brows, as if challenging her to say something in return.

He'd been watching her? Her heart thumped in her chest. What was he expecting her to say? Did he expect her to compliment him in return? She didn't even know him. She hadn't even let go of the idea that he could be the Dollmaker yet. She could be part of some sort of twisted plan. He was different enough to seem crazy. Who married someone on a whim? He did seem to have anger problems, with his abrupt mood swings. And there was one other thing.

"Why do you make dolls?" she blurted out.

His face fell, before he masked his expression. "I hope that isn't an accusation again."

She shook her head. "No, of course not." Though her heart said differently.

He tucked his lips inward before he sighed. "It was my mother," he said. "She had the most exquisite doll collection when I was growing up. It was her most prized possession—other than Gideon, my sister, and me. I saw how happy it made her, and I suppose I wanted a part of her to live on if I created the same thing. I haven't told you, but it's why I would do anything to live in my childhood home—here in the Hemsworth manor. I want to spend the rest of my life here. I want to be close to her."

He wanted to live here? Would he take her to live here?

She couldn't. Not with Arthur.

She focused on his mother. *She* was the reason he created dolls. Guilt swept through her for thinking him a psychopath. He wasn't murdering people. He was only keeping his mother's memory alive.

She rubbed her forehead. "I'm so sorry."

"Don't be. She lived a good life. She loved her children, and she'd want us to be happy."

Sebastian kept surprising her. The more she learned about him, the more she discovered what made him tick. He was a kind soul, albeit a bit tortured. Both the brothers were.

"And you really didn't—" She broke off. She was afraid to ask this next question. "Sophie, you didn't try to take her for your own?"

Sebastian leaned forward and linked his slender fingers together. His face darkened and he ground his jaw. "She came after *me*," he said softly. "I didn't touch her. And deep down, I believe Gideon knows it."

He spoke the words quietly, but there was an intensity to his voice that scared her. She didn't dare ask another thing about it.

He slowly rose from his chair, his body unfolding. "We'll resume tomorrow. That is, unless you'd like to continue the investigation with Gideon instead?"

She paused, thinking. Did she? She and Gideon had been in this together since the beginning. But she didn't want to let Sebastian down. He had shared a piece of himself with her tonight, and she realized she *wanted* to work with him. Plus, Gideon wasn't in any state to work.

"We can work together," she said. "It's time we put this to rest."

His mouth gave a small twitch before he left the room.

The next day, Dawn rose early to check in at the clinic. She and Sebastian weren't meeting until later, and as much as she was ready to find Rose *now*, she needed to bide her time. So she walked through the town square, a bitter wind chilling her skin, a coating of snow over the cobblestone roads. She was grateful for her lace-up boots and the velvet coat around her back. The streets were silent, the sun obscured by gray puffy clouds.

When she opened the clinic door, Dr. Miller was inside, his back to her, rifling through the books on the shelves. He grunted in frustration and swiped a few to the floor.

Her eyes widened and her mouth dropped open.

"Dr. Miller!" She rushed forward and threw her arms around him. "You're out. They released you!"

Dr. Miller spun around, a crazed look in his eye. His gray hair was poufed out to the sides, wild, like he'd been pulling at it all morning. He'd clearly bathed, as the fresh smell of lye soap wafted off him. His clothes were in a sorry state, though, his wrinkled shirt untucked from his trousers. He pushed Dawn off him, muttering under his breath.

Dawn stumbled back. "What is it? What's wrong?"

"What's *wrong*?" He flung his arm outward, swiping a line of bottles onto the ground. They crashed, glass exploding everywhere. "Everything's gone! I need something. Everything. I need . . ." His hands shook. "Drugged me, they did, and now look at me. I *need* something."

Dawn eyed the bare shelf where the opium was kept. "You're addicted."

"Yes!" He collapsed onto a chair and set his head in his hands. "My body feels like it's on fire. Yet I'm so cold. And I can't stop this itch inside."

She knelt next to him, taking his hand in hers. "It's going to be all right. I can't believe what those monsters did to you. I don't even know how you're sane right now."

"I'm not."

"At least you're alive. I was so worried." She squeezed his hand. "You're going to be all right. We'll get through this." She squeezed his hand again. "But this makes me wonder *who* is stealing from us?" Her eyes shot up to the empty shelf again.

Dr. Miller's shoulders shook and he dropped his head down into his lap. "I don't know, but maybe I should be grateful." He started to weep. They shared space quietly for a moment before he sniffled and straightened. "I won't let them win. MacLarin and the others are too keen on finding this killer and pinning the murders on *anyone* who crosses their path. And you should be scared too." He gave her a direct look. "Your name is being tossed around. Arthur Hemsworth has made mention of your 'dark abilities.' I wouldn't put it past the authorities to come question you."

Dawn froze. She opened and closed her mouth.

"Think about it," he continued. "You clearly have medical knowledge. It was obvious to everyone that you didn't want Rose to get married. You've already been found at someone's deathbed."

"But that's ridiculous!" she burst out. "Kill Rose because I didn't want her to be married? And Frederick's death was nothing like the other murders!"

He shrugged. "They let me go. They have to pin the murders on someone."

Heat pounded behind her eyes. She'd done nothing but try and stop all of this, and now she might be *accused* of being the actual Dollmaker?

"I'm going to get to the bottom of this." Dr. Miller stood, shaking, and grabbed his coat.

"Wait, Dr. Miller—" She shook her head. "I don't think it's wise for you to be out. Not until . . ."

Not until the withdrawals stop.

Dr. Miller turned and placed a hand on her head. "Bless you, child, for coming in here today. You watch out for yourself."

He buttoned up his coat and headed for the door.

⚬⚬⚬ ⚬⚬⚬ ⚬⚬⚬

Later that morning, after cleaning up Dr. Miller's mess, Dawn set out toward the theater; it was still too early to meet up with Sebastian.

She couldn't get Dr. Miller's words out of her head.

They have to pin the murders on someone.

She shivered, scrubbing her arms. The authorities wouldn't come after her, would they? The thought was absurd. She was a healer. The town should've known that. And MacLarin had seen her *help* Angelica, so why would she be a threat?

Dawn hoped to catch Angelica in the rehearsal hall. She needed to make sure her wound wasn't infected and that she was staying off her feet. Dawn was sure she'd be at the theater watching the other girls rehearse—not wanting to leave them alone with Caldwell.

As she stepped into the courtyard she noticed all the leaves had fallen off the trees, bits of frost covering the mushy leaves on the ground. She walked along the pathways, everything muted in the cloudy light. A breeze skimmed along her shoulders, the cold air crisp on her cheeks. Memories flooded in of everything that had happened here. Watching the tree limb fall onto Frederick. Attending the ballet with Gideon. Entering the side passageway to Sebastian's lair. She couldn't believe all of it had happened within the span of two weeks.

Slipping inside the hallway, Dawn removed her gloves and rubbed her hands together, warming them. Music drifted down the hall and the melody loudened the further she traveled.

She peeked her head inside the studio, where a sea of white tutus swirled around. The girls were running in a circle, arms stretching, necks long.

Angelica sat off to the side, silently counting the steps. Her arm was still bandaged up but she was doing the movements with her hands, watching the girls intently. Caldwell stood up front, sweat dripping off his hair, his shirt open to his waist. Muscles rippled along his abdomen.

Dawn darted her gaze away. She suddenly wondered what Sebastian would look like in such attire.

"Stop!" Caldwell yelled.

The dancers paused and the music ceased. Chests heaved, sweat trickling down the girls' lovely faces.

"You have no energy! You look like dying swans. Perfection. I expect perfection!"

He marched up to the girl right in front of him and gripped her chin roughly. He pulled her face up close to his and narrowed his gaze. The girl stiffened, her eyes wide.

"If you want to be here, then get it right," he growled in her face. He shoved her away. "And you." He stormed over to the next girl and gripped her around the waist, yanking her up against him. "You have no passion. I need passion." He reached up and gently slid his fingers down her face. Her lips trembled and her breaths pumped out fast, but she clearly couldn't move.

Dawn froze, her feet rooted to the floor. Her gaze shot to Angelica, who sat on the edge of her seat, glaring at Caldwell. Her eyes were two tiny darts, her face a permanent scowl. Dawn felt the same anger—like she could pounce on Caldwell any second.

Caldwell continued to approach every girl, criticizing them. Dawn hovered in the doorway, every inch of her alive. She couldn't just stand here and do nothing. He needed to be stopped. Dawn started forward, mouth opening, when Angelica sprung up from her chair.

"Stop."

Angelica's voice ricocheted through the room. Everyone paused.

Caldwell slowly turned. He straightened his shoulders, dark brows lifting in surprise. His mouth curved up to the side.

"You can't treat us this way," Angelica said, trembling. "I won't have it anymore. We *all* won't have it anymore." Her voice shook, but her hands were clenched into fists.

Caldwell pushed the dancer next to him aside and she stumbled into the girl adjacent to her. He stalked toward Angelica, his eyes narrowing.

"I think you're a bit confused," Caldwell said darkly. "You see, I'm the one in power. You belong to *me*. I mold you into the beautiful creatures you are to become. You wouldn't be anywhere without me, and if I choose, you would be out on the street. I can do a lot more harm than just kicking you out of the company."

Angelica faltered back a step but kept her chin lifted.

"No," she said. "We won't have it. We're putting our foot down. All of us." Her eyes skated to the rest of the dancers, but they all stood unmoving.

Caldwell let out a laugh, the deep sound bouncing off the studio walls. The pianist hid behind the large instrument, clearly also afraid to stand up to Caldwell. Caldwell stopped in front of Angelica, glaring.

For a moment, Dawn thought he was going to strike her—hit her, attack her—but he only lifted up her hand and set it on his chest, rubbing it.

"We'll have a talk about this later," he said, eyelids lowered.

Dawn marched forward. She couldn't stay silent any longer. She strode over and stepped between them, placing her hands on Caldwell's shoulders. She shoved him and he stumbled back a step, confused. He blinked, taking Dawn in.

"What . . ." He swallowed. "Can I help you, Miss Hildegard?" He ran a hand through his sweaty hair, straightening his shirt.

"Actually, it's Mrs. *Hemsworth* now," she said.

She didn't want to tell him *which* Hemsworth—if he thought she was married to Gideon, he might be more afraid.

Caldwell kept his jaw together, a tic jumping in his cheek. "I hadn't heard."

"I think you need to listen to these girls," she said. "And I think I need to speak to my husband."

The girls started to stir behind Caldwell, exchanging glances.

More sweat ran down Caldwell's brow. "That won't be necessary," he said tightly.

"Oh, I think it is," Dawn replied. "Don't you girls think?"

The girls continued to peer at each other, their wide eyes full of fear, until a brunette in the back stepped forward. She wrung her hands. "I . . . I think he should leave. We want a new director."

"Yes." Another girl tentatively stepped forward. "We won't put up with him anymore."

Angelica sat back on her heels and smiled. Caldwell's gaze flicked around the room from girl to girl, his face contorted in anger.

"I won't have it!" he bellowed. "Get back in line!"

The girls started to group together, pressing their lips together tightly, their eyes narrowing. Such anger seemed foreign on their perfectly painted faces, but they kept their glares fixed and their chins lifted.

"Out!" another girl said. "If you leave now, we won't ruin *your* life. I wonder what the police would do if we all came forward and said *you* were the Dollmaker."

"You wouldn't," Caldwell said.

"Wouldn't we?" another girl said. "We're sick of being treated like objects. Like we're not human beings with real feelings and desires. You diminish who we are and make us uncomfortable. You use your power to make us feel small."

"You're a sick man," another voice popped in.

"We want you gone," another girl reiterated.

They all nodded in agreement, continuing to advance on him. Caldwell backed away, eyeing the door behind him.

"This is preposterous. How dare you?"

Dawn watched with her arms crossed, a small smile on her face. Even though the girls threatened to go to the authorities, Dawn knew they wouldn't need men to fight this battle. Caldwell was backing out on his own. She could see the resolve in his eyes.

"Fine," Caldwell spat. "If you don't say anything, I'll leave you alone."

Dawn wished they could do more. But no man would lock Caldwell up for being too forward with women. It was all they could do to get rid of Caldwell, but it would be enough. For now.

Caldwell disappeared and everyone in the room seemed to exhale at once. The girls squealed, clapping and hugging one another, their eyes bright. Angelica moved over to Dawn and laid her head on her shoulder.

"Thank you," Angelica whispered. "We couldn't have done this without you."

"No," Dawn said. "It was your spirit that stopped this. I just . . . I just wish we could stop him for good. Who's to say he won't go to another ballet company and do the same thing?"

Angelica nodded. "I know. But at least we've won this fight."

23

Bridge of Air

Dawn walked home in a daze. The events of the day repeated over and over again in her mind. The look on Caldwell's face . . . the girls' expressions when he left . . .

Her heart bloomed at the thought of those women sticking up for themselves. Maybe there was hope for them after all. Maybe miracles did happen. Maybe the Dollmaker would face the fate he deserved.

Dusk was falling fast, the last rays of light slipping through the clouds. The nighttime chill was settling in the air, and Dawn tugged her coat closer around her, white breath puffing from her lips. A few gas lampposts had been lit, their light reflecting on the cobblestones.

Thoughts of her parents drifted to her mind and she shivered. Even though they'd abandoned her, she wondered how they were doing. They hadn't contacted her since the wedding. Did they miss her at all?

She shoved them from her mind. They didn't matter. It was her and Sebastian now.

She was to meet Sebastian back at the house. She hadn't asked him what he was doing all day—she only knew they were meeting that night. And that she trusted him. They were going to put an end to all of this.

Her footsteps clacked on the stones as she passed the town square heading toward her new neighborhood. The cold pushed her forward, seeping through the back of her coat. Chills rippled up and down her legs.

At first she thought it was just the air that sent itching chills along her back, but soon she felt the presence of someone else on the street. She kept her gaze forward, head straight, but she could feel the presence growing closer, the person's eyes pressing into her back. Not again.

Her thoughts crashed together at once, alarm bells clamoring in her head. It could be Caldwell, out for her blood. She had helped ruin his career—maybe he'd followed her, wanting to get his revenge. But her obvious thought was that it was the Dollmaker. She'd escaped his clutches once, and now he was back. She wasn't engaged, so maybe she was safe—but she *was* the one behind the article coming out the next day. Tomorrow all the women in town would know the Dollmaker was targeting engaged women. She'd ruined his upper hand.

But a new feeling settled in the air—it was an intensity she only felt when she was around Sebastian. Sparks seemed to crackle between her and the entity, and she stopped in the middle of the cobblestone road, the dark buildings towering around her. Silence beat in the air, her heartbeat heavy in her chest.

"You might as well come out," she said. "I know it's you." Her voice echoed out into the night. "I was just coming to meet you."

Sebastian stepped onto the road, his hands in his pockets, head cocked to the side.

"It's not safe for you to walk alone," he said.

"You really do more harm stalking me and scaring me to death than actually protecting me."

He smiled and took a step forward. He kept his hands in his pockets, his gait smooth.

"I just wanted to make sure you were all right. You can't be too careful," he said dryly. "Especially when someone is out to get you." The dim light glowed on his face, highlighting the deep grooves and facets that angled his features.

She stared back at him, her lips parting. "Is that what you've been up to? You've been investigating without me? But *who*?"

"It's Gideon."

Her world screamed to a stop. "*What?*"

"I saw him sneak out from the manor not an hour ago. He had a crazed look in his eye, Dawn. And I saw him carrying a knife."

She shook her head. "It isn't Gideon. There's no way. The Dollmaker killed Sophie. Gideon wouldn't kill his own fiancée!"

"I'm not so sure," Sebastian continued, his head still cocked to the side. "I've been watching him. He's been disappearing at night. He's been on these drugs, perhaps he's half out of his mind and doesn't know what he's doing. He . . . he also loved my mother's doll collection. Maybe he has a sick fascination with it. I've had my suspicions for a while. It's why I didn't want to leave you alone with him."

This was too much. She shook her head again. "I won't believe this."

"Dawn." He edged closer again and gently wrapped a hand behind her head. He leaned down and put his forehead to hers, their lips inches apart. "I wouldn't accuse my brother if I didn't think he was a threat to you. I couldn't bear it if anything happened to you."

She held her breath, frozen at his proximity. Her heart was pounding through her entire body. Could Gideon really be the Dollmaker? Sebastian made some good points. Had she been investigating with the murderer all along?

Sebastian was close. Too close. She was married to him, but it felt so foreign to be this close to a man. Heat rushed to the surface of her skin, tiny fireworks exploding on her nerve endings. Suddenly all she could think about was kissing him. What would it feel like? Would he be gentle? Rough? Demanding? Kind? She couldn't move.

Rose.

She shoved thoughts of Sebastian out of her head.

"So, what do we do now?" she breathed.

He slowly backed away, lowering his hand from the back of her head. "I take you home. You wait it out. And I'll find my brother."

Objection rose in her throat, but she stuffed it down. There was no point in arguing with him. She'd lived in this world long enough to know that if she wanted something done, it couldn't involve a man.

Besides, Sebastian seemed to follow her everywhere. If he didn't want her searching for Gideon, then he wouldn't let her. She would have to find out the truth another way. Like she always did.

"Okay," she said, playing his game. "I'll let you take me home."

<hr />

Dawn quickly set to work. She lit the lamp in her room, scurrying around to gather her things, the night pitch black outside her window. A plan was still formulating in her mind, and she didn't quite know how she was going to pull it off—all she knew was that she wasn't going to sit around all night and let Sebastian stalk his brother. With Sebastian's volatility and Gideon's addled state, someone could get killed.

Gideon couldn't be the Dollmaker. She needed to find the real culprit and save Gideon from his brother. She would cut off her own hand if she had to.

A knock sounded on her door. She paused.

Mrs. Hampshire stepped in, her thin body ramrod straight, her mouth turned down. Why was she awake at this time of night? The old woman lifted her chin and stared Dawn down at the same time. A crinkled piece of paper was clutched in her hand.

"You received this," she said. She held out the letter, which Dawn eyed suspiciously. Mrs. Hampshire studied her carefully, as if deciding whether or not to trust her.

"What is it?" Dawn slowly moved forward and took the crumpled page from her hand. Her eyes scanned the contents.

My masterpiece is almost complete.
I have almost all my pieces, but I am missing one thing.
You.
Your hands represent perfection. The miracles you create, the lives you save, the talent that is in those fingertips.
You should be grateful that I've chosen you.
Sincerely,
Me.

Dawn's hands trembled as she gripped the page. She read the letter two more times, her eyes wide. "Where did you get this?"

"It arrived on the doorstep not five minutes ago."

She turned it over, searching for any clues. The paper was flawless, unmarked except for the neat scrawl on the front. Her legs shook and she forced herself over to the divan by the fire. She abruptly sat down, the letter fluttering to her feet.

"I want to help," Mrs. Hampshire said.

Dawn stared out in front of her. "There's nothing you can do."

"Isn't there?"

Dawn pinched the bridge of her nose, leaning back. "The Dollmaker clearly knows who I am. I just don't fit his modus operandi. I'm not engaged nor am I a perfect ballerina."

"Your wedding was spontaneous. It was done in secret. Perhaps he doesn't know."

"He seems to know everything. He's always a step ahead. And my . . ." She peered down at her hands before wrapping her arms around her stomach. "What if my fate is sealed?"

"Don't be ridiculous," Mrs. Hampshire snapped. "I haven't known you long, my dear, but I've seen enough to know that you don't give in to what seems impossible. I also know Sebastian would never link himself to someone who wasn't extraordinary."

She shook her head. "What if I'm fooling myself?" Her confidence was wavering. "This letter says I create miracles, and I claim to be a doctor, but I'm a nobody. The Dollmaker has us all beat. I'll never be able to stop him." Her voice had softened to a whisper.

"Dawn." Mrs. Hampshire moved across the room and set a hand on her shoulder. The touch was warm through her sleeve. "You're right that men rule this world, that we women are lucky if we get any satisfaction in life. But this Dollmaker won't overcome you. You know why I have hope? Because of what happened at the theater earlier today."

Dawn paused. "You heard about that?" But her voice trembled, still locked on the thoughts of the Dollmaker.

"Of course I did. We servants have our own form of communication. Word spreads fast. I know you were a part of that."

Dawn sighed, though it did nothing to relax her shoulders. "So what do I do?"

"You need to stop hiding who you are. You've skulked in the shadows long enough. Stop pretending to not be the lady you are. You think that if you dress well and have money, you're giving in to the image of what society expects you to be. You can be a lady *and* a doctor. You can be a wife *and* a doctor. You can be a mother *and* a doctor. And you can also stop this Dollmaker. Maybe only a woman can do that. The men in this town haven't gotten anywhere. We need your smarts, your intelligence, your spirit. Use the freedom you've been given and use it for the better."

Mrs. Hampshire's words cut off and her voice echoed through the room. The fire crackled, the flames reflected in the windowpane. Something new welled up inside Dawn, swelling in her throat, burning her eyes. She stared at Mrs. Hampshire through tears, her vision blurring. She was right. Dawn didn't need to be afraid of the Dollmaker. He hadn't been able to harm her yet—she could still evade him, find out who he was, stop him.

She eyed the dresses hanging in her wardrobe. "Thank you, Mrs. Hampshire. I know exactly what I need to do."

⚬⚬⚬ ⚬⚬⚬ ⚬⚬⚬

Dawn stayed awake all night, staring into the thick darkness of her room, her mind spinning. Mrs. Hampshire's words had sprung new life in her, thoughts and ideas sprouting in her head like little blades of grass.

When morning came, she slipped on a silk red dress Sebastian had given her. The material felt foreign on her body as it hung down at her sides, fine trimming on the edges. She passed by her mirror and paused. Her hands spread over the silk and lace, the stitching smooth and detailed underneath her fingertips. It shimmered in the morning light as it glided along her body.

It looked just like the dress the doll in Sebastian's lair had been wearing. She analyzed the detail further. He had made the doll for her.

Another wave of emotion swept through her. Sebastian really did care. Dawn flattened her hair up into a bun against her head, little curls framing her face, and applied a light amount of makeup. She was a lady *and* she was a doctor. She was also a woman who wasn't going to let the Dollmaker hurt her or anyone else. And if she were to meet her death that day, she wouldn't do it looking like a frumpy vampire. It was daring to wear the vibrant color out in town—the deep red reminded her of the Dollmaker's bloody victims—but she wanted to be seen. She *wanted* to show him that she wasn't afraid.

She pulled on a new pair of lace gloves that stopped at her wrists but stuck with her usual silk scarf—she wouldn't feel like herself without it.

Mrs. Hampshire gripped her hands as she stood in the doorway and squeezed them tight. "Good luck. I have full faith in you."

Dawn headed into the square, the sun shining overhead and providing a bit of warmth in the crisp air.

People turned their heads as she passed, before averting their gazes. Inside the ribbon shop, mothers were holding up trimmings to inspect the quality, but their eyes darted out the windows every few moments. A heaviness hung in the air, the streets quiet as people walked quickly past her.

Down the way, Nora hovered outside her shop with a basket of plants in hand. She was speaking with MacLarin, who lifted his head as Dawn approached. His wide shoulders towered over Nora's thin frame. He said a few more words to Nora before he bowed in Dawn's direction.

"Mrs. Hemsworth." He eyed her with suspicion. "How's your . . . doctoring? Help anyone new lately?" His voice darkened. "I couldn't help but notice the fine stitching you did as you helped Miss Williams the other day."

Visions of Angelica's arm came to Dawn's mind, how she'd stitched it up nicely. *Was there accusation in his voice?* She eyed him carefully, her lips pressed together.

"It's nice to see you too, Officer."

MacLarin crossed his beefy arms. "Be careful," he said. "It's dangerous for young ladies to be out." His eyes narrowed and he nodded to Nora. "We'll speak later." And he departed down the street.

Dawn's heart rate picked up. MacLarin thought she was guilty.

How long would it be before he arrested *her* for the murders?

She glanced at Nora. It wasn't the first time she'd seen MacLarin speaking with her.

Nora lifted a brow, appraising Dawn. "You've been avoiding me."

"I have," Dawn said honestly.

Nora's lips twisted upward. "I'm curious as to why."

Images from the night of the séance surged to her memory. The sweet smell that wafted in the air was still heady in her nose. Realization dawned and her eyes widened. She didn't know how she hadn't recognized it before now. Just as with Gideon. "You've been using drugs to make people see what you want them to see. It was opium I smelled it in the air that night!"

Nora let out a chuckle that resonated down the street. "Is that all? Yes, I use opium in the air. It *enlightens* my customers. That's hardly a crime, is it?"

"It's still a lie."

Nora's lips twitched. "You may think I'm completely without sight, but I'm not. I *did* tell you that you would find your true love. Is that not true, *Mrs. Hemsworth*?"

Dawn peered closer at Nora, her mouth tight. She didn't know *how* Nora could predict she was to marry Sebastian, and she didn't know how she felt about "true love," but she'd been right about her meeting him. Perhaps there was more to Nora than she thought.

She cleared her throat, letting it drop. "I know you're the one giving drugs to the prison," Dawn said. She glanced at where MacLarin had left. "I didn't put it together until just now."

Nora blinked, her expression faltering for a moment before she tucked her lips inward. "And why would you think that?"

"You stole from the clinic, and I'm sure you're getting your supplies from other places. You're clearly not afraid to use opiates for your own purposes. You watch me. You know my schedule. You know when I close up shop."

Humor lit Nora's eyes. "You're a smart one, aren't you? I'm not going to try and hide it, as I know there's nothing you can do about it. Do you think I make enough money selling my herbs? Customers are hard to come by these days, even with contacting the dead. I steal from you, and I sell to MacLarin. We have a deal, and he pays me well."

"You need to stop," Dawn said firmly. "You're putting men in harm's way. You're killing them."

Nora eyed her and slowly lowered her arms. "Why are you really here? I have a feeling it's not just to berate me about my life choices."

Dawn paused, swallowing hard and sighing. "I need you to help me," she whispered.

"So you're here to blackmail me into helping you, is that it?"

"Something like that." She twisted her mouth.

Nora released a long laugh, and passersby gave her odd looks. She finally calmed, wiping her eyes. "I like you, Dawn Hildegard Hemsworth. All right, I'll bite. What do you want from me?"

"I want you to use your supply of opiates one last time."

She squinted. "So you chastise me for using them, and now you want me to give them to you?"

"They were mine to begin with."

"True . . . but for what purpose could you use them?"

"We're taking him down," Dawn said. "I want you to burn them in the air like you did that night. Do your magic or whatever it is you do, so we can catch him off guard. Make him see things. Weaken him. Help me get the truth out of him."

"And by him, you mean . . ."

"The Dollmaker, yes."

Nora eyed her suspiciously for a moment before her face relaxed into a smile.

"I'm in."

24

Black Sheets of Rain

The letter wouldn't leave Dawn's mind. She sat in the clinic rehearsing the words over and over, not able to stop the dread that had taken root in her stomach. She faked bravery, thinking she could defeat the Dollmaker by using Nora to trick him and make him weak, but the truth was, he frightened her. And the more she thought of the words in the letter, the more terrified she became.

Her hands.

She peered down at her hands, analyzing the lines on her palms. She turned them over and studied the ring on her finger. The simple gold band shone dimly in the light of the setting sun. She couldn't live without her hands. They were what allowed her to do everything she could do. That is, if the Dollmaker didn't kill her first. He was breaking his usual behavior just to find her, and she knew he would stop at nothing until he got what he wanted. She closed her hands into fists and waited in silence.

She watched the light shift overhead until beams of the fading sun slanted through the window. She knew the Dollmaker had to be watching somewhere—she was sure he knew her every move—but she wouldn't back down now. She had a plan.

She was going to fulfill it.

The door jingled as Sebastian stepped inside the clinic. His crisp and put-together appearance seemed to fill the space. Instead of his usual coat he wore a clean white shirt with a dark vest, a handkerchief in his pocket. His black pants were tailored perfectly to his hips and legs. He stared her down, intensity in his gaze, until he finally spoke.

"I know what you're doing. And I won't allow it. You think Gideon is going to seek you out and find you."

She shook her head. "Not Gideon. The Dollmaker. The silhouette who has been attacking these women was larger. I know you think it's Gideon, and it's a good deduction, but my gut tells me you're wrong."

"All the facts are there, Dawn. You can't ignore them."

She stared up at him and rose from her chair. She began to pace around the small clinic, wringing her hands.

"Have you been able to find him?" she asked.

Sebastian sighed, running a hand over his face. "Not yet. I think he might be in an opium den. He's not on the streets and he hasn't returned to any of his homes. Or maybe he has another location where he tortures his victims?"

A shiver rocketed through Dawn, but she wouldn't believe it. She *knew* Gideon. He was her friend. He was suffering, yes, but she couldn't believe he would be committing these murders. He wouldn't have sent her that note.

"You continue looking for him," she said. "And we'll just wait and see what comes up."

Sebastian narrowed his eyes darkly, his mouth pressed tight. "You can't believe I'm that obtuse. I'm not letting you out tonight."

She blinked. "What do you mean?"

"I mean I'm taking you back to the Hemsworth manor, where you can't do anything stupid." He stalked toward Dawn, keeping his dark gaze connected with hers. "I know you're meeting Nora at the graveyard tonight. I confronted her and she told me everything. She said you were going to visit your brother's grave to draw him out. Really, Dawn? Did you ask Nora to spread rumors of your whereabouts, hoping to lure the Dollmaker to you? How idiotic *are* you?"

"I'm smart enough to finally do something once and for all," she bit back. "Something must be done! And I'm the one who needs to do it."

"I *forbid* it," he said. "And you're *not* going to object." He gripped her arm and started to lead her to the door. "And if I had a sane mind, I would *never* let you out again!"

Fury built up inside of her to a level she had never felt before. She yanked herself free of his hold. Her breathing sped up and she stared back at him, not willing to look away. "You *told* me that you would trust me. That you would give me my freedom. Are you really going to tell me what to do and where to go? Please don't force me to do something I don't want to do."

"I'm your husband. I'll do whatever it takes to keep you safe. That is the number-one priority."

He reached for her again but she backed away. "I thought you were different. I didn't think you were like the other men in this town."

He paused. A muscle jumped in his cheek. "Well, maybe I'm not different," he said. "Maybe I'm only here to disappoint you. Regardless, I'm not going to let you die tonight."

He gripped her once more, this time his hold tighter than a vice, and pulled her from the clinic.

"Sebastian, stop! Please!"

"Stop arguing!" he said. The crisp air attacked her face. "You don't get it, do you? You're mine! *Mine*. And you *have* to obey me!" He whirled on her, chest heaving.

Dawn blinked back at him, tears in her eyes, heart hammering.

She couldn't believe it. He had turned into the one thing she'd been most afraid of.

"I hate you," she whispered.

His expression faltered before hardening once more. "Fine, then hate me."

His car waited on the road in front of them and he forced her inside. He hopped into the driver's seat and took off down the street. They sat next to each other in silence, his gaze burning a hole through the dim light in front of him. She couldn't look at him. She stared out the window, more anger and hate building up inside of her the farther they traveled. They didn't speak over the heavy rumble of the engine. All she could hear was her pulse thumping in her ears.

When they reached the Hemsworth manor, she hopped out without letting Sebastian touch her and marched up the front steps. She let herself inside, brushing past the butler into the marble foyer. She stormed upstairs and locked herself in a room.

Tears burned in her eyes as the seconds ticked by. She wasn't sure if Sebastian had left or if he was still at the manor, but it didn't matter. She wasn't going to try and reason with him anymore. If this was the husband he was going to be, then their life together was going to be an unhappy one. He had started to make his way into her heart—she'd let him in—and now she didn't think she could ever trust him again. He'd said he'd give her freedom. She thought he'd be different.

And now she was trapped in a marriage—living her worst nightmare. What was next? He'd take away her dream of a clinic? Were his promises all just a ruse to get her to marry him? And what about Rose? She had failed her.

If she allowed herself to be dominated by this man, she would never save her friend.

No.

Dawn wouldn't let herself be subject to his rule. She'd rather lose her hands than let a man rule her. She needed to escape. She needed to follow through with her plan. She didn't care what Sebastian thought. She suddenly wished she had a mother to comfort her. One who treated her like a mother should. Like how Mrs. Cook did. Her biological mother hadn't even checked in on her since she'd been married. And did her father even care? All they cared about was money, and if she could provide it for them.

She waited until her emotions calmed and the tears had dried from her eyes before she started to plot her escape. She realized Sebastian couldn't keep her from what she wanted to do. He'd only *delayed* her. He didn't have power over her—not anymore, anyway—and *nothing* was going to stop her from finding the Dollmaker.

Hearing a few sounds clanking from the kitchen below, she glanced at the bedroom door. The servants were still moving about, but she should be able to escape without them noticing. They might not even know she was there, unless Sebastian had told them to keep an eye on her.

She still wore her red silk dress, which only reminded her of the doll in the lair. Her coat was draped over her arm, ready to be put on when she slipped outside. She cracked the door open and stepped out into the hallway. It stretched long and dark, a few oil lamps burning on the side tables. Paintings hung on the walls: large portraits of men who stared Dawn down as she passed by. Their eyes seemed to follow her, judging her for sneaking out. A proper lady would stay in her place, not skulk down the hallways at night.

She crept quietly, the floor squeaking in a few places, but the servants downstairs didn't seem to notice—sounds of their work continued to drift up to the second floor.

When Dawn turned the last corner to go down the stairs, she cringed at what she saw. Arthur Hemsworth stood blocking the way. His veiny hands gripped the gold knob at the top of his cane, his black suit tight against his body. He licked his lips at the sight of her, smiling.

"Good evening, my dear." His voice was scratchy, like he hadn't used it since the last time he'd seen her. "I heard about your arrival, and thought I'd give the new bride her congratulations. How is your new husband treating you?"

Dawn stayed at the top of the stairs, her feet glued to the soft carpet. Brocade wallpaper surrounded her and she felt the urge to rip it down.

"I really need to go. If you'll excuse me." She headed down the stairs, intending to march past him, but he planted himself firmly in front of her.

"I'm sorry, but I can't let you leave just yet." His gaze flicked to her neckline and back to her face.

"Please. I'm leaving."

She started to brush past him but his old hand reached up and snatched her around the waist. He pushed her to the side until her back hit the wall. She struggled to push him off her, but he was surprisingly strong for an old man.

He kept her pinned.

"Stop it!" she ground out, squirming underneath him.

He licked his lips again and leaned in so his face was only inches from hers. His foul breath wafted into her face. "You were mine, and I still claim you as mine. My nephew has no hold on you, and now he's abandoned you for my taking."

Dawn, still pressed against the wall, stared at him with wide eyes. A frightening thought zinged through her brain: She wondered if Arthur Hemsworth could be the Dollmaker. Was he here to end this once and for all?

His hand slid up her rib cage, stopping just underneath her chest. He grinned wickedly and started to inch his hand up further.

"Stop!" Dawn yelled. She stomped onto the top of his foot, hard enough to do some serious damage.

He screamed and stumbled back, catching himself with his cane. She'd made a promise to do no harm, but in this moment she was willing to break that vow.

"You witch!" he yelled. "You deserve to live a life of misery with that nephew of mine. Not right in the head, he is. He grew up obsessed with his mother's doll collection. Always closed off, hiding in the shadows. He was a strange young boy who grew up to be a crazed man. I hope he finishes you off like he did the rest of them. You don't deserve to live!"

Every part of her froze. She could hardly breathe. "You're saying Sebastian is the Dollmaker?"

"I know he is! Why do you think he's so set on blaming it on his brother? Why do you think he rarely shows his face? He's hiding from the world. Hiding his secret."

Arthur's words echoed through her whole being. She couldn't believe it. Or could she? She had suspected him for quite a while. But he'd shown her a kindness and vulnerability that couldn't be the qualities of a murderer. No, Arthur had to be lying. Sebastian didn't want to control her, he wanted to protect her. Even though she was still angry with Sebastian, she would defend him.

She narrowed her gaze. "Sebastian has more humanity and kindness than you will ever have. He's shown me respect while you take what you want, *whenever* you want it. It's why no one could ever love you!"

Arthur's face twisted in fury, and he sprang at her once more. She reacted on instinct. Her hands reached out and connected with his chest, shoving him backward. He stumbled, his cane slipping, and he tipped over the stairwell. His thin body bent in half as he tumbled downward, limp like a dead fish. His head hit the floor hard, and he lay still.

Dawn stared, wide-eyed, heart racing. She screamed.

What had she done?

Footsteps echoed down the hallway—people were coming. She bolted down the stairs and dropped next to Arthur, feeling his bony body. His mouth was open and slack, his eyes staring blankly up to the ceiling. His chest was frozen, unmoving. Blood spilled out from behind his head onto the white marble. She hovered over him, unable to move as she stared at his lifeless body.

Servants rushed out from the kitchen and the butler emerged from the parlor. They each paused, staring down at their master. Hands flew to mouths and a few cries escaped. Heads snapped to her. She scrambled to her feet.

"I'm so sorry," Dawn said. "It's too late. I'm so sorry."

She rushed to the door, disappearing outside before she could say another word.

Her feet pounded on the cobblestone roads, swallowing up the ground beneath her. She wove in and out of the streets, the lamp-posts' light blurring in the corners of her vision. Rain started to fall, pricking cold on her skin. She'd dropped her coat back at the manor and the water quickly soaked through her dress. Her feet splashed in puddles with fervor, racing along the ground as quickly as possible. She tried to shove Arthur from her mind. She had to focus on her plan with Nora. She'd been delayed long enough, and nothing could stop her from following through.

Her argument with Sebastian resonated over and over again in her mind. She couldn't believe the person he'd become. She could still feel his grip around her arm, still see the anger in his face. She continued to run, blinking through the raindrops that fell in her eyes. But she'd defended him. She knew deep down that he was a good person. She'd felt it. She'd seen it.

Nora was ready and waiting for her. The trap was set. She was going to face the Dollmaker within the hour, and this would be over one way or the other.

The buildings around her became scarce and eventually disappeared completely. The graveyard sat just outside of town, tucked beneath large trees, tombstones sticking up from the grass. A light fog churned in the air, swirling around her head and curling along the ground. Nora had chosen a different location for the fire. Dawn could see it was near her brother's grave.

She slowly approached, thinking that if her brother were alive everything would be different. Would she still be a healer? Or would she be married to someone else? She'd probably just be a wife right now, maybe even with a child. Would she be locked in a loveless marriage like she was with Sebastian? Maybe that had been her fate all along.

Her brother's grave came into view, just a few feet from the fire. Smoke hung in the air and her feet crunched on the frozen grass as she approached the tombstone. She paused in front of it, moonlight trickling down. She knelt on the ground and her heart slowed as she stared at the tombstone.

JOSEPH ELIJAH HILDEGARD

1906–1913

Only seven years old. She ran her hands along the stone, her fingertips trembling. Even if her life were to be different, at least he'd have had the chance to live. So many people were robbed of their lives way too young. Fevers. Plagues. Accidents. You never knew what would happen. Mankind was fragile, and people needed to live the best lives they could while they had time. She knelt in silence for a few moments until the fire drew her attention. She rose from the ground, brushing the bits of frost off her dress, and approached the warmth.

The fire roared in the black night, its flames licking up toward the sky. She didn't smell any opium in the air, so Nora must not have started the plan yet. A shiver zipped through Dawn as she approached, wondering if the Dollmaker was here. Was he watching her in the shadows? She crept forward further, her jaw chattering.

She just needed to get him close enough to the fire to incapacitate him. If there was enough opium in the air, his defenses would diminish and they'd be able to apprehend him. She peeked into the darkness around the fire where Nora said she'd be waiting, but she wasn't there.

Her footsteps were soft in the quiet, the fire immediately warming her face. A chill rocketed down her and she circled the fire, squinting. *Where was she?*

"Hello?" she called out. "Nora? Are you here?"

The fire continued to crackle and burn, the soft sound the only noise in the dark night around her. She knit her brow as she continued to search. Smoke stung her eyes.

"Nora?" She tried one more time.

She stepped around the fire once again and paused.

Everything screeched to a halt.

Nora lay on the cold ground, blood pooled on the grassy earth. A knife was stuck in her chest, piercing right into her heart. Her eyes were wide open and blank, her lips slightly parted. A letter was stuffed into her lifeless hand, the light from the fire playing off its crisp white surface. Dawn stood paralyzed, unable to believe her eyes.

Nora was dead.

Dawn couldn't comprehend what she was witnessing. Her healer instincts were paralyzed for a moment before reality flooded in and she quickly knelt by Nora's side. Dawn knew she was dead but still checked for a pulse. Nora's flesh was cold and unmoving.

Dawn's eyes shot to the note and she leaned over to retrieve it. She couldn't open it fast enough.

Funny, how you think you can trick me.
You will die on my terms.
Meet me at the theater.
Your death will await you there.

Dawn slowly lowered the note, her whole body beginning to shake.

She peered out into the dark that circled the fire before turning her gaze to the knife in Nora's chest. She zoned in on the silver blade. Gideon had left the house with a knife.

Dawn pushed to her feet, still gripping the letter. She would face the Dollmaker tonight. Even though this plan had failed, even though Nora was dead, nothing had changed.

He wouldn't live to see tomorrow.

25
Nighttime Madness

The rain had stopped, but Dawn was still soaked to the bone. The wind bit her cheeks as she ran, the cold sticking to her skin. She entered the city again and wove in and out of the buildings, trying to get to the theater before anyone stopped her. Knowing Sebastian, he'd find her and march her back to the Hemsworth manor. He could be stalking her right now.

As she sprinted through the city, all the people she'd been involved with the last couple of weeks came to the forefront of her mind. She thought of Angelica and how the Dollmaker had attacked her. Did he still need her? Or had he replaced her arms with someone else's? She thought about Dr. Miller and what he had suffered. Would the doctor ever be all right again?

And what about Rose?

She thought of Chester. If she ever found Rose, Dawn would plead with her to forget about him. Even if he said he had changed, she didn't want Rose to trust him. She wouldn't believe a man like him could ever change.

And Nora . . .

She couldn't think about that now.

Sebastian and Gideon pushed all her other thoughts away, but she forced herself not to think about them too. They had both betrayed her—Sebastian with his controlling nature, and Gideon with his lies about who he really was. But she couldn't hate them. A small part of her still believed they were both innocent.

Dawn rushed into the theater's courtyard, her chest pumping up and down. The smell of rain still hung in the air, thick and heavy. The moon was swallowed up in clouds, making the courtyard extra dark, only small bits of light cutting through the fog that had crawled onto the ground.

She moved toward the towering theater, shivers rippling down her body. She wrapped her arms around her soaked dress, peeking up through the strands of her hair that were plastered to her face. She didn't know if Sebastian would be inside—or if Gideon would be inside—but something about being here in this moment called to her like an invisible siren.

She cut across the grass, weaving through the mucky leaves, until she reached the steps of the theater.

A pointe shoe lay before her on the ground, bits of red staining the ribbons, a pool of blood soaking the middle of the shoe.

Dawn halted, staring down at the morbid sight. The rain had clearly soaked the shoe, diluting the blood. She peeked up at the theater's doors. One was slightly open, revealing the darkness within. She peered down at the shoe again and shook her head, trying to clear it. She was an aspiring doctor.

She wasn't afraid. She would do this for Rose. For Angelica. For all the other young women out there. And for herself.

She slowly crept up the steps, moving past the shoe and into the theater.

Inside, silence echoed around her. The foyer was deadly quiet, with a few lamps burning softly down the side hallway.

Someone was in here.

Dawn moved quietly through the foyer and stepped into the hallway, the lamplight glowing on the gold-trimmed walls. Her footsteps were soft on the red velvet carpet as she crept forward, her wide eyes searching for any sign of movement.

At the end of the hallway, she paused. A soft cry sounded from inside the theater, sobs echoing. The voice cut straight to Dawn's core.

She couldn't believe it.

She thought she'd never hear that voice again.

"Rose!" Dawn cried.

Relief exploded through her chest and tears gathered in her eyes. Her heart took off as fast as her feet and she pushed herself through the curtain that led into the theater. She wove her way through the audience seating, peering in the dark. Then on the stage, where a single spotlight fell, she saw her.

Rose sat in the middle of the stage on a single wooden chair. The spotlight cascaded down onto her, making her look like a ghost. Her pale features were washed out, her lips dry, her eyes swollen. Dawn rushed down the aisle, sprinting for the stage.

"I can't believe you're alive!" She raced up onto the stage. Her heart was leaping in her chest, excitement coursing through her. Dawn looked Rose over. She wasn't tied down. She was just sitting there, body shaking, eyes wide. "What's going on?"

Rose continued to sob, not meeting Dawn's gaze. Instead, she stared out at the theater, terror in her eyes. Dawn's brows pushed together and she slowly turned.

Hanging from the chandelier was a body, swinging slightly back and forth, hooks underneath its arms held up by wires. The body comprised a series of different limbs stitched together. It was wearing a tutu with a bodice cut down to the navel. She could see the stitches along the torso that connected the two different halves together. Different arms were sewn into the chest and shoulders, and legs were sewn into the hips and other joints, including feet. One foot wore a pointe shoe; the other foot was bare, blood dripping down from the ankle. The body was complete, save for a head and two hands. Dawn stared in horror at the "masterpiece"—it was clearly a work of art, sick and twisted as it was.

"It's almost complete," said a voice to the left.

Dawn spun around, her body stiffening.

A shadow emerged from the wings, stalking forward, footsteps soft. The spotlight burned Dawn's eyes and it was hard to see. She squinted through the light as the silhouette walked closer, slow, calculated.

That silhouette. It was the same silhouette she'd seen in the courtyard that night.

"I knew you'd come."

The voice seemed familiar, but recognition hadn't hit yet.

The shadow continued forward until Mrs. Cook came into view. Dawn blinked, unable to believe what she was witnessing.

Mrs. Cook wore a loose white blouse, a brown skirt, and an apron. A bonnet sat on her head, a few gray curls escaping. The dim light highlighted her pudgy face, her round figure a silhouette against the wings. Mrs. Cook moved further into the light and placed a hand on Rose's shoulder.

"She's a good girl, waiting her turn," Mrs. Cook said. "She knows she's next." She slowly circled Rose, dragging a finger along her face and down the back of her neck. "I haven't seen a face this pretty since my Sophie. She will make the perfect finish to my masterpiece. Along with your hands." Her eyes caught Dawn's, but Dawn couldn't move.

She stayed paralyzed, watching Mrs. Cook.

Her mind couldn't catch up. She expected Caldwell or MacLarin, Gideon, or even Sebastian to emerge onto the stage; she could hardly believe what she was seeing.

"What are you . . . Mrs. Cook, *what* are you doing?" She hadn't seen her since she'd married Sebastian. "You can't possibly be . . ." She broke off. She couldn't say it.

"The Dollmaker?" She let out a laugh. "Of course I am, dear. Do you know anyone else with such masterful stitching skills? The scarf I made for you is the favorite thing you own, is it not?"

Dawn fingered the scarf around her neck, and she swallowed.

"Do you think my skills would be wasted on such material things?" Mrs. Cook laughed. "I was a nurse during the war. I was a healer, like you. You have no idea how many men I stitched back together. Limbs blown apart, arms and legs amputated." Her eyes glazed over in memory. "I'll never forget the images."

"I don't . . . I don't understand." Dawn could hardly speak, her voice stuck in her throat.

Mrs. Cook glanced at Rose before addressing Dawn. "You really are blind, aren't you, child? Didn't you notice the murders started at the same time I came to work for your family? Even the failed attempts? Do you think that tree branch fell on its own that day? Poor Frederick wasn't the target, his new wife was. The limb was meant for her. I wanted her arms. Such beautiful arms."

Dawn's thoughts still couldn't catch up. She couldn't believe what she was hearing.

"Why?" she choked out.

"Back in New York, I was Sophia's nanny. She grew up with me. I raised her. And Gideon didn't even recognize me. Shows how much attention he paid to *servants*. No one loved Sophie more than I did," she said. "She was like a daughter to me. Her parents only cared about marrying her off to Gideon, but I cared about her dance career. I wanted her to be happy. I was the one who was devastated and abandoned when she died, not them." She paused, hurt washing over her face. The stage lights highlighted the rash that spread across her nose. "I found her, you know. Dead in the street. She was murdered by a bitter suitor who had wanted her hand in marriage before she was promised to Gideon. But her murderer didn't go far. I caught up to him and I punished him. I cut out his tongue so he couldn't scream for help. I watched the fear in his eyes right before I stabbed him in the heart. That's when I hated all of her suitors. I hated him for killing her. I hated Gideon for wanting to take her away from her true love. Getting married was her demise, and without that engagement, she would still be alive today. So that's when I knew."

"You knew what?" Dawn could hardly recognize her own voice it shook so much.

"That I could save all women from being married off like Sophie. That I could punish men and stop them from having the women they wanted." She gripped the sides of her face, and her nails dug into her skin. "I couldn't heal all those men in the war. So many of them died. The images..." Her eyes glazed over. "The body parts..." She lowered her hands. "But then, I was glad those men were hurt. Because men are why Sophie was murdered.

"Sophie was perfect. No one had her face, her hair, her perfect body, down to her fingertips. She needed to live on. She couldn't be gone from this world completely. I needed to re-create her so she could be remembered. And I decided to do that while saving other girls like her from the fate she almost had to endure. It was better to die than to be tied to a man."

"Young girls who were engaged," Dawn said.

She nodded. "I killed young women about to be married to save them from evil—to save them from marriage. I knew I was also hurting the men who loved them. They deserved to be punished."

Dawn couldn't wrap her mind around this. "You aren't paying homage to Sophie! This..." She waved her hand up to the mutilated body hanging from the chandelier. "That isn't conserving her memory. That is just plain murder!"

"No." Mrs. Cook looked wistfully up at her creation. "This one will be the most perfect of all. With Rose's face and your hands, it'll give tribute to my Sophie. She would be proud."

Dawn's stomach lurched. She took a step back, trying to keep her eyes off the rotting body swinging in her peripheral vision. "Sophie wouldn't want this. She would be disgusted."

Mrs. Cook's wistful look faded as she took Dawn in. "You know *nothing* of what Sophie and I had. She looked at me like a mother, and I loved her as my daughter."

"So you cut off her *hand*?"

"As a symbol to Gideon that he couldn't have her. No one could. The world has received my message." She smiled with pride in her eyes.

"I won't let you hurt Rose. I won't let you hurt anyone else."

Rose continued to sob, watching the exchange, tears falling down her puffy cheeks.

"Stop crying!" Mrs. Cook snapped. "You're ruining your beautiful features. I can't have my Sophie looking like a puffball!" She took a shuddering breath before she said, "We'll start with you first." She smiled at Dawn and pulled out a long blade from a pocket in her apron, slowly moving forward. Light sparkled in her eyes as she passed through the stage's spotlight. Dawn edged back.

"You don't want to do this." Dawn held up her hands. "We can get you help. We can fix this."

Mrs. Cook continued to inch forward, the spotlight glinting on the sharp blade in her hand. Dawn's heart was pounding against her ribs. She tucked her hands behind her, hiding them.

"I won't let you do this," Dawn said, but her voice trembled.

"You don't have a choice." Mrs. Cook leaped forward and Dawn jumped out of the way. Her blade sliced down through the air and Dawn bolted toward Rose. Mrs. Cook hobbled after her, surprisingly fast for her size.

She leaped forward again, slicing down with the blade once more, and Dawn pulled Rose out of the chair.

"Run!" she yelled at Rose, shoving her forward. Rose stumbled but couldn't move. She stayed paralyzed on the stage, continuing to sob.

Mrs. Cook jabbed the knife forward again, slicing Dawn's arm. Dawn hissed, flinching, her mind going blank for a moment. Mrs. Cook used the opportunity to dart in and grip Dawn around the throat. Her large hands squeezed tight and Dawn froze, unable to move, unable to breathe.

Mrs. Cook stuck her face close to Dawn's and said, "I can't wait to watch the light fade from your eyes."

Dawn struggled, her mouth opening and closing, her throat sealed off like cotton had been stuffed down inside it. Black spots sparkled in the corners of her vision. Her entire body went numb as the pressure around her throat intensified. Her eyes bulged and she struggled desperately to find air, but no relief came. Mrs. Cook chuckled, the sound echoing distantly in Dawn's ears. Darkness closed in before Mrs. Cook yelled out, and there was a large thud as something banged on the floor. Dawn crumpled, her breath finally unobstructed. Dawn's eyes opened to Rose on top of Mrs. Cook, pinning her to the stage floor. Rose had snatched the knife and was holding it up to Mrs. Cook's throat. Dawn coughed, blood rushing back into her head, her vision slowly clearing. She wobbled back to a standing position, setting a hand on her forehead.

"Keep her there, Rose." Dawn coughed again.

Rose's hand shook, but she kept the knife to her throat. "I ought to kill you right here and now." Fire had ignited in Rose's eyes, her full lips pressed into a thin line. "Shall I cut off your head like you planned to do to *me*?"

Footsteps pounded from the wings and Gideon and Sebastian emerged onto the stage. They stood, long and dark, looking so similar with their carved faces, hollow in the dim stage light. The two brothers' gazes shot from Dawn, to Rose, to Mrs. Cook.

"Looks like you didn't need us," Gideon said.

Dawn glanced from one brother to the other. Sebastian had found Gideon. They stood side by side, looking so much like brothers. A softness hung between them, like they'd resolved some of their issues.

They bolted forward at the same time. Gideon yanked Mrs. Cook up, holding her tight to his side. Mrs. Cook struggled but Gideon kept her pinned.

"You're not going anywhere," Gideon said. "Nor are you going to hurt anyone ever again."

Rose's hands trembled and she dropped the knife, but her face spread into a wide grin.

Sebastian rushed forward and took Dawn's face in his hands. "I was so worried about you. I couldn't handle it. After I found Gideon, we rushed back to the manor to find you gone. We found our uncle. The servants told us what happened. It's all right—I hope you don't feel guilt. Everything is all right."

Dawn stared back at him, her heart heavy in her throat. She couldn't speak.

Sebastian continued. "I thought . . . I thought . . . I'm so relieved you're alive. Dawn, I'm so sorry. I don't know what came over me. I was such an idiot. I only wanted to protect you. I promise I will *never* act in such a manner again. Will you forgive me?"

Dawn searched his eyes, seeing the passion and sincerity behind them. His hands were tight on her face, and the feeling that usually settled around them softened her shoulders. She had been wrong about Sebastian. She'd thought he was trying to control her, but he'd only been protecting her. Did that mean he truly cared? It felt foreign that anyone should care about her that much. She'd grown up without parents loving her. She was only a paycheck to them; they couldn't wait to get rid of her, ever since her brother's death.

But Sebastian, he didn't make her feel smothered. He made her feel alive. He made her feel as if she could do anything. Even for the short time that she'd known him, he'd given her a peace and renewed energy she didn't know she needed.

Sebastian really cared.

"I'm sorry too," she said. "I should've had more faith in you."

Gideon was pulling Mrs. Cook off stage. "You're going straight to prison," he said. "Where I hope you rot for eternity."

A laugh escaped Sebastian's chest and he pulled Dawn in tight, holding her. His arms stayed wrapped around her for a long time. She breathed in his lavender scent, the pleasing smell relaxing her further.

"Let's take you home," Sebastian said. His voice rumbled through her whole being, and he looked at Rose. "Let's take you both home."

26
Death Proof

Gideon had taken Mrs. Cook to MacLarin, where she was admitted into prison. He hadn't at first believed that Mrs. Cook was the culprit, but with Rose's testimony, she would either spend the rest of her days behind bars or in a mental institution. The thought sent a wave of relief through Dawn, but it also left her unsettled. She didn't want Mrs. Cook harmed—she had been a healer, after all. Mrs. Cook was a woman stricken with grief, a woman mad from the effects of the war and unable to accept the loss of Sophia. But the thought of all those girls dying . . . it was too much. She'd made multiple "creations" in the last couple years, too many deaths to count. She needed to be off the streets. She needed to be punished.

Sebastian had escorted Rose home, where her great-uncle had nearly fallen over in relief. If Rose's parents had been alive, they would've been beside themselves. After getting Rose settled, Dawn and Sebastian drove back to their home, but she needed time to clear her head.

Things hadn't ended well the last time they'd spoken, and she wasn't sure how to respond. Even though everything was over, she was still married to him. She still had to have a life with him. She was still linked to him, and he could do whatever he wanted with her. How did he really feel?

He'd never been physically close to her—they hadn't even kissed—and she realized she wanted that. She *wanted* him to want her. The feeling was foreign, and she tried to tell herself that just because she wanted a relationship with Sebastian, it didn't have to take away her desire to be a doctor. Being married to him didn't steal her identity.

But she couldn't live in a loveless marriage, could she? She hadn't grown up seeing her parents love each other. Did marriages exist where two people actually cared for each other? Every time she was close to Sebastian, there was a feeling between them that seemed to lift her from the earth—seal them in some sort of bubble. Was that love? Or was love a choice? She could choose to love Sebastian, right?

Sebastian had brought her home without a word, but she couldn't stay there. Not now. She needed to walk. She needed air.

She wandered down the street, not looking back, early-morning light falling over the city. A light fog snaked on the ground, dancing along the undisturbed cobblestone roads. Dawn didn't know where to go, but she walked with a new feeling of security.

Mrs. Cook was off the streets; there was no more harm lurking in the shadows. The papers would soon scream about the killer being found, and young ladies would feel safe to go out and about— and also to marry. Soon something else would be the talk of the town—perhaps it would be that a new female doctor had opened her own practice. The thought sent a rush of anticipation through Dawn. Could she do it?

Then her thoughts turned to Rose.

Dawn had spent the last two weeks searching for her, praying that she was still alive, and she'd found her. Rose was a fighter. She didn't know what she'd had to face with Mrs. Cook, but she had come out on top. Now, Dawn only prayed Rose would have enough strength to walk away from Chester. She deserved to live her dream as much as Dawn did.

Then there was Arthur. Dawn still had to deal with the guilt of having killed an old man. She hadn't meant to—the whole thing had happened so fast. But the fact hadn't changed. She had *killed* a man. Sebastian's uncle.

Was Sebastian upset? He didn't seem to be. But would it cause another rift between them?

There was also Gideon. Now that everything was over, he needed to find a way to deal with his anguish—his addiction would only lead him to his death. Same with Dawn's father and his drinking. Were all men subject to such addiction?

At least Gideon had Sebastian in his life now. The previous night at the theater, they had stood side by side as if in unity. Gideon had to know, deep down, that Sebastian hadn't betrayed him. Perhaps the brothers' bond could be healed after all. Just as Dawn's relationship with her parents could possibly be healed? She shook her head.

No, that would never happen.

Dawn turned down another street, her thoughts still jumping from one thing to the next. A deep sadness hovered around her the further she walked. She needed to face Sebastian. She wanted to see him. But would he come for her? Follow her? Tears burned behind her eyelids. If she wanted to see him, she should just go to him. She didn't need to wait for a man to chase her down, but she was paralyzed.

Then an eerie feeling settled in the air. She stopped in the middle of the street and spun around. A chill rippled through her as she peered into the foggy air before her. Lamplight sliced through the white fog, and she stood with her feet planted firmly on the ground. She could feel him watching her. Like he always was.

"You look lovely this morning." His voice cut down the street. Another series of chills rocketed through her. She should've known he'd find her. "Even after the night you had."

She slowly took a step forward, squinting. The fog parted and his silhouette came into view. Sebastian leaned against a lamppost, the light above him carving out his features. Fog swirled around his ankles; his arms were crossed.

Dawn placed a hand to her chest. "Sebastian."

"I like the sound of my name off your tongue." His voice had a tease to it, but it also sounded inviting. Her heart began to speed. He cared.

Sebastian pushed off the lamppost and glided toward her. Dark shadows curved over his indented cheeks and deep set eyes. A small smile played on his lips as he stopped in front of her. "I'm so relieved that you're all right."

Dawn stood breathless, staring up at him. More fog snaked around his head. "I'm so glad that Rose is safe," she said.

He nodded, silence settling between them for a moment.

Her heart still wouldn't slow. She didn't know why she had tried to hide from him. There was a comfort in the air that always surrounded him.

"We need to speak about what comes next," Sebastian said. "Do you still feel the way you did when we last spoke? Do you really feel as if I want to control you?"

She searched his face, the worry in his gaze, the way his hair was stark against his pale skin. How could she have ever thought that? With the feeling that wrapped around them, she knew all he cared about was her happiness.

"No," she whispered. "I think I'm beginning to see who you really are."

His brows rose. "And who is that?"

"You're incredible," she whispered.

Something changed in his face. His guard dropped and he looked so vulnerable, her heart cracked. Warmth lit his eyes, and his smile lifted his lips once more. He took her hand and slowly bowed before her, one foot forward, his head dipping downward.

"If you would do me the honor, *Mrs.* Hemsworth, I would like to invite you to a party."

"A party?" Her heart fluttered in her chest. "Whatever for?"

"Our wedding celebration," he said. "We never had one. And I think it's a great thing to celebrate indeed. We'll have it at the manor. Now that my uncle—"

"Stop." She held up her gloved hand. "You'll never be able to forgive me. I'm so sorry. I promise you that—"

Softness glowed in his gaze as he lowered her hand. "It's all right, Dawn. He was a wicked man. We've all been released from his presence. Now there can be lightness in the home once more. That is, if it's where you choose to stay." He gave her a shy look.

Live in the Hemsworth manor?

No.

Not where Arthur had resided. Not when his ghost would haunt the halls. It was such a large home, and away from town, and she needed to be close to her patients. But she knew how much it meant to Sebastian. He'd said he wanted to live in his childhood home. But could she? It was too gaudy. Too big. It wasn't who she was at all. But . . .

"I'll . . . I'll think about it," Dawn said, even though she already knew.

He gave a firm nod. "Good. We have a celebration to plan."

<hr>

Dawn enjoyed working with Mrs. Hampshire. They had remained in the home, planning the party. She helped with the guest list, the menu, the table settings, the decorations. The staff needed to be ready to serve a couple hundred people, as Dawn wanted to invite more than just the elite to her party. She wouldn't have the celebration for only those who had money.

She wanted Dr. Miller's patients to be there—they were more like family than Sebastian's third cousin who lived in a huge estate out of town.

Mrs. Hampshire arranged for Dawn to have a new dress made, and for the first time ever, she was delighted to be measured and fitted for her own personal wardrobe.

The dress was a deep purple silk, with sequins that cascaded from top to bottom. It hung loosely down her frame, stopping right below the knees. A matching headband would adorn her head with the same sequins as the new pair of earrings Sebastian had given her earlier that day. She didn't normally care for such things, but it was nice to feel like a lady.

It didn't take away from who she really was.

She didn't see Sebastian very much for the next few days because he said he was attending to special business, and he trusted Dawn and Mrs. Hampshire completely when it came to planning the party. But whenever she saw him in passing, he would give her small reassurances, like a squeeze of her hand or a full smile.

In the late afternoon, Dawn sat in the parlor, sipping her Earl Grey. Her feet ached and a headache began to creep up to the top of her head. She needed lavender—that would help. She closed her eyes, enjoying the silence, when Graham announced the arrival of a "Mr. Hemsworth."

Her eyes shot open and she immediately thought of Sebastian, but Gideon stepped into the room. He wore a gray pin-striped suit with a red handkerchief in his pocket, his black shoes shiny.

Dawn rose from her chair, a hand on her heart. "Gideon."

He'd been gone all week. She hadn't seen him since that night.

Gideon held a bouquet of flowers, a wry smile on his face.

"For you," he said. "I wanted to thank you."

Dawn traveled across the room and took the flowers from him, inhaling their fresh scent. She waited to see if the scent would mingle with the sweet smell that usually emanated off him, but there wasn't a hint of opium. She peered up at him through the flowers. He had more color than the last time she had seen him, his cheeks not as hollow.

"How are you feeling? Where have you been?"

He ducked his head, running a hand over his sleek hair. "With Dr. Miller. He's been helping me. We've been getting through our addiction together. I've been free from it all week. Every day I feel stronger."

She took him in deeper. There did seem to be a lightness about him—the usual tension that thrummed through him was gone.

"Does Sebastian know?"

He nodded. "Sebastian has been a great comfort to me. When he found me that night, I realized how much I'd been lacking in my life. I had lost Sophie, but I hadn't lost him. I should've turned to him. And Sebastian was right. I knew deep down that he hadn't betrayed me with Sophie. She'd had other suitors—I should've seen what I didn't want to admit. She was a tease. A flirt. I probably didn't mean anything to her at all. It was easier to blame Sebastian than to see the truth." Silence stretched for a moment before he motioned with his hand toward her chair. "But enough about me. Sit." Half of his mouth curved upward.

Dawn placed the flowers on the nearest side table and sat back down in her chair. It was hard to picture the two brothers as soft toward each other.

Was all this hardship necessary for them to heal? Maybe that's what it took to overcome this huge trial. They needed to walk through darkness to find the light.

Gideon lowered himself into a seat across from her, elbows on his knees, wringing his hands together. "You saved my life," he said quietly. "Not only with the drugs but with . . . but with Sophie too. You were there for me, you helped me, and you never stopped caring."

Dawn started to open her mouth, but Gideon stopped her.

"Like I said, I haven't had a drop of opium since that night—for over a week. My head is clear for the first time in ages. I feel all right with Sophie's loss. I have hope for a new future."

Dawn placed her hands on her cheeks. She peered at him through tears that built in the corners of her eyes. "I'm so glad."

Gideon let out a deep breath, and his face relaxed into a genuine smile. Dawn lowered her hands.

"I want to court Rose," he said abruptly. "When she heals. When she's had enough time to process everything that's happened. Are you all right with that?"

"Rose?" Dawn's mouth fell open. "But isn't she engaged to—"

"Chester? Not anymore. Last night she made her objections quite clear to her great-uncle, and he's already given me his permission. But I wanted to ask you too."

Dawn sat back, eyeing him. "I only have one condition."

"To let her dance? I've already thought about it. I've seen how Sebastian has supported you. I want the same with Rose."

She exhaled a deep breath. "You and your brother are quite surprising."

He nodded thoughtfully for a moment, before his lips lifted. "Speaking of my brother . . ."

Heat rushed to Dawn's cheeks. "Yes?"

"It seems as if you're a good match."

Her eyes fluttered downward as she stared into her lap. "Yes. I believe . . . I believe I'm quite taken with him."

"I'm glad."

She couldn't hold back the smile on her face. "It looks like the both of us might be all right after all."

"Perhaps," Gideon said with a smile. "Now, about some tea. Is that Earl Grey I see?"

27

Darkness 'til Dawn

The day of the celebration, Dawn traveled to the Hemsworth manor early to help the staff prepare for the eventful evening. She tried to help with the place settings, the food, the live music, and the flower garlands that were to decorate the main entryway, but no matter how hard she tried, the staff would whisk her away, telling her they had everything handled and that she needed to go rest and prepare.

After disappearing into her room, she was grateful for the reprieve. Dawn pulled up a chair and set it by the window, where she peered out into the frosted gardens below. It had snowed all morning, the world a white wonderland beneath her. Ice covered the walls of the manor and snow covered the walkways. White fluff was crystallized on the dried roses and the dull glow of the sun was muted by thick clouds.

The whole scene seemed to sparkle in front of her, and she tried to imagine what her first Christmas would be like with Sebastian. She imagined Christmas trees with real electric tree lights on the branches. Tinsel and mistletoe. She could imagine the entire manor decorated from top to bottom and presents underneath the trees.

She had never had a Christmas like that; she'd only dreamed of what it would be like to be immersed in a fairytale. She'd always told herself she didn't need such things—and she didn't—but a new life started to form in her mind, a new life full of warmth and laughter.

Time passed, the room chilled, and a maid came in to start a fire. After a flame sparked and the wood started to burn, she left, and warmth immediately radiated through the air. The sun had descended, the last bits of light filtering in through the window.

A knock sounded on her door, and Dawn turned. Rose poked her head inside, a silver headband around her blond curls. It matched the glitter on her eyes.

"Rose."

Her pink lips lifted to the side as she quietly shut the door behind her. "Dawn."

In a heartbeat, the two girls rushed forward and clasped each other in a hug. Dawn breathed in Rose's light perfume, the scent mingling in her nose. All the tension drained from Dawn's shoulders as she hugged Rose tighter.

"I was so worried," Dawn said. "You have no idea. I've been so sick. I haven't been all right. I—"

"You never gave up on me," Rose whispered. "Thank you."

They pulled back, keeping a hold on each other's arms. Moisture filled Rose's eyes, and Dawn took in the lines of her lovely face.

"You're my best friend," Dawn said. "Are you all right?"

Rose dropped her arms and spun around, emotion in her voice. "I will be. I'm not sure when, but I will be."

Dawn nodded, silence stretching between them.

"We have so much to catch up on," Rose said. She moved over to the window, peering down at the frosted world below.

They did. Sebastian. Gideon. Dr. Miller. The murders—but they couldn't talk about them now. Not until Rose was strong enough.

"We have plenty of time," Dawn said.

Rose turned, and a small smile spread over her lips. "We do."

The door was flung open and Mrs. Hampshire strode into the room, holding Dawn's new dress, her usually stern face soft.

"It just arrived," she said. "I was beginning to worry."

Dawn slowly moved forward and ran her hand over the purple sequined material. "It's perfect."

"Come on. Let's get you ready." She turned to Rose. "She'll meet you downstairs."

Bits of light reflected in Rose's eyes as her smile deepened. "I can't wait to get to know Sebastian better." She squeezed Dawn's hand as she exited, shutting the door behind her.

Mrs. Hampshire set to work, laying the dress out on the bed. She instructed Dawn to undress and Dawn obeyed, peeling off her layers of clothes down to her chemise. They slid the dress over her head, straightening the boat neck on her shoulders. The mirror in front of her was clean and polished, her reflection crisp. She swished the skirt side to side, anticipation fluttering in her stomach at the thought of dancing with Sebastian.

Mrs. Hampshire pushed Dawn down into a chair facing the small mirror attached to the vanity, and twisted her charcoal locks up into a chiffon, tight against her head. She curled a few pieces in front, pinning them to her head before placing the headband on. It shimmered in the firelight.

"You have lovely skin," Mrs. Hampshire murmured, applying rouge to her cheeks. She applied lipstick and liner until Dawn could barely recognize herself in the mirror. It was her, but also a new version of her. She was beginning to find two sides of herself merging.

After Mrs. Hampshire finished the final touches to her makeup, Dawn blinked, the firelight in the corner warming the side of her face. She couldn't believe a party was being thrown for *her*, that she would actually be accepted into society. And as a healer, no less. Hopefully.

Voices drifted below in the foyer and music from a small band soared up the stairwell. The jazzy swing made Dawn's insides sing, and her body itched to move.

Mrs. Hampshire left and Dawn stayed in her room, her hands placed over her stomach. She paced from side to side, her mind suddenly full of too many thoughts. Could she do this? Could she face all those people below? The last time she had entered a party, she'd been scoffed at and thrown out on the street. But did having a name and status suddenly make her have worth in their eyes? She was a Hemsworth now. That shouldn't have mattered.

Maybe she didn't want to attend the party.

But Sebastian's face appeared in her mind. His dark eyes and chiseled features. His unruly hair and soft demeanor. This was for him. It was to celebrate their marriage together. It must've been a big deal that he was stepping into the spotlight after being in hiding for so long. She needed to think of him.

Opening her door, she went out and descended the stairs, stepping through the main foyer and into the ballroom. The smooth marble floors glinted underneath the chandeliers, bright and sparkling. Diamonds dripped all over the room, from the chandeliers to the necklaces around women's necks. A swirl of colors churned through the space, bright dresses swishing to and fro, a sea of dancers swaying with the music.

Angelica danced with a tall sandy-haired man, and a few of the other ballerinas also danced with their partners. Dawn recognized some of Dr. Miller's patients, including Mrs. Smith, who had had a baby just weeks before. She had a glow about her, like she was relieved to be out of the house.

Dawn stepped deeper into the room, her eyes searching for Sebastian. Gideon stood with Rose across the way, Rose playing with the necklace at her throat, her blond hair pinned perfectly to her head. Her silver headband matched the silver dress, which hung just below her knees. Dawn's heart ached at the sight of her. She seemed to be doing okay. She was out in public. She was conversing. Maybe she'd be all right after all. Gideon gave Dawn a nod.

Dawn looked over the large space at the mural on the ceiling bearing intricately painted cupids and women and flowers. She stood alone in the midst of the dancing and laughter, conversations buzzing around her. Warm smiles were tossed in her direction, and she marveled that she was ever considered a "witch" in this town. Finding the Dollmaker had cleared her name and her reputation.

Two figures loomed up behind Dawn and she stiffened.

"Well, I'll be. I never dreamed of you catching a man like this. Especially with your ... hobbies." Her mother's voice resonated next to her, scratching at her skin.

"Now, now, dear," her father said. "Congratulate our daughter. She has, after all, secured us our future."

Dawn slowly turned. Sights and sounds swirled around her, but all she could focus on were the two bodies in front of her.

"To think that this is all ours," her mother said. "To think of the dresses I'll have. The jewelry I'll get to wear."

"And I'll be free of debt," her father said. "With more money to spend than I could imagine."

"Stop," Dawn whispered. She faced them head on. "I won't allow it."

Her mother laughed, folding her arms in front of her. "Sorry, dear, but this is why you exist. Your only purpose in life is to secure our future. Especially after everything we've given you. Raised you in a home, put up with your endeavors, forgiven you for—"

"Killing my brother?" Dawn interrupted. She shook her head, and tears welled in her eyes. "I spent years believing you. Years of thinking you were right." She clenched her fists and lifted her chin. "Sebastian was right. I think I became a healer just to prove you wrong."

Her mother started to rant again, but her father placed a hand on her arm. "Let her believe what she will. All that matters is that we won in the end."

Dawn felt a gentle hand place itself onto her back, and Sebastian dipped his mouth close to her ear. "Let me handle this."

Her shoulders softened with his sudden presence, and she released a breath, nodding.

Sebastian moved up next to her, his eyes narrowed, his presence dark. "You will both leave now," he ordered.

Her mother blinked, her red lips parting. Her father lifted a quizzical brow.

"You're not welcome here," Sebastian continued. "And you're not welcome in Dawn's life. I will pay you, yes, I will give you enough money for you to go on your merry way, but you will *not* be a part of your daughter's life. The only good thing you have done for her was to bring her into this world. After that, she owes you *nothing*. You will leave, and when you depart, you will not come back. If you do, I will take away your funds and I will cut you off. Are we clear?"

Every part of Dawn warmed—her heart, her mind, her body. Sebastian had said the words that she desperately needed, and even if that was the only thing he did for her for the rest of her life, it would be enough.

Her parents both gawked for a moment before her mother gripped her skirt. "Come dear, we don't want to be part of this celebration anyway."

Sweat shone on her father's brow and he tugged at his collar, but he nodded, and the two disappeared out the ballroom door, giving Dawn one last look.

Dawn slowly turned to Sebastian, who stared down at her with his mouth quirked upward. His gaze roamed over her, taking in her hair, sliding down her body to the bottom of her T-strap heels.

"You look exquisite," he said. "I'm quite certain I've never seen anyone more beautiful than you."

Heat colored her cheeks, and she resisted the urge to touch them. Her eyes fluttered downward before she peeked up at him again.

"Thank you," she whispered.

"I will always defend you," he replied.

They stayed staring at each other for a moment, no words spoken between them. They didn't need words. They only needed each other, only needed to be close. She longed to close the distance between them—the air floating between them was too much space.

"Would you like to dance?" He held out a hand and gave her a small bow, his white shirt crisp against his black collar, his finely stitched coat and slacks perfection.

Dawn looked around the room at the swirling colors and glittering lights. She had learned to dance as a child but had never done it in a public forum. The music sailed through the room, the band's rhythm thumping in her chest.

"I would," she breathed, slipping her hand into his.

Sebastian pulled her onto the dance floor, a large smile on his face, his teeth flashing white. The jazzy music resonated around them, twirling through the air. She started to dance with a fast tempo, but Sebastian drew her in, holding her close instead. He began to move from side to side in sort of a half waltz. Even though the music beat heavy around them, she felt as if she were trapped in a bubble. The steps overtook her, and their own personal melody seemed to carry her around, guiding her feet. Sebastian wouldn't take his eyes off her. She felt as if he were devouring her with every heartbeat.

"Say something," Dawn finally said, out of breath.

They continued the dance, and Sebastian's mouth flicked upward. "I want to be with you. I want to have children with you—only you. And although odd circumstances brought us together, I know I want to spend the rest of my life with you."

She couldn't look away. His words sent electric currents through her skin. "I think I want the same thing."

"Think?"

They continued to swirl around.

She nodded, squeezing her eyes shut for a moment. "It's only that ..."

A low sound rumbled from Sebastian's chest. "I've already taken care of that for you."

Her eyes popped open. "What do you mean?"

"I've purchased your own clinic for you. It's what I've been working on these past few days. Dr. Miller has helped me. He's very excited for you."

Dawn halted, her feet suddenly glued to the floor. The world continued to churn around her, but Sebastian stayed strong and still in front of her.

"You have?"

"Of course. I wouldn't have it another way. The only other thing we have to decide is where you want to live."

The music continued to soar around her, floating around her head. But her mind was clear. She knew what she needed to do.

"You gave me my practice," she said. "I want to give you your home. I know how important it is for you to live here. To be close to your mother's memory."

Sebastian swallowed, and a lump bobbed in his throat. "You're sure?"

She nodded quickly, her own throat swelling.

His hands lifted to the sides of her face and he pulled her in close. He set his forehead to hers, and they stayed standing in the middle of the ballroom, the music still surging around them. "I'm going to kiss you now, is that all right?"

The words jolted through her, and all of her senses came alive at once. Before she could answer, his lips crushed down on hers, somehow forceful and gentle at once. His mouth moved over hers for a moment and she fell into the kiss, giving herself completely to him. Her mind spun; the only thing holding her up was his grip around her back. He gave her two more soft kisses and pulled back. What once was her worst fear had become a dream.

"What do you want to do now, Mrs. Hemsworth?"

Dawn stayed locked in his gaze for a moment before her breaths slowed and her head cleared. The dancing and laughter came back to her at full force as she realized they were still standing in the middle of the room.

"I want to leave," she said. "Perhaps you can show me your mother's doll collection?"

A combination of humor and warmth lit in his eyes. "I would love nothing more."

Acknowledgments

To my mom and dad, for providing the most magical childhood for me. To Boo, who helps me live that magic every day. To Jason Matthews, who taught me everything I know. Thanks to my agent, Marisa Corvisiero, but also to Karen Grencik, Victoria Lea, Natalia Aponte, and Kelly Peterson for helping me along my path. So much thanks to my editors at CamCat, Bridget McFadden and Helga Schier, and to Sue Arroyo for taking a chance on me. I'm indebted to Cortney Pearson, Wendy Higgins, Evelyn Skye, Ryan Dalton, Jolene Perry, Tammy Theriault, Nyrae Dawn, Tiana Smith, Elizabeth Briggs, David and Melissa Hoffman, John Macdonald, Jen Conroy, Leigh Fallon, Dorothy Keddington, and Kevin and Rhonda for being my first supporters. To Julie and Stacey Orlob who ingrained ballet into my soul, so I could write about it. To Matt Bellamy, for inspiring all of my stories. So much love to my four kids who give me light and laughter every day. And finally, to the love of my life, Aaron, for always sticking by me. Without you, I wouldn't have stories to tell.

About the Author

Morgan Shamy is a former ballerina turned writer. She has been immersed in the arts since the young age of four. She has accomplished much in her dance career, including performing in various roles alongside a professional ballet company for over seven years and dancing on prestigious stages like soloing at Carnegie Hall.

Morgan has taught hundreds of girls in her many years of teaching, during which some of her students received full-ride scholarships to dance academies. She is also an accomplished concert pianist and was the first woman in Utah to receive the 75 pt. Gold Cup in the Utah Federation of Music piano solo/concerto competition.

Morgan discovered her passion for writing when her three-year-old son was diagnosed with cancer. That experience sparked her desire to share art and magic through words on the page.

She currently lives with her X-Games gold-medalist husband and four children in Salt Lake City, Utah.

If you enjoyed
Morgan Shamy's *The Dollmaker*,
you'll enjoy
Marcy McCreary's
The Murder of Madison Garcia.

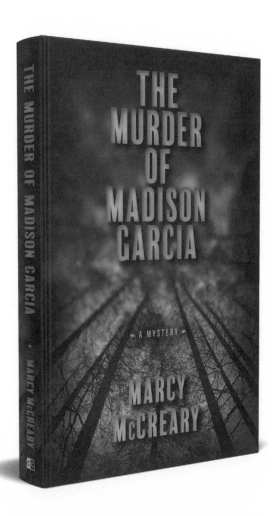

1

SUNDAY | JUNE 30, 2019

I SLID underneath the bubbles. My knees poked out above the surface. One. Two. Three. Four. Five. When I came up for air I heard "Radiate"—my phone's ringtone. I lifted my body, turning toward the sound, and my boobs collided with the edge of the tub. Damn, that hurt. I inched my fingers across the floor but the phone was unreachable, resting on the far edge of the bathmat. I gave up and submerged my body back into the warmish water. *If it's important they'll leave a voice mail.*

With the tips of my fingers sufficiently wrinkled, I reached for the towel that lay crumpled on the toilet lid. With the towel secured around my midsection, I picked up my phone. A missed call from my daughter Natalie. I hit "Recents" to call her back and noticed an incoming call from the night before. A red phone number, indicating a person who was not in my contact list. Boston, Massachusetts, was displayed below the number. Probably one of those spam calls—a request for my social security number or a plea from a political fundraiser. There seemed to be a lot of that lately with the presidential campaign heating up. The American people had taken sides—lefties, centrists, right-wingers—and it wasn't pretty. *It never used to be this way.* Or maybe it was, but social media and cable news were exaggerating and exacerbating the divisiveness. Made me think of that Stealers Wheel lyric: "Clowns to the left of me / Jokers to the right / Here I am stuck in the middle with you."

After applying a fair amount of goop to tame and defrizz my curls, I slipped into my black yoga pants and gray drawstring hoodie. I settled on my bed, opened my laptop, and googled "reverse look-up." Curiosity is a strong motivator to get to the bottom of things— and as a detective, it was hard to pass up the chance to solve this little mystery. I entered the phone number into the rectangular box at the top of the screen. The results page displayed the name Madison García, a resident of Brooklyn, New York, not Boston, Massachusetts. I opened my Facebook page and typed "Madison Garcia" in the search box.

There was one Madison García living in Brooklyn. But the page was private. And her profile picture was a black cat. When I clicked on the name, I was greeted with a handful of pictures she must have designated shareable and therefore accessible to the public. There were people—mostly millennials—in the photographs, but no one I recognized. All personal info was hidden.

"Susan, you up there?"

"Yeah!" I shouted, closing the lid. "I'll be right down!" I plucked a tissue from the box on the bedside table and blew my nose, then headed downstairs with the laptop tucked under my armpit and the box of tissues in my grip.

"Feeling any better?" Ray asked.

"Fucking summer cold. Just popped a DayQuil." I shook the tissue box. "And I got these bad boys."

"You look like shit." A beat later he added, "And I mean that in the nicest way."

"Good save," I said before I blew my nose with more force than necessary. "What's your plan today?"

"I'm heading into the station soon. Chief assigned me to work on those bungalow robberies. Seems we have a serial cat burglar in the area." Ray put on his serious face and wagged his finger. "You are to stay put. I'll pick up dinner tonight."

"Yes sir," I said, military salute included.

My phone rang and we both glanced at it. I thought it might be the Boston/Brooklyn caller. I swiped to answer. "Chief?" I bobbed my head a few times as Ray shot me dirty looks. "Got it. On my way."

"Susan, is this your idea of staying put?"

"Eldridge tells me we got a dead body over at Sackett Lake." I blew my nose again in my semi-used tissue. "Besides, it's just a little summer cold." I coughed up some phlegm and headed back upstairs to change into real clothes.

<hr />

A POLICE vehicle and an ambulance were parked along Fireman's Camp Road. I spotted Officer Sally McIver and her partner, Ron Wallace, at the edge of the parking area. Two paramedics stood beside a black Lexus, the only car in the small Fireman's Camp parking lot.

Sally waved as I got out of my car. Ron held up a roll of police tape and shook it like a tambourine. I looked out toward the lake and took in the scene. From this distance, the dead woman in the car simply looked like she was daydreaming, staring out at the placid water without a care in the world. I retrieved my packet of protective outerwear from the trunk, then joined them.

"What can you tell me?" I asked Sally.

"You sound like shit," she replied.

"Top of the morning to you too."

"That guy over there tapped on the driver's-side window," she said, pointing to a gray-haired gentleman with a German shepherd by his side. "Thought she might be sleeping or something. When she didn't respond, he opened the door. Saw the blood. Then he called 9-1-1. Ron and I got here about five minutes ago."

One of the paramedics approached us. "Multiple stab wounds to her torso. I noticed a bathing suit in the backseat. Perhaps here for a swim and was robbed?" He shrugged, then sighed, clearly not thrilled with how his day was starting out. "All yours." He turned and headed back to his partner.

There wasn't much we could do until Gloria and Mark showed up. Gloria Weinberg was our forensic photographer. Back in the Borscht Belt days, when the Catskills resort hotels were in full swing, she took pictures of the guests, who would then purchase their portraits encased in mini keychain viewers. Now she photographed crime scenes . . . and the occasional wedding.

And once, the crime scene around a murder victim whose wedding she had photographed. Mark Sheffield was our crime-scene death investigator. He had joined the Sullivan County ME's office last fall—wanted to get away from the grim murder scenes of the city.

Wait until he got a load of this blood-soaked tableau.

I turned to Ron. "Let's get a perimeter going. From this area here all the way around to the water," I said, sweeping my arm across the landscape to indicate the area I wanted cordoned off. I wiped my nose on my sleeve. "Sally, run the plates. I'm going to have a little chat with the man who found her."

I approached the gray-haired man and introduced myself.

"Benjamin Worsky," he said in response.

"Okay, Mr. Worsky. Just a few standard questions, and you can be on your way."

"It's no trouble. None at all. In all my years, never thought I'd come across a . . . a dead body. Poor woman."

"When did you happen upon the car?"

"I left my house at seven o'clock on the dot. I'm a man of habit. Seven on the dot every morning to walk Elsa." He petted the top of Elsa's head. "It takes me ten minutes to walk from my house to this spot, so I would say I spotted the car around seven ten. But I didn't think anything of it and continued my walk past the car. But when I came back this way—and I'm thinking that would be around seven-thirty because I walked another ten minutes and then turned around—the car was still here."

"Why did you approach the car?"

"I'm not really sure. Perhaps a sense that something was wrong." He looked down at Elsa, who looked up at him. "Elsa was a bit agitated. Maybe it was that. So I peered in and the driver didn't look well." He frowned and raised his hand to his heart. "I tapped on the window just to ask her if she was okay and when she didn't answer, I opened the car door. That's when I saw the blood and called 9-1-1."

"Did you touch anything?"

"Just the car door handle."

"Did you see anyone else around, either when you came through or off further on your walk?"

"No. But you might want to visit with a woman who lives up the road a bit. She walks along the lake every morning at six o'clock. She might be able to tell you if the car was here at that time."

"Yeah, that would be great. Her name?"

"Eleanor Campbell."

"I know her. The woman with the birds, right?" I chuckled softly, recalling Eleanor Campbell's birds driving Dad crazy when we were working the Trudy Solomon cold case last year. She was a character you didn't easily forget.

"Yeah, budgies, I believe," Mr. Worsky replied.

"Okay, great. If you can just give your address to that officer over there," I said, pointing at Sally, "then you're free to go."

"I don't mean to step out of line here, but you sound awful." Mr. Worsky tugged at his whiskers. "You should really be in bed."

———

A BLUE Honda Accord pulled into the parking lot. The blaring rock music ended abruptly when the ignition cut out. Mark's lanky legs emerged first. When he fully stood, he maxed out at six feet, six inches. His nickname was Pencil, and he seemed to have no qualms about that.

He had a penchant for wearing khaki pants and tan shirts and his hair was the color of graphite. He was such a good sport about his nickname that at last year's Halloween party he wore a tan T-shirt with "No. 2" emblazoned on the front. He opened the trunk of his car, pulled out a pair of overalls, and suited up.

"Good morning, ladies! What brings you out on this fine, fine day?" Mark winked. He looked over at the black Lexus. "Ah. Has the scene been photographed yet?"

"No. Still waiting on Gloria," I said, checking my watch. "Thought she would've been here by now. She lives just a little ways up the road." As if on cue, Gloria's Chevy pickup rumbled up the road. "The gang's all here." I coughed into the crux of my elbow.

"You sound like shit," Mark said. "Bad cold?"

"Yeah, I'm on the back end of it." He nodded and lifted an eyebrow in that way people do when they don't believe you. So I added, "No longer contagious."

We watched as Gloria pulled off the tarp and lifted her gear from the rear bed.

"Sorry for the delay, guys. I was over at Horizon Meadows." Gloria laid her camera bag on the ground and slipped into her protective wear. "My sister was in a bad state this morning. They're moving her to Level Six care." She knelt and removed two cameras.

She hung one of the cameras around her neck and held the other. "There but for the Grace of God go I."

We all nodded.

"I'll start with a few global photos," Gloria said, snapping the shutter to capture the entirety of the crime scene from a distance.

I donned my PPE, then trailed behind Mark and Gloria as they walked toward the victim. As we neared the body, she threw out a question over her shoulder, "Is this how you found everything?"

"Minor scene contamination," I replied. "A passerby opened the driver's-side door and the paramedics checked for life. But we haven't touched a thing."

"You sound like shit," Gloria said.

"That seems to be the consensus today."

The humidity was setting in, further irritating my sinuses and making it harder to breathe. My hands were also a sweaty mess. On days like this it was hard to tell whether my palmar hyperhidrosis was the cause of my sweaty palms or whether the clammy air was simply making my hands wet. I dragged my palms along the front of my pants to sop up the moisture. Then I slipped on my bright blue latex gloves.

We stood bunched together at the open driver's-side door while Gloria laid her duffel bag on the pavement and unpacked her yellow number markers and photo scales.

"Do we have an ID on the woman?" Mark asked.

"Still working on that," Sally replied, as she zipped up her white Tyvek coveralls.

Mark crouched down next to the body. "What a fucking blood-bath."

"Looks like someone stabbed her and walked, drove"—I looked out at the lake—"or swam away." I peered over his shoulder to get a closer look. "Mid-to-late twenties. Maybe early thirties?" I sniffled, trying to suction back the escaping mucus. "I suck at guessing ages."

"I'm getting a late twenties vibe," Mark said.

"No signs of a struggle. Perhaps she knew her attacker. A date gone sideways?" I inferred.

"I don't see a purse," Sally said, cupping her hand like a visor over her eyes and gazing into the passenger's-side window. "There's a duffel and a bathing suit on the backseat."

"Try the door," Mark said.

Sally opened the passenger door. "Not locked."

"How about the rear door?" I asked.

Sally opened a rear door. "Not locked."

Gloria moved around the rear of the car to take midrange and closeup photographs of the items on the backseat.

Sally's phone pinged. She glanced at it, then said, "Car is registered to a Samantha Fields, a doctor who lives in New York City. Should be easy enough to find someone who can provide a positive identification." She drummed her fingers on her cheek. "Unlocked doors. No handbag. No phone. I'm thinking robbery."

"Or someone trying to make our job harder by making us think it's a robbery," I suggested.

Mark leaned over the body to get a closer look at the stab wounds. "Three wounds ... here, here, and here," he said pointing to each incision. "What's this?" he muttered, mainly to himself. "Well, lookee here." Mark reached down into the footwell and pulled out an iPhone. He held the phone up to the woman's face and the device sprang to life. "Here you go," he said handing me the phone.

I hit the green-and-white phone icon on the lower left corner of the phone. "Holy shit. This is *not* Dr. Samantha Fields."

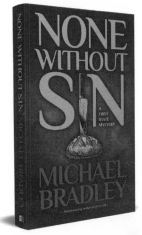
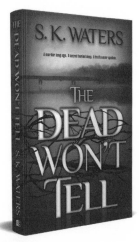
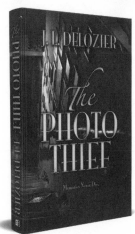

CamCat
Books

VISIT US ONLINE FOR MORE BOOKS TO LIVE IN:
CAMCATBOOKS.COM

CamCatBooks   @CamCatBooks   @CamCat_Books